The Rutherford Cipher

The Rutherford Cipher

a novel by
William Rawlings, Jr.

HH
HARBOR
HOUSE

AUGUSTA

THE RUTHERFORD CIPHER
By William Rawlings, Jr.
A Harbor House Book/2004

Copyright 2004 by William Rawlings, Jr.

For information address:
      HARBOR HOUSE
      111 10TH STREET
      AUGUSTA, GEORGIA 30901

Jacket Design by Jane H. Carter

Library of Congress Cataloging-in-Publication Data
Rawlings, William, 1948-
  The Rutherford cipher / William Rawlings, Jr.
    p. cm.
  ISBN 1-891799-03-7 (hardcover : alk. paper)
  1. United States--History--Civil War, 1861-1865--Fiction. 2. Inheritance and succession--Fiction.
3. Treasure trove--Fiction. 4. Unemployed--Fiction. 5. Diaries--Fiction. I. Title.

  PS3618.A96R88 2004
  813'.6--dc22

                 2004015179

Printed in the United States of America
10 9 8 7 6 5 4 3 2 1

The Rutherford Cipher is a work of fiction. The characters and events in this novel are entirely imaginary and are not meant to represent any person or persons living or dead. The town of Walkerville and the County of Adams in the State of Georgia exist only in the mind of the author and are not based on any specific place.

Any comments regarding the manuscript are appreciated. My email address is rawlings@pascuamanagement.com.

                                   William Rawlings, Jr.

For Elizabeth and Sarah,
remember who you are.

Acknowledgements

The greatest inspiration for this book came from my great-great-grand-father, Solomon Newsom, (born 1805) whose meticulous records before, during and after the Civil War gave me a direct connection to that turbulent time in American history.

My aunt, Elizabeth Newsom, who served as family and county histori-an, made it all come alive for me as a child.

My wife, Beth, has been my helpmate and staunchest supporter. Her forbearance has made this all possible.

I want to thank my numerous "readers" and critics, without whose suggestions these pages would be far less enjoyable. Special thanks go to Ken and Diane Saladin, Wade Register, Becky Burgess, Layne Kitchens, Carole and John Barton, Jessica Heldreth and Mary Eleanor Wickersham, among many others.

Heatherly Dukes was most kind in arranging a tour of the Savannah River Site, and in giving general information on the activities there.

George Scott's enthusiastic support makes all the hard work worth-while.

Again with this book, I appreciate the interest and encouragement of Randall and Anne Floyd of Harbor House.

A special word of thanks is due my muse, Laura Ashley, to whom I will always be 17.

Author's Note

One of my goals as an author is to write believable fiction that could have happened, even if it didn't. The story of the Lost Confederate Gold is one of the most enduring of Southern legends, having given rise to scores of late night tales and boyhood dreams of hidden riches. Like one of the characters in this novel, I spent countless hours as a teenager searching for buried treasure with my military surplus mine detector, only to be rewarded with the occasional horseshoe or lost penny.

For the record, there are varying and sometimes conflicting accounts of the chaotic final days of the Confederate government. The so-called "treasure train" with the bullion and specie that remained in the Treasury, as well as about $450,000 in gold reserves from the Richmond banks, did follow Jefferson Davis and his Cabinet south as they fled the embattled capital in early April 1865. Details of the exact holdings of the Treasury vary widely, leaving an author ample leeway to create a bit of parallel – and possible – history. To a reader interested in a more factual account I recommend An Honorable Defeat, William C. Davis' history of the last days of the Confederate government (Harcourt, 2001). One of the most readable accounts of the escape and subsequent capture of President Davis, as well as the fate of the remaining members of the Cabinet, was skillfully recorded by A. J. Hanna in his 1938 book Flight into Oblivion, reprinted in 1999 by The Louisiana State University Press.

For the reader seeking a deeper understanding of the world of ciphers and their military and civilian use, I highly recommend Simon Singh's wonderfully written work, The Code Book, published by Doubleday (1999).

While the plot, characters, and situation remain fictional, many place descriptions were drawn from first-hand experience and research. Non-fictional information regarding the Savannah River Site was gleaned from public sources.

I welcome readers' comments and will try to answer all correspondence. Please e-mail me at rawlings@pascuamanagement.com.

William Rawlings, Jr.
Sandersville, Ga.
March 2004

CHAPTER

One

THE SERVICE WAS OVER AT EXACTLY 11:08 A.M., an observation remarkable only for the fact that it had started promptly eight minutes earlier. It seemed to me a rather brief benediction for a life of 86 years. The minister — more commonly the preacher in this part of the South — was in his late 20s, about my age. His hair was a greasy shade of black combed back over the tops of his ears. He wore a colorful polyester tie that clashed with his somber gray suit. I really don't remember much of what he said, except he obviously didn't know my Aunt Lillie very well. His comments were generic, something about a life well-lived, a home in heaven and the like. He had incanted a bit and read something from the Bible, a Psalm, I think. By the time I realized it, he was walking over to those dozen-odd of us family members who rated the opportunity to sit under the shade of the Davis Funeral Chapel tent as shelter from the midday August sun. We were in the Walkerville Old Cemetery, dating from the 1840s. Only those families whose forebears had had the vision or money to buy large plots more than a century ago still used it, and a funeral there usually meant the death of one of the town's more prominent citizens. So it was with my aunt.

The preacher was moving down the line, grimly shaking the hand of each member of the deceased's family. The protocol of these things required you to stay seated until he had spoken personally to everyone. He reached me and offered a limp hand "I'm so sorry about your aunt's passing" he said.

I wanted to reply that for God's sake she was 86, but instead smiled — equally grimly — and said, "Thank you for everything. I'm Matt Rutherford."

There was a brief flash of recognition in his eyes.

"You're Matt? Miss Lillie was asking for you right before she passed."

Maybe he had met her after all. He continued, "But she was a bit confused those last days in the hospital."

"Thank you," I said again, and he turned his attention to my uncle who was seated next to me.

Momentarily we rose, giving the rest of the mourners a chance to speak to the family. It seemed to me a large crowd for a woman of my aunt's age, but she'd been well-known. My mother had observed earlier that while Aunt Lillie had outlived most of her contemporaries, she had a huge circle of friends. As we trooped toward the cars parked in the shade under the huge magnolias, several people came up to greet me. The conversations were all basically the same.

"Matt, how are you? How's California? You in town for a while?"

"Great, thanks." I'd smile broadly. "I'll probably be here for a few weeks. I'm taking a little break from my job." I lied.

"You at your momma's place?"

"For the moment." I'd smile again. What I didn't bother to tell them was that I was out of a job, broke and had no immediate prospects for either employment or income.

We had almost reached the car when I heard someone call my name. I turned to see Nick Morgan. He had been my father's closest friend and my family's lawyer since long before I was born. Gray-headed, he was lean, tan and muscular in the wiry sort of way that made you think he could hold his own in a barfight.

My father had been killed in a hunting accident when I was six years old. Nick was given charge of the trust funds that supported my mother and paid for my education. When I was in college and graduate school, we'd spoken often. I hadn't heard much from him in recent years.

Nick smiled. I smiled. He spoke. "Matt. How are you?"

"Great, considering." I didn't know if he knew my situation.

"Anne tells me you're going to be in town for a few days." Anne is my mother. "Did you get to speak with your Aunt Lillie before she died?"

"No, I didn't." I was waiting to see what he wanted.

"Have you seen your cousin, Lance? I thought I could catch you both here at the funeral."

Why did he want Lance?

"No," I replied. "I got in late yesterday afternoon. My mother said he was at the hospital right before Aunt Lillie died. I would think he'd be here at the funeral."

We both looked around at the scattering crowd.

"Me, too. I called his place in Columbia and his roommate said he had come over here to see his aunt, and that after she died, he called back to say he was staying for the funeral."

"Did you check with Jack and Maggie?" My father's younger brother, Jack, and his wife, Maggie, are Lance's parents.

"Yeah. They said he was staying at their pond house out on the farm. There's no phone in the cabin, so I rode out there yesterday afternoon. His car was there, but no one was home."

"He'll show up."

"Well, I need to speak to the both of you together."

"Why?" I asked.

"It's no secret now. You two were Lillie's sole heirs. She appointed me co-executor, and we need to discuss her estate."

I was truly surprised. I had never been especially close to Aunt

Lillie; after all, she was pushing 60 when I was born. She was my father's sister, and I had never really considered her a close relative. I leaned against a small oak tree. I felt light-headed.

"What do you want to do?"

"Well, we need to secure her house as soon as possible, and then you two need to sit down and divide up her material estate — the silver, furniture and all that. I'd be glad to help you, but I don't even have an inventory of what she had. Otherwise, dividing up her liquid assets should be no problem. I don't think we're going to have a problem with the IRS, but we do need to file an Estate Return."

"Do I have to pay taxes on the estate?" I had left California because I hadn't been able to pay the lease on my condo.

"You'll owe some, I'm sure. But the estate is fairly liquid. She had about three-quarters of a million in CDs and securities. Plus, I understand there's still a pretty good annual income from her *War Diaries* book. I don't think there will be much of a problem."

I involuntarily flinched.

CHAPTER

Two

NICK SUGGESTED WE WALK TO HIS OFFICE. The oppressive heat would normally have made me refuse such an offer, but the thought of financial salvation had an amazing anesthetic effect. The Law Firm of Morgan and Wystant was located on the city square in a renovated storefront, its nineteenth-century cast-iron facade dolled up to something that looked vaguely like Williamsburg.

The office itself was a bit down at the heels, the front door was scuffed, and I noticed the wood at the bottom of the bay window facing the courthouse was badly in need of a fresh coat of paint.

Not that it mattered in a town this size. Nick could have practiced out of the back of his pickup truck and still have been immensely successful. He was by all reports a very good, fair and generally honest lawyer. He led me into his book-lined conference room and motioned for me to sit down.

"I'm surprised you didn't know your aunt had left things to you. She wasn't especially secretive about it."

I was still in a bit of shock.

"Well, I have been living on the West Coast and a little out of touch. I was thinking about it on the way over here. She didn't have many other relatives — maybe her options were limited."

"No, she was very specific." Nick was ruffling through a large file cabinet he had unlocked with a formidable-looking key. He extracted a slim folder and laid a blue-backed legal document on the table. "And, too," he continued, "the fact of the matter is that you boys are the last of the Rutherford line. She's been the unofficial family historian since long before your father was born. I imagine she wanted the family records preserved, and was maybe hoping one or the other of you would take an interest in her historical stuff. She was pretty well-known for that, you know."

I couldn't care less, I thought.

Looking at the cover of the will, Nick squinted, "She updated her will, I think, here it is, two years ago." He started to slide it across the table but hesitated. "Look, we've got to have the reading of the will in the presence of all the heirs, so I really can't do much until Lance shows up. Here, let me just go over it with you informally."

He unfolded the document and slipped on a pair of half-frame reading glasses. "It's a very simple three-page will. The first page says basically that your aunt considered herself of sound mind and directs that her legal debts be paid." He turned to the second page. "The next page leaves directions for her funeral, and the last page specifically names you and Lance as her sole heirs. In fact, she was so specific she had me put a clause in that says if either of you predecease her or are physically or mentally unable to take control of her assets, the other one gets everything." He paused, looking over his glasses. "I tried to get her to explain to me why she wanted that provision but she wouldn't." He looked back at the document. "And finally, if both of you died or couldn't take control of the estate, then all of her personal effects and the entire contents of her house are to go to the Adams County Historical Society and the remainder of her estate goes to the First Methodist Church. It's plain and very simple."

"I don't know what to say," I lied.

A thousand thoughts were racing through my mind. At least I'd have enough cash to tide me over until I could find a halfway decent job somewhere. I may be a fool, but my ego won't let me flip burgers at McDonald's, no matter how hungry I get.

Nick stood. "Before we do anything else, we need to go over to Lillie's house and make sure things are all locked up. She'd had someone try to break in the house a few months ago and ended up installing a burglar alarm system. When Lance gets here, we'll do all this again for the record, but it would ease my mind if we could check on things. Maybe one or the other of you could stay over there at night."

My heart leaped. Anything to get away from the embarrassment of staying with my mother.

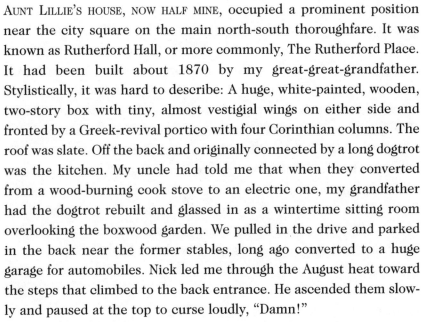

AUNT LILLIE'S HOUSE, NOW HALF MINE, occupied a prominent position near the city square on the main north-south thoroughfare. It was known as Rutherford Hall, or more commonly, The Rutherford Place. It had been built about 1870 by my great-great-grandfather. Stylistically, it was hard to describe: A huge, white-painted, wooden, two-story box with tiny, almost vestigial wings on either side and fronted by a Greek-revival portico with four Corinthian columns. The roof was slate. Off the back and originally connected by a long dogtrot was the kitchen. My uncle had told me that when they converted from a wood-burning cook stove to an electric one, my grandfather had the dogtrot rebuilt and glassed in as a wintertime sitting room overlooking the boxwood garden. We pulled in the drive and parked in the back near the former stables, long ago converted to a huge garage for automobiles. Nick led me through the August heat toward the steps that climbed to the back entrance. He ascended them slowly and paused at the top to curse loudly, "Damn!"

"What's the matter?"

"Some son-of-a-bitch has broken this door in!" He pointed to the shattered door jamb. "Well, hell, let's go in and call the police. I hope her phone still works." He pushed open the shattered door.

The back door opened into a small vestibule beyond which a second set of doors opened into the main hall that ran from the front to the back of the house. I recalled that the plan was rather simple, basically a wide stair hall in the center and several rooms on either side downstairs, with the same basic pattern repeated upstairs. Nick punched a code into the keypad of an alarm system. "Well, this is strange. The alarm system is off." As he opened the frosted-glass, inner door, a hot blast of foul-smelling air rushed over us.

"God! What is that smell?" Nick said, putting a hand over his mouth and nose.

The odor was overwhelming, like rotting flesh. "I'll bet some kids broke in and trashed the kitchen." We turned to our right and back through the glass sitting room toward the kitchen. The smell stayed in the house.

"Not here," I stated, obviously.

We walked back toward the main part of the house, through the dining room and into the wide hall toward the front. The smell grew stronger. The huge sliding panel doors that opened into the two front rooms were closed. Nick tugged on the one on our right, sliding it effortlessly into the wall. The ornate parlor was undisturbed. We looked at each other. I grabbed the handle on the door leading to the library and pulled. The stench was overwhelming. I could hear the buzzing of insects. I eased it open a couple of feet and we peered in.

The fly-covered body of my late cousin, Lance, lay bloated in the center of the Tabriz carpet, its delicate hues stained dark by the dried blood that had gushed from a gaping wound in his head.

CHAPTER
Three

THE POLICE HAD ARRIVED PROMPTLY. Lance's parents were notified. My mother sent word that she'd be at their house.

Nick and I were told to wait in the yard while the cops did their work. We sat on white-painted cast-iron benches under a massive oak, watching the parade of official cars and vans that came and went. We were interviewed by no fewer than four officers, each asking the same questions, each wanting to know why my cousin would break into his aunt's house. I explained to them that I'd been back in town for less than 24 hours and had no idea about what went on. I gave them what few facts I knew, which they evidently didn't believe, as they'd come back and ask me to repeat one part or another in greater and greater detail.

They asked Nick to come in and tell them if he noticed anything obviously missing from the house.

From our vantage point in the yard, I noted that the tall floor-to-ceiling windows in the house had been opened and someone had placed a fan in one of them. The odor of death escaping into the afternoon sun added to the weight of the heat.

Finally, the coroner and the medical examiner arrived, traveling together in an official gray Ford with its county government tag and a small forest of stubby antennas sprouting from the trunk area. I knew them both well, or at least I had before I'd left home more than a decade ago.

The coroner, Zeke Chappel, was a tall, balding man whose primary occupation was that of an insurance agent. His chief qualification for the coroner's job was that he had been able to convince the voting public at election time that he was less incompetent than his opponents. His salvation was Dr. Winston Guillard, an intense and analytical, local general practitioner who took his unpaid, appointive office most seriously. Between the two of them, Chappel handling the politics and Guillard doing the real forensics, they made a reasonably good team. They spoke briefly to Nick and me, and then headed up the wide back steps to the crime scene.

After about half an hour they emerged, Dr. Guillard peeling examination gloves from his hands. A surgical mask hung loosely around his neck and he was carrying a large black bag. They conferred briefly and then walked over to where we were sitting. Chappel spoke first. "A real mess in there," Chappel said. "Nick, how long did you say it had been since you know for certain that anybody was here?"

"At least three days, so far as I know. Today's Wednesday. Miss Lillie died late Saturday night and I came over before church Sunday morning with Jack and Maggie to pick up a burial dress for the funeral home. As far as I know, I'm the only one she'd given the alarm code to; she was real peculiar about that after the attempted break-in. I sort of rode through the yard Monday afternoon for a look-see. I suppose I could have missed it, but the back door didn't look broken then."

"Did you go in?" Guillard asked.

"No. In fact I didn't even get out of the car. I was on my way home from work and I just pulled in the back yard, looked around and left."

"And when was the last time anybody saw or heard from the Rutherford boy?" Chappel asked.

"Apparently on Sunday morning about 9 o'clock. He called his roommate in Columbia, South Carolina, to tell him he was staying over for the funeral today. He didn't really get along with his parents, so much so that his daddy, Jack, told me that he usually would stay at their cabin in the country whenever he came to town."

"What about his job? Did he call his employer?"

Nick shrugged. I spoke. "He didn't work. At least not on a regular basis, as far as I know," I said.

They looked at me curiously.

I continued, "You really had to have known Lance to know what I mean. He was a dreamer, always hoping for something big to come along. He was smart, maybe a genius even, but I can't really say that he was lazy. It was that, how do you put it? He was always looking for an angle. Some easy way to reap the rewards without having to put out the effort to get them. He kept talking about 'luck' and making 'just one big score.' Know what I mean?"

They nodded. "What about the burglar alarm? It apparently was disarmed," Chappel said.

"Like I told the police," Nick replied, "I *think* I set it when I left last Sunday morning. I guess I could have forgotten. Only Miss Lillie and I knew the security code. I had changed it for her after the alarm was installed and even the burglar alarm company didn't know what it was."

The back door of the house opened and two EMS workers emerged, each wearing surgical masks and gloves. They manhandled a stretcher laden with a thick, black, rubber body bag down the steps. Chappel said, "We're taking the body to the morgue at the hospital. I've called the GBI. We're going to send it to Atlanta for a forensic autopsy."

Nick spoke. He seemed suspicious. "How long do you think Lance has been dead? Any theories about who killed him?"

It seemed strange to me that he would ask.

"There're quite a few questions that need answers, Nick. Maybe we can get some more information about the murder weapon, for one," Guillard replied.

He opened his black bag and extracted a heavy object wrapped in a clear plastic evidence pouch. I noted that the top was sealed with bright red tape labeled "EVIDENCE" and a white card marked "Chain of Custody" was firmly taped on one side. He held it out.

"What is it?" I asked.

"Apparently what the killer or killers used to hit him on the head," Guillard replied.

He handed me the pouch. It sagged with the weight. Inside was a rectangular-shaped object, about a quarter the size of a standard brick. It appeared to be thickly covered with what could only be dried blood, under which could be seen a dull black finish.

"What is it?" I asked again.

"A paperweight or bookend or some such, I think. Another one, I guess its mate – if it is a bookend – is still lying on the floor in there. The police checked it for prints, but it was clean. The room is pretty much a wreck."

"Oh," I replied and handed the pouch to Nick who gave it a cursory examination and gave it back to Guillard.

Chief of Police Roger Mathis walked up. "We're about finished in there. You fellows need anything else?" he asked Chappel and Guillard.

They shook their heads no.

Mathis turned to Nick. "It looks like we're through here then, Mr. Morgan."

"What do you think, Roger? Robbery gone bad, or what?" Nick replied.

"Right now I don't know. We've got a lot of work to do. There are a lot of things that don't fit. There was evidently a struggle. The room got pretty well trashed and a front window got smashed, which accounts for the flies." He turned to me. "Matt, you're not planning to leave town, are you? We may have some more questions for you."

Wondering what he meant, I assured them that at this point, I was here for the foreseeable future.

"That's good," Mathis replied. "I'll probably give you a call in a couple of days. I want to talk with you about some specific things."

Turning back to Nick, he said, "guess we'll hand things back over to you, or whoever."

Nick looked at me. "I hadn't really thought about it, but it looks like Matt here is now the legal owner."

If you want to know the truth, I hadn't thought about it either. The whole thing was too much, too soon. Lance and I were never at all close, but he was my cousin. I had to think of his parents, my mother, the family. I realized that they were all looking at me. "Thank you," I said, and shook everyone's hands. "Thank you for everything."

The last police car left as Nick and I climbed the back steps once again. The house was cooler with the fan in the front parlor, creating a good cross breeze through the long central hall. A faint smell still lingered in the air. Tentatively, we walked to the library and peered in.

The room had been totally ransacked. The position of the body was roughly outlined in masking tape on the carpet, its cephalic region surrounded by a dark irregular stain. The front and side walls were dominated by huge windows, now open to the August afternoon heat. A large fireplace with an ornately carved mantle dominated the outside wall opposite the door. Built-in book shelves raised most of the way to the 12-foot ceiling. Beyond this, nothing was intact. A carved, walnut chest had been pulled away from the wall, apparently in a search for something. Leather-bound volumes lay in jumbled heaps under the bookcases. An embroidery-covered, Biedermeier-style sofa had been pulled up to one side and apparently used as a stepping stool to reach the highest shelf. Pieces of smashed porcelain, apparently at one time displayed on the shelves, lay in heaps. We were silent.

Nick gently moved a jagged piece of an elaborately painted Meisien vase with his foot. "Goddamn," he said softly. He walked over and silently began picking up the books and putting them in stacks.

The afternoon sun, filtered by the summer leaves, was shining through the tall, west-facing windows. An object lying in the middle of the floor caught my eye. It was rectangular, perhaps the twin of the bookend that had been used as the murder weapon. I stepped into the room and picked it up.

It was heavy, like its mate, but unstained except for the fingerprint dust of the police investigator. I turned it over in my hand, studying the surfaces. It looked like an ingot, poured while molten into a mold and stamped on the surface with some sort of identifying marks. I examined the marks closely. There appeared to be some kind of a figure – a man on a horse surrounded by what? A wreath? To the side was stamped "C" and an "S" followed by some illegible letters or numbers. I looked closely at the figure again. I'd seen it somewhere before.

I realized that the object had been painted, and that the thick coats of dried paint obscured the details. I reached in my pocket for my keys, and with a sharp edge scratched at the paint. Underneath, there was shiny metal. I studied the horseman and wreath design again, searching my memory and failing to identify it.

I started to ask Nick about it, but thought better of it and laid the bookend on the chest. I began to help him stack the books. I picked up a copy of one of my aunt's books, *A History of the War Between the States*. Something stamped on the cover attracted my attention. The figure on the bookend – it was the same man on a horse surrounded by a wreath. It was exactly the same and appeared to be a seal of some sort. Curious, I opened the book to the title page and again saw the same figure with the legend, "Great Seal of the Confederate States of America."

My heart was pounding, but I was reluctant to say anything to Nick. I stood up and leaned against the chest. "This has been enough for one day. Let's call it quits," I said.

CHAPTER

Four

I SAW THAT I HAD SOME PRIORITIES. Nick gave me a ride to my mother's house. I picked up my car, a leased Explorer, and drove to Lance's parents' house.

The mood was somber. Friends and neighbors came and went. Casseroles and plates of fried chicken accumulated in the kitchen. Jack and Maggie received everyone in the living room, with lots of tears and hugs.

After what I thought was the minimal amount of time I would be expected to stay, I said my good-byes and drove back to my mother's to pick up a change of clothes, some tools and one of my father's long-unused shotguns. It was nearly 7 p.m. when I arrived back at Rutherford Hall. The yellow crime scene tape was still strung across the front walk, and cars passing by on Main Street slowed and stared. I took it down.

Lance's murder was not an act of random violence. Clearly he had not been alone, and judging from the fact that only one room had been ransacked, they must have been looking for something in particular. Whoever killed him had evidently not returned to the scene of the crime. That would imply that they had found what they were looking for, or had been scared off and planned to return later. I was not going to take any chances. After some searching, I discovered a big ring of keys hung on a nail in the kitchen pantry, and tested each one until I found one that fit the massive front door lock.

In the waning light I managed to find some boards in what at one time must have been the tack room of the stables and nailed them over the outside of the shattered window in the front parlor. I nailed the broken back door shut, and set out to find the instruction booklet for the burglar alarm. After an hour, I gave up and called the number on the red "Warning: Alarm System in Use" sticker on the back glass.

After much explaining, a very annoyed technician named Mike showed up 45 minutes later to check the system and show me how to reprogram the entry and exit codes. I offered him a beer that I had found in the refrigerator and tipped him my last $20.

I had no idea what I was going to do. The idea of sleeping in the house where my cousin had lain dead for three days didn't appeal to me in the least, but then nothing whatsoever had gone well in my life for the last year.

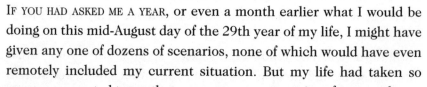

IF YOU HAD ASKED ME A YEAR, or even a month earlier what I would be doing on this mid-August day of the 29th year of my life, I might have given any one of dozens of scenarios, none of which would have even remotely included my current situation. But my life had taken so many unexpected turns that one more strange series of events almost seemed normal.

I was born in Walkerville. For the most part had a happy childhood, at least until I was 6. My father was a lawyer, landowner and heir to the Rutherford name. He was Matthew Rutherford IV, so naturally when his son (and as it turned out, only child) was born, I was christened Matthew (no middle name) Rutherford V.

My father died accidentally on a cold November day in 1980. He and Nick were duck hunting on one of the lakes on the family's river property. We had a big playful black Lab, Sugar, he took with him to fetch the ducks. The dog was my friend. Years later I learned that my father and Nick had finished hunting and had pulled the boat up on the bank, leaning the shotguns on the thwarts to keep them off the wet interior of the hull. Somehow Sugar in her eagerness to get out of the boat had placed her paw on the trigger guard of the Browning 12 gauge, at once pressing the safety off and pulling the trigger that released a fatal blast of No. 4 lead into my father's chest. He died almost instantly.

My dog and my father never returned home.

As a family, we were not poor. My father had inherited well, as had his father before him. We owned several thousand acres of good timberland and what I presumed were other assets. On his death, all this was put into a series of trusts whose stated purpose was to provide income and support for my mother and me, and "to preserve the corpus of the Rutherford estate for future generations." I was never allowed to know their value. His life insurance took care of the mortgage on the house and left sufficient funds to allow my mother to maintain her lifestyle. As the only child, I was due to inherit the land held in trust on my 35th birthday. I planned to sell it.

My mother was 30 when my father died. She grieved for years. As a child, one never understands the world of adults. Despite this, I did recognize that after an appropriate amount of time had passed her friends tried to get her to start looking again. She refused. The only man who came close to being a regular visitor at our house was Nick. Beginning perhaps a year after the accident they dated for a while, and then apparently broke up. I never asked any questions and she never volunteered any explanations.

Growing up fatherless in a small Georgia town probably influenced my career choice. Unlike my father and the generations for more than 100 years before him, I had developed no great love for the land. My cousins hunted and fished; I read. They developed outdoor skills; I developed a love of words. It was not that I wasn't athletic. I played wide receiver on our high school football team the year we went to the state finals (and lost). My one goal in life was to escape Walkerville and Adams County.

In August 1991, two months before my 18th birthday, I left home to enroll at Duke University in Durham, North Carolina. I majored in English – a degree that Nick and my mother reminded me had no practical value in the real world. I made my obligatory visits home on holidays and for a couple of weeks in the summer, but I was determined not to end up in some tiny backwater Georgia town following in the footsteps of my father and grandfathers before me. Despite whatever misgivings he might have had, Nick made sure the checks to pay for my tuition and living expenses arrived promptly on the first of every month.

I took summer courses and completed my degree requirements in three years. With a Phi Beta Kappa key on my chain and as a *summa cum laude* graduate, getting into a master's degree program in linguistic anthropology at the University of Oregon in Eugene was no problem. I figured a couple of years there, then two more for my doctorate, and I could write my own ticket to a tenured professorship on a college campus far from rural Georgia. My master's thesis was entitled *Archaic Syllabification: The Persistence of Pre-Great Vowel Shift Word Forms in Regional American English.*

Two weeks before my orals, and one month before I was formally granted my degree, I got a call from Luke James, one of my fraternity brothers from Duke. Luke was a bit of a nerdy type, but a master of computers and information systems. In college we had long discussions fueled by too much beer about his wild idea of storing the entire world's accumulated knowledge in some vast central supercomputer. All literary and scientific writings would be reduced to some common abstract mathematical language which could then be accessed through a translation interface in any of the world's myriad languages.

"Imagine," Luke said, "how it would promote world peace if everyone could, with a few strokes on a keyboard, read or even hear the same basic documents in real time in their own language?" I thought he was a crazy dreamer, but we were 19 at the time. Five years later, he was president and CEO of Linguafont Technologies Inc., in which capacity he called to offer me a job.

Luke had made it. Not like we had envisioned in our beery ramblings all those years before, but in a form that was practical and salable. "Linguafont has many accounts, but our No.1 customer is the U.S. government," he explained. "There are lots of people out there who wish harm to America and her interests. The military, the NSA, the CIA – they all collect huge amounts of raw data from phone taps, satellite intercepts, e-mail and so on. Their computers churn away to separate the wheat from the chaff, but ultimately, the important stuff has to be classified, collated and shared between agencies, departments and even governments. That's where we come in.

"Matt, I need someone who is educated, articulate and polished enough to act as our spokesperson with both government and corporate clients. Heck, I've still got the same pocket protector I had in high school. You've got the right people skills and the perfect background in linguistics. It's an ideal fit."

I had listened silently. I was on the verge of saying thanks-but-no-thanks when Luke added, "And the base salary is $150,000 per year, with a signing bonus, moving expenses and our stock option package that should be worth big bucks when we go public."

Three months later, I was living in Palo Alto.

CHAPTER

Five

LINGUAFONT TECHNOLOGIES DID WELL. Unlike many dot-coms, we actually had a product to sell. Luke and his team of twenty-something-year-old software engineers had expanded on the original idea of storing vast amounts of text, voice, video, and electronic data in its original form, and then providing almost instant access and search capacities when a request for a particular reference or pattern of words was requested. We could extract useful data with some accuracy from voice or text forms in 42 languages. The generals and the spooks loved it. Corporate types were a bit slower to catch on, but the prospect of covert but legal industrial espionage always hovered in the background.

As executive vice-president for communication, I was showered with perks: a corner office, layers of assistants and secretarial staff, a Jaguar XJ-8 company car and memberships to three of the best local clubs with an unlimited entertainment budget. Rent was astronomical in the Bay Area, so the company picked up about half of the $2,800-a-month lease on my condominium.

Brandi, a Stanford senior whose parents were entertainment executives in Malibu, became my live-in girlfriend. She was blond, blue-eyed and totally in love with northern California. The two things we had in common were her love of my lifestyle, which kept me at one media party or another five nights a week, and sex.

Linguafont had planned to go public in spring 2000, but that idea was scuttled with the crash of the NASDAQ and the following dot-com meltdown. Despite all the carnage around us, we survived and even prospered. By mid-2001 our gross sales exceeded $200 million and we were once again tooling up for a public stock offering in the fall.

The company was doing well. I was doing well. At 27, I had made it. My job was public relations, and I didn't hesitate to let everyone know about it. I scheduled news conferences with each new success. I churned out press releases by the dozens, making sure each time the *Adams Sentinel*, my hometown newspaper, received a copy.

Then, September 11, 2001, happened. We huddled that afternoon in the glass-lined conference room watching the CNN live feed from New York. The consensus from a business standpoint was that we'd make it through this crisis, too, and that our products would be even more in demand. We were right, but to a degree and in a way we had never envisioned.

On October 16, the company was purchased by an agency of the Department of Defense. Luke called a mandatory emergency staff meeting with his top executives and vice-presidents – about a dozen of us. He was accompanied by a somber-faced, military type disguised in a dark business suit. In essence, Linguafont Technologies had been declared a vital national asset and had been sold to the government through the purchase of all of the closely held preferred stock. Luke was at once elated and sad. He was angry and overjoyed. He was also very, very rich. We were all given six months salary and benefit continuation and offered the services of an excellent outplacement firm.

I was not worried. After all, I'd helped take the firm to the top and within six months surely I'd have another equally lucrative opportunity laid at my feet.

I was such a fool.

The Jag was the first to go. They picked it up over my protests November 1 after determining that company vehicles were not normally considered a "benefit," hence I was not entitled to its use. I leased a used Ford Explorer for six months, figuring I could ditch it for something better in a month or two when I was back at work.

I met twice with representatives of the outplacement firm. They were cheery, encouraging types who offered to help me rewrite my résumé and enroll me in glorified self-esteem classes that were designed to give me the confidence and ability to survive the job search. I wrote them off and began calling in favors from the various business contacts I'd made over the past couple of years.

I still had the club memberships, or so I thought. The dues were paid annually in advance, and I had always had the option of charging non-business meals and entertainment to my personal account. I'd invited the CEO of a successful software firm and his wife to dinner at the North Bay Yacht Club. I knew his vice-president for public and governmental affairs had just resigned, and I made it clear that I wanted to talk about the position over an informal dinner. He was agreeable. We were seated by the maitre d', ordered drinks, and then were politely informed by the manager that my membership had "lapsed" and that we would have to leave. We ended up having a superb dinner at a nearby Tuscan restaurant, but the evening and my chance were blown.

On November 15, I received a late notice from the management company stating that I had only made partial payment on the current month's rent. I called and explained to them that I sent in a check for my part and my former employer took care of the rest, and was scheduled to do so for six months. They'd already checked with Linguafont, they said, and that I was mistaken as that particular "benefit" was not included in my package.

By Christmas, I had sent out more than 200 résumés and had half a dozen semi-serious interviews. The consensus seemed to be that I had been overpaid, was underqualified for most jobs, and that a master's degree in linguistic anthropology did not imply a particularly useful skill set for most of the jobs in high tech. One interviewer actually burst out laughing when he read the title of my master's thesis.

Brandi moved out, having become involved with a Cisco Systems senior vice-president old enough to be her father.

I tried dumbing down my résumé by simply omitting the time I spent in graduate school. The next interviewer picked up on that immediately, and observed that the last applicant he saw with a two-year hiatus in his history had been serving time in federal prison for embezzlement. I stuck the master's back in.

By the first of February, it occurred to me that my job prospects were poor in a market flooded with out of work dot-commers, and that I should return to my long-lost plan for a life in academia. I had burned too many bridges at Oregon to call my graduate professors.

I got on the Internet and searched for every post-secondary school in North America with a department of anthropology or linguistics. I sent out roughly 500 more résumés. The problem with this tack was that any department head who gave my job history more than a cursory glance would figure out I had been untrue to my calling, had sold out to the lure of quick money and did not intend to spend the next 40 years churning out dry tomes on the glottic variations between phonemes in Bantu and Swahili. And they would have been right. By the first week of April, I had received eight phone calls, five letters, and eventually two invitations for interviews.

One invitation came with the offer of paying my interview expenses, including air fare and lodging. Unfortunately, it was at the School of Native American Studies in Whitehorse, in Canada on the Yukon River roughly 400 miles south of the Arctic Circle. I declined the offer.

The other was for a community college near Little Rock, Arkansas. They were planning to start a department of anthropology and were looking for a candidate with strong administrative skills. In late April, I flew from San Francisco via Salt Lake City to Little Rock and picked up a rental car for the 45-minute drive to the school. The interview went well.

Three weeks later, I received an offer to start with the fall semester, beginning work August 15. They offered me $42,500 a year. I took it.

My last paycheck from Linguafont Technologies had arrived April 15. I had some savings, but not enough to last me much beyond the summer and my new job. I decided to stay in my leased condo in Palo Alto and move directly to Arkansas about the first of August. Having nothing much to do and no cash to do it with, I took up writing short stories and submitting them to *The New Yorker, The Atlantic Monthly* and other serious literary periodicals. I collected a stack of rejection letters. By the first of July, I had maxed-out both my Visa and MasterCard, and accepted half a dozen "special introductory offers" for plastic credit from the dozens that seemed to arrive in my mail weekly.

After the Fourth of July, I returned to Arkansas; this time I drove. I had extended the lease on the Explorer for another six months. I found a two-bedroom, one-bath apartment near the school for $460 a month and paid the deposit and a month's rent in advance to start with the month of August. By now I was almost completely out of cash, but estimated that with my credit cards I could hold on until my first paycheck arrived in September.

I gave notice and had reserved a U-Haul for a one-way trip from California to Arkansas when the certified letter arrived. Due to "the evident lack of student interest in the subject as evidenced by very poor advance registration for the proposed Introduction to Anthropology Series, and to funding uncertainties on the state level," plans for the new department, and my job, had been cancelled. They enclosed a check for $1,000. I cashed the check, closed out the condo, put my furniture in storage, and headed home to Walkerville to catch my breath. As I was packing my last bag, my mother called to tell me of Aunt Lillie's death.

CHAPTER

Six

I DON'T WANT TO IMPLY that I didn't know my Aunt Lillie. It seemed everyone knew Aunt Lillie. If Walkerville had ever produced anyone who might pass for a celebrity, it was Lillian Stembridge Rutherford, author, historian and prolific writer on all things Southern, especially as they related to the Civil War. Many times I'd be in some far-flung part of the country on Linguafont business and have the conversation go something like this:

Client: "So you're originally from Georgia? You know, I took a course in college based on the Civil War diaries of some soldier from a little town named Walkerville."

Me: "You mean *The War Diaries of Capt. Matthew Rutherford?*"

Client: "Yeah, that's it – wait, that's your name. You're not by any chance related to…?"

Me: "My great-great-grandfather."

Client: "Wow! That's amazing. What's it like to grow up with all that history? How does that…?"

Me: "All that happened in a time long ago and in a galaxy far, far away. To answer your question, I don't know. I never thought about it."

And then I'd change the subject.

In truth, I had thought about it and had answered the same series of questions so many hundreds of times that once I had seriously, albeit briefly, considered changing my name. To me the War Between the States – to use the preferred Southern term – was ancient history. It had no more bearing on my life and existence than did hundreds of other wars that had caused millions of deaths and been fought over causes whose time had passed before the first shot had been fired.

The first edition of *The War Diaries of Capt. Matthew Rutherford* had been published in 1962 as part of the centenary remembrance of the Civil War. Dozens of magazines and publishing houses had cashed in on the craze, publishing elaborately illustrated articles and fancily speculative books about what happened or what might have happened "if..." *War Diaries* was unique and different. Unlike most of the rehashed and embellished speculation that characterized the more popular books, this was first hand, and previously unknown.

In its first iteration it was a simple book. Published as a quasi-scholarly work by the University of Georgia Press, *War Diaries* consisted only of an introduction by Aunt Lillie followed by photographically reproduced copies of Capt. Rutherford's journals on the left side of a double-faced page, and a typeset copy of the same on the right in order to allow for easier reading of the text. The work was unique for several reasons. My great-great-grandfather was apparently reasonably well-educated and quite determined to record not only the facts, but also his thoughts and interpretations as they fit into his world at large. Secondly, he was faithful in recording his journal to the point of compulsion, never going more than three days without an entry, and always catching up the details when he had more time. Finally, his war experience began as that of a common soldier, took him through several of the major battles in the eastern states, documented his rise in rank and responsibility, and at the end of the war found him in Richmond as a personal adjutant to General Breckinridge, whom Jefferson Davis appointed as Secretary of War in the waning days of the Confederate government.

The book was an instant success and propelled its author to some degree of national recognition. The initial press run was 10,000 copies. It sold out in a matter of weeks. Eventually more than a 100,000 copies of the first edition were printed and sold. I heard my aunt was approached about the movie rights, and that there was interest in making a television series entitled *Captain Rutherford's War* based on the characters in his journal. She refused to discuss either of these possibilities.

The second and best known edition of *War Diaries* began as a collection of lecture notes from a course taught by Andrew Bradley, at the time an assistant professor of history at the University of Georgia. Using the basic journal entries as a point of departure, and Captain Rutherford's interpretations as representative of the thinking of the day, he crafted a curriculum that covered the historical facts of the Civil War while not losing the perspective of its effects on an individual, his family and his world. The course was wildly successful and taught in multiple sessions each quarter. By the early 1970s, Bradley had risen to professor, and with my aunt co-authored the second edition: *The War Diaries of Captain Matthew Rutherford: A History of the American Civil War from a Soldier's Perspective*. This work was even more successful in its design as a college level textbook and remains in print, now in its eighth revision. My aunt received the lion's share of the royalties.

The popularity of the Rutherford-Bradley edition of *War Diaries* spawned dozens, if not hundreds, of courses at colleges around the country. In a moment of foolish weakness during my sophomore year at Duke, I signed up for "History 206: The American Civil War and the Common Man." I figured it would be a crip course; after all, it was based on the life experiences of one of my relatives, and I already knew, or so I thought, the basic facts. Not only was I singled out by the instructor for almost daily questions or requests for comments, I was referred to derisively as "Reb" by a few of the northerners in the class and verbally abused by several black students as the verifiable descendant of a slave owner. I completed the course with an A and swore never to discuss *War Diaries* again.

Aunt Lillie, meanwhile, went on to become a frequent contributor to the *Georgia Historical Quarterly* and other scholarly journals, an invited speaker and panelist at academic conferences, and in her late 70s, president of the Georgia Historical Society. Well-educated but never married, she was the youngest daughter of my grandfather, who was 48 years old at the time of her birth. When he was disabled by a stroke in his late 60s, she helped her mother manage the family lands and businesses. She had lived in Rutherford Hall all her life.

She was said to have been a beautiful woman when she was younger, and the numerous framed photographs sitting on tables and consoles around the house confirmed that. Slim, high-cheeked with long blond hair that she kept braided up on the back of her head in the fashion of the day, Aunt Lillie could be seen living what must have been an adventuresome life. Here she was on the back of an elephant attended by a mustachioed mahout. In another she was surrounded by a group of unnamed muscular men in athletic garb with the five-ringed Olympic flag flying in the background next to the Nazi swastika, and the brief notation, "Berlin 1936," penned in the lower corner. There was a group of several frames that featured a dark-haired man, one of which was signed, "All my love, Alex." The last one in the series showed him in military uniform with three other men standing in front of a B-24 on whose nose was painted the face of a blond and the name, "Lucky Lillie."

But she grew old, and died. All that she was, or had been, was now gone, leaving only her memories, an old house, photographs – and the journals of Capt. Matthew Rutherford.

ON ONE LEVEL, WE ACCEPT DEATH as the logical end of life. On another, we deny its inevitability and sometimes its proximity. At night we brush our teeth, placing the toothbrush back in the cup for the morning. We put out the cat, secure the doors and plan for the morrow while waiting for sleep. Sometimes death arrives suddenly and unexpectedly – as with Lance. At others, there are swells and surges before the final wave that carries one to eternal darkness.

I thought about how it must have been with Aunt Lillie. Surely, at 86 she realized that her time was limited. According to my mother, she had been physically and mentally active until the end. On the day of her funeral she had been scheduled to speak at a seminar at nearby Georgia College in Milledgeville on "Central Georgia in the Reconstruction Era: The Emergence of 20th Century Southern Political Thought." On the Wednesday before her death, she had awoken with right-sided weakness and garbled speech. The ambulance was summoned and she was admitted to Adams Memorial Hospital with the working diagnosis of "a stroke." She seemed to improve a bit Thursday and Friday. At times she seemed lucid, and at others confused. Lance had come to visit her Saturday morning. That afternoon she suffered a massive extension of the stroke and died within minutes.

There seemed to be something vaguely obscene about my presence in Rutherford Hall. I was intruding on someone's most intimate space. In my aunt's bedroom the clothes that she had worn the night before she left for the hospital were still lying on the chair. Her nighttime water was on the bedside table, leaving white rings as it evaporated from the glass. I walked throughout the huge house, making sure all the windows and doors were securely locked. I checked the refrigerator and tossed out the outdated milk and moldy leftovers neatly stored in foil covered bowls. Taking my pick of one of the upstairs bedrooms, I made sure the bedside phone worked, set the thermostat down to 72 degrees, and went to bed with my father's loaded shotgun within easy reach.

CHAPTER

Seven

DESPITE ALL, I SLEPT WELL. I was awakened at 7:30 a.m. – 4:30 a.m. California time, according to my internal clock – by the jangling of the front door bell. I threw on my khakis and a T-shirt and stumbled down the stairs to find a middle-aged black woman in a maid's uniform standing on the front porch. "Can I help you?" I asked.

She looked embarrassed. "Mr. Rutherford, I'm Eula Mae Miller. I know you don't know me, but I've worked for Miss Lillie for nigh on 20 years. I always come on Monday and Thursday, and well, I ..." She looked like she was about to cry.

I stared at her blankly, barefoot and half awake.

After a pause, she continued. "I don't know if you're going to be needing any help. See, I got four children, and I really got to work. I came over here last Thursday and the place was locked up – she did-n't give me no key, see – and then I heard that Miss Lillie was in the hospital, so I went to see her up there. She was talking a little funny like she couldn't find the right words. But I did understand her to say she was getting better. She told me that things would be fine and that she'd pay me for Thursday, but I didn't have to work none that day, and that I should be there just like usual on Monday. I came back to

see her on Saturday morning and she was doing just fine and, and ..."
At that point she broke down sobbing. I opened the door and invited
her in.

"Listen, Ms. Miller," I searched for the words, "I don't know too much
of anything at this point – in fact, I'm not sure how long I'll be staying
here. But how about this? I'll certainly honor whatever Aunt Lillie
promised you about last week, and I'll pay for this past Monday, too."
She brightened. I was being benevolent with my new-found wealth.
"Why don't you just plan on helping me out for a week or two, until we
can get things settled? After that, we'll see. Does that sound OK?"

The strength came back into her voice. "I really 'preciate that, Mr.
Rutherford. I'm not a person to beg, but if I don't work ..."

"I understand." I cut her off. "And call me Matt, please."

We were standing in the front hall. I pointed to the wreck that
had been the library. "Good Lord in heaven!" she gasped. "Was that
where?"

"Yes." I walked in the room and quickly began peeling the masking tape outline of Lance's body from the rug. "Think maybe you
could help me clean up this mess?"

She smiled, "Yes, sir, Mr. Matt," and headed back to the kitchen for
the broom and dustpan. I followed her, searching for coffee.

Three hours later the library had returned to some semblance of
normalcy. Much of the porcelain had been broken, and after debating
between us, we decided there was no use in trying to salvage it.
Several leather-bound volumes were ripped beyond repair, and two
small tables had been smashed in the scuffle. We put the broken
tables and anything that we thought might be repaired in separate
piles next to the hearth. The local laundry assured me that they
understood how to clean "them fancy Oriental rugs" and sent a man
over to pick up the carpet.

Shortly before 11 a.m., the phone calls began. The first was from
Max Floyd, an editor in the textbook division of Macmillan
Publishers. He explained he had just heard about Miss Rutherford's

death and how sorry he was and how he wanted to be sure the heirs intended to stay with Macmillan, etc. He was obviously protecting his income. I thanked him and told him we'd be in touch. Between noon and 4 p.m. I had half a dozen more calls: two from auction houses that wanted to handle the disposition of Aunt Lillie's estate, two from museums wanting to make me aware that they would like to acquire, either by gift or purchase, the originals of Captain Rutherford's journals, one from a collector of Civil War memorabilia stating basically the same thing, and one from Professor Andrew Bradley, who called to say he'd been out of the country and had just heard about "dear Lillie's" death. I thanked him and told Eula Mae to quit answering the phone.

With help from Uncle Jack, I'd found a local carpenter who could repair the smashed window and back door that afternoon. By 5 p.m. it was finished, complete with a coat of primer. He promised to return the next morning to put on a final coat of paint.

The phone continued to ring. I called the telephone company, had Caller ID added to the number and found an answering machine with Caller ID display on sale at Wal-Mart for $69.95. I used my plastic credit to buy it.

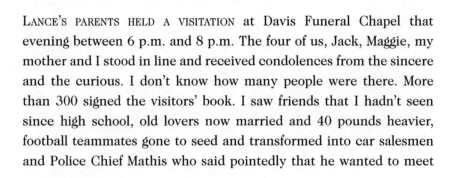

LANCE'S PARENTS HELD A VISITATION at Davis Funeral Chapel that evening between 6 p.m. and 8 p.m. The four of us, Jack, Maggie, my mother and I stood in line and received condolences from the sincere and the curious. I don't know how many people were there. More than 300 signed the visitors' book. I saw friends that I hadn't seen since high school, old lovers now married and 40 pounds heavier, football teammates gone to seed and transformed into car salesmen and Police Chief Mathis who said pointedly that he wanted to meet with me at his office at 10 a.m. the following morning. No options, just be there.

I slept less well Thursday night.

At 10:20 the next morning I was shown into Chief Mathis's office. I had arrived on time and waited while he talked with someone on the phone. I couldn't hear most of the conversation, but I knew it was about Lance's murder.

Mathis was cordial but formal. "Matt, I appreciate you coming down here to the station. You know in a town this size, we don't get that many murders. To be truthful, in the 15 years I've been here I can't recall any of our more prominent families being involved in something like this. Yeah, we get our Saturday night shootings and the occasional armed robbery gone bad, but this whole situation is different." He paused and stared at me to gauge my reaction. I said nothing.

He continued, "I didn't know your father, but I do know your mother, and your uncle and, of course, I knew Miss Lillie. I guess I first met you when you were in high school." I nodded.

"From what I know of things you come from a real fine family. But right now, Matt, I've got to be honest with you. You're the No. 1 suspect in Lance's death," Mathis said.

He watched my expression passively as the color drained from my face. "Mr. Mathis, if you're somehow implying ..."

"Just let me finish," he cut me off. "You may or may not want to talk with me without a lawyer here."

"You're not seriously thinking about charging me with murder?" I was incredulous.

"No, not at this point. But I wanted to give you a heads-up. Listen. You don't have to say a thing. Let me just go over the facts with you and *then* you can decide what you want to do. I want to tell you where we stand with the investigation. This is not a secret, and your lawyer – if you think you need one – will be entitled to this information anyway."

"But ..." I started to protest.

"Matt. Just listen to me for a minute, and then you can talk all you like." He took a long drag from his coffee mug, settled down in the chair behind his desk and propped his foot on a half-open bottom drawer. "You know times have changed. I guess 30 years ago when I first got into this business we'd still be doing things the same way they did when your aunt was a little kid. But now we've got computers, and the Internet, and DNA testing and so on. Amazing. Despite all that, some things never change. In a case like this, the first things you look for are motive and opportunity. Well, you combine the old and the new and what do you know? You can rule a suspect in or out in no time flat.

"First, motive," he continued. "It didn't take my investigator very long on the Internet to figure out that you're in bad shape financially. Credit cards maxed out, late paying bills. Your credit rating has gone to hell in a hand basket since you got yourself fired last fall."

I was beginning to get angry. "Hold on just a minute, Mr. Mathis. I was not fired; I got laid off with most of the rest of upper management when my company was sold. And ..."

"Whatever. The bottom line is that you're broke and in bad need of money. We made a few inquires and it looks like despite all of your efforts you just can't seem to land a job. Your aunt had made no secret of her plans to leave you her estate, or so says our Mr. Morgan. But you were going to be forced to split it with your cousin. Is that motive enough for you? All told his death is worth several hundred thousand dollars to you. Lance was a harmless nobody, and so far as we can tell, nothing was stolen from the house, Mathis said.

"Now, opportunity. You'd be surprised what results you can get from a search warrant scanned and e-mailed to your cell phone company, or your credit card companies, or whoever. I will certainly admit that your story about being in California when your aunt died is probably true, assuming it was you using your cell phone. On the other hand, somebody made several calls to local numbers here in Walkerville after she went into the hospital. Why so?"

I suddenly felt like I was being forced to find excuses. "I was trying to decide whether or not to store my furniture there or haul it back here in a rental truck. I ended up deciding to leave it there."

Mathis continued. "Maybe so. Or you could have been searching for someone to do the dirty deed. But here's the kicker. You say you left California on Sunday morning. We know your mother called you there Saturday afternoon after your aunt died. You also say you didn't arrive here until late Tuesday. Given this heat wave, the medical examiner couldn't really tell when your cousin died – could have been as early as midday Sunday or as late as midday Monday. There's no record of your using any credit card to buy gas or meals or stay in a motel. Where were you between the times you spoke with your mother and finally arrived here on Tuesday?"

"I'd gotten a check as a settlement for my cancelled employment contract. I paid cash, and I slept in the car at rest areas. I'm broke, remember. You said it," I replied sarcastically.

I was mad now.

"Of course, we could also speculate that you drove straight through, which would have put you here during the time frame we figure for Lance's murder." He stared at me, waiting for a response. I sat silently. "Son, we've got some more investigating to do, but I'd consider getting me a good lawyer if I were you. It seems like you've got a lot of explaining to do."

CHAPTER

Eight

I STRODE PURPOSEFULLY OUT OF THE POLICE STATION and stood for a moment facing the city square. The ornate Victorian spires and cupolas of the Adams County courthouse loomed above me. I took a deep breath, tried to calm down and think. Being as objective as I could, given the circumstances, I realized Mathis was just doing his job. His interpretation of the facts, while wrong, was not totally illogical. I knew that I had nothing whatsoever to do with Lance's murder, but would the police try to blame me for it because on the surface I seemed to be the most likely suspect? I headed for Nick's office.

Nick sat behind his desk and laughed. I had told him what happened. Catching his breath, he said, "Those stupid assholes! They are so desperate to make an arrest that they twist their interpretation of the facts to suit whatever preconceived theory they like the most." He leaned forward and assumed a more serious face. "Matt, this is a problem, of course. You and I both know you didn't have anything to do with the murder, and Mathis will eventually figure that out. For the moment, let's not do much of anything. If they contact you again, just refer them to me and I'll handle things. I suspect what will happen is that the forensics reports will start filtering in over the next few days and they'll realize you had nothing to do with it."

He was wrong. As we sat in Nick's office, deputies and investigators were serving my mother with a warrant seeking possession of "any clothing, including, but not to the exclusion of other items, shirts, pants, belts, underwear, socks, and shoes worn by Matthew Rutherford V during the time frame including August 3 through August 6, 2002." With all that had been happening, the laundry had not been done. They hauled away my dirty clothes after giving my mother a receipt.

I arrived back at Rutherford Hall to find an unmarked police car parked in the yard. The investigator was polite, almost apologetic. He presented a warrant, searched through the few things I'd brought over from my mother's and took away my tennis shoes.

I DIDN'T LEAVE THE HOUSE for the rest of the day. The phone calls continued. I didn't answer any of them, letting the machine pick up instead. About a third were expressions of condolence from various out-of-town friends, another third wanted to "inquire about the estate" or something similar, and a third didn't leave any message.

I brooded about how to approach Jack and Maggie. Lance's funeral was the next morning, and I wanted to avoid any possible public confrontation. At dusk I drove to my mother's house. She cried and told me she loved me and didn't believe for a minute that I'd do something like that. Her reaction made me realize she thought the accusations might be true. I drove to my uncle and aunt's house. They both hugged me, and said the "rumors" that were being put out by the police were ridiculous. They said I had their love and full support. I felt better.

At 10 a.m. Saturday, we were once again in the Old Cemetery. Lance's plot was a dozen feet away from Aunt Lillie's plot. The flowers on her grave were wilting in the heat; only the potted yellow chrysanthemums retained their blooms in full glory. This time the crowd was huge. The same minister said essentially the same words, and again, for the second time in less than a week, we suffered through the same ritual.

As we were heading for the cars, a short, purposeful looking man in wire-rimmed glasses approached me and stuck out his hand. He looked somehow familiar, but I didn't know why. "Matt, we haven't met. I'm Doug Smith, commander of the local chapter of the Sons of Confederate Veterans. I wanted to tell you how sorry I am for all your family's losses. Miss Lillie had been real good to us. Do you reckon I could come around and talk with you sometime about some things?"

For some indefinable reason, I liked him immediately. "Uh, sure, I guess. What do we need to talk about?" I couldn't understand why I seemed to think I knew him. And then it came to me. Douglas E. Smith, your friendly State Farm Insurance agent. His picture in the same wire-rimmed glasses over a half-crooked smiled was on half a dozen billboards all over town.

"It's about her historical research. I helped her with it a little bit ..."

"Doug, I've probably had close to two dozen phone calls about Aunt Lillie's papers, and my great-great-grandfather's journals. I really don't think we've decided quite yet what to do with all that."

He smiled and held up his hand. "Gosh, I'm sure you've been pestered. I don't want to buy them or own them or anything like that. I just want to be certain that all of her research doesn't get lost to future generations. I know you've got a lot going on, but if you could call me when you get a free moment, I'd like to talk with you." He reached in his pocket and handed me a card that read *Douglas E. Smith, CLU,* next to a silver-wreathed "Select Agent" designation under a red and white State Farm logo. "My numbers are on the card. You can reach me 24 hours a day." He smiled again and was overtaken by the crowd.

WE WENT BACK TO JACK AND MAGGIE'S HOUSE for a covered dish lunch. I made my excuses and drove back to Rutherford Hall. If I was going to make it through this situation I found myself in, I had to get my thoughts organized. I brewed a strong pot of coffee, poured myself a large mug with lots of sugar, and sat down on the glass-walled porch overlooking the garden to think.

My life was in a mess. As if having my career crash and burn was not enough, I'd foolishly wasted the better part of a year thinking that a job would materialize if I just got the word out about my sterling qualifications. I had run home penniless with my tail between my legs and, within 72 hours of my arrival I'm the prime suspect in a murder. All those bumpkins whom I had grown up with, who'd taken dull but solid jobs at local factories, or as truck drivers or carpenters or plumbers, while I launched salvo after salvo of self-praising news releases for the local newspaper, were now quietly laughing at my fall.

The suspicion of murder was clearly the most pressing problem. The job and the money, or lack thereof, would eventually work themselves out. But even if I was never formally charged with Lance's death and the crime was never solved, the suspicion would remain. That would follow me for the rest of my life. For practical purposes, the only acceptable solution would be the arrest and conviction of the murderer or murderers, or barring that, complete exoneration of me as a suspect.

I tried to think like the police.

First, opportunity. There was practically no way that I could prove my whereabouts for the time I was driving from Palo Alto to Walkerville. I'd taken my time, paying cash for my gas and my food, most of which I picked up at fast food drive-thrus. I'd folded down the back seat of the Explorer and slept in it at rest areas. As if that were not bad enough, I'd cleaned out the car at the last rest stop where I spent the night in Alabama, discarding McDonald's and Wendy's bags and with them the receipts that might offer a reasonable alibi.

Second, motive. That seemed to offer some hope. True, one might think I had a motive if you assumed that I was aware of the potential inheritance and the details of the will. I wasn't but couldn't prove that. But how would that figure in Lance's (or someone's) trashing of the library of Rutherford Hall? He had to have been looking for something. And the phone calls. True, there were a few offering condolences, but the majority were seeking to buy or otherwise acquire items from her estate, the most notable of which was Captain Rutherford's diaries. They were surely valuable, but that couldn't explain Lance's murder.

There had to be something more. Something that was not obvious. There had to be something worth killing for. I needed information, and I wasn't really sure whom I could trust. I thought for a while longer and picked up the phone to call Douglas E. Smith, Select State Farm agent and commander of the local chapter of the SCV.

CHAPTER

Nine

I DIDN'T LEAVE THE HOUSE for the remainder of the day Saturday, politely refusing phone invitations from both my mother and Uncle Jack to accompany them to church Sunday morning. I spent the time going over every room in the big old house, opening drawers and closets, and generally trying to understand what could drive someone to murder.

A 14-foot-wide stair hall stretched from the front to the back of the house. The twin parlors, or more properly, the sitting room and library, were on the front corners. Behind the library was a bedroom that had been converted into Aunt Lillie's study and workspace. Across the stair hall was a large formal dining room that was adjacent to a butler's pantry and the passageway to the kitchen. Some years after the house was built, small-story wings were constructed on each side. In each upstairs wing and by the downstairs bedroom, there were huge, tiled bathrooms with ceramic-footed tubs. This was evidently done when Walkerville constructed a city water system that allowed for indoor plumbing with real running water. On the dining room side, the space was used for china storage. Upstairs, the wide hall was repeated, but the rear opened onto a shuttered sleeping porch. There were four large bedrooms, each with a massive poster bed and armoire. Aunt Lillie had slept in the one over the library; I had installed myself in the one above the dining room. Each major room had a coal-burning fireplace which was vented by one of the two pairs of massive chimneys on each side of the house.

I saved the study for last. It was a big room, about 20 by 20, with a fireplace on the outside wall between two windows. There were two doors, one off the main hall and another leading to the bathroom and dressing room. I noticed that above the original ceramic-handled mortise lock, a new and shiny brass deadbolt had been installed. I surveyed the room. Despite her age and whatever infirmity accompanied it, my aunt had kept a very neat and modern office. She apparently did most of her writing at a library-sized table that sat on a worn oriental carpet in the middle of the room. A recent model computer sat in front of her leather task chair, with cables snaking off to a high-volume laser printer and a scanner next to it. A series of neat stacks of papers, photocopies and correspondence was scattered about – she evidently was a "pile" person, moving her chair around the table to work on whatever project was in each stack. On one wall were five four-drawer filing cabinets plus another smaller table with a fax machine and professional sized photocopier. On the opposite wall a large, roughly constructed bookcase held hundreds of volumes on Southern history and the Civil War.

I spent the better part of an hour basically surveying what was what. The filing cabinets were not locked. Four of the five held lecture notes, photocopies of articles and related research material. The fifth was devoted to her personal financial records. I flipped on the computer. It was a Dell, only a few months old, and powered by a Pentium IV chip with lots of RAM. After a bit of searching, I discovered that she had Internet access via a broadband line. I logged into her e-mail server and was rewarded with 279 new messages – mostly spam – with endless ads for generic Viagra, penis enlargers and low-rate mortgages. Half a dozen were legitimate, all referring to one or another of her current projects, and all dated before her death. I found dozens of text files on her hard drive and on diskettes, but a quick perusal of the file names gave no indication of anything other than ordinary historical research. I decided to put off examining the files in more detail until later and shut off the computer. After hours of searching I still had no clue to indicate anything that might be connected with Lance's death.

I waited until 10 p.m. to venture out to the grocery store. The truth was, I was embarrassed to be seen in public. After all the energy and effort I had expended by way of my incessant news releases to the local paper touting my many successes in the world of high-tech, I had come home a total failure. The additional fact that I seemed to have been designated as the prime suspect in my cousin's murder didn't help. I didn't want to see anyone. I didn't want to have to make excuses. I was rapidly coming to the conclusion that I was pretty much a loser, and that maybe, just maybe, I was the last one to figure it out.

CHAPTER
Ten

DOUG ARRIVED PROMPTLY AT 2 P.M. Sunday afternoon. We talked. He was intelligent, educated and, like Aunt Lillie, was an expert on Civil War history. I couldn't help but like him. Even though he was half a dozen years older than me, he was technically of a younger generation. His great-great-great-grandfather had served as Captain Rutherford's lieutenant before being killed in the battle of New Market, Virginia, in May 1864. I explained the situation to him, holding back nothing.

"Looks like you've gotten yourself into a mud hole. You asked what somebody could be looking for? Well, there're lots of things. You know Miss Lillie kept the originals of diaries in the bank vault. But even if you stole them, they're so unique that you couldn't sell them on the open market. I doubt that's what they were looking for. After someone tried to get into the house several months ago, she said she was going to move all of her jewelry down to the bank, too, so that's out. And you said that as far as anyone can tell, nothing was missing. Maybe everybody is looking in the wrong direction. I'll bet someone is looking for the Rutherford gold."

"Rutherford gold? Not that again." I grew up hearing rumors and fanciful stories about how sometime long ago one or another of my ancestors had discovered or otherwise acquired some hoard of buried gold—all fantasy, I had been assured.

He seemed surprised. "Matt, just how do you think your family got it's money?"

I had never thought of it. We were comfortable, sure, but it never occurred to me to ask. "I presume they inherited it."

"Yeah, well, duh, as the kids say. That's pretty obvious. But did you ever trace it back to see who the first Rutherford with money was? It was Matthew the first, your great-great-granddaddy. I used to help Miss Lillie with her research. The courthouse is full of records going back to the early 1800s. I got curious about it one day and looked it up. Matthew was 21 years old in 1860. He'd finished what passed for college in those days but was still living at home on the farm with his father, William C. The tax records for that year and the 1860 census both show that they were scrounging out a living on 320 acres of rocky ground up in the northern part of the county. The old man stays home, and Sherman comes through and burns him out in November 1864. Meanwhile, the son goes off to war and comes back in 1865 a rich man. By the early 1870s, they owned close to 5,000 acres of land between the two of them, Matthew the first had earned – or bought – himself a seat in the Legislature, and they were suddenly on top. Sorta makes you wonder, doesn't it?"

There were so many variations on the rumor I had long ago ignored them all. "Now, let me get this straight. Are you saying that he stole something, or what?"

"Man, I can't believe you haven't figured this out! You're damned right he stole something–like a big chunk of the gold from the Confederate Treasury."

We talked for two more hours. *The War Diaries of Capt. Matthew Rutherford* spanned the time from his enlistment in the Georgia Guard in 1861 until about a month after his reassignment to Richmond with General Breckinridge in January 1865. Although Captain Rutherford apparently kept a journal beyond that point, the explanation was that it had been lost in the fog of war during the evacuation of Richmond, the Confederate capital. In April 1865, the entire Confederate Government packed up and fled south, hoping to make it to Florida or even Cuba from where they could continue the conflict. With them, they carried the gold and silver from the national treasury, as well as the gold from the vaults of the Richmond banks. Some of the gold coin was spent for provisioning and to pay the troops, and in the end, some was recovered. Much of it, however, seems to have simply disappeared.

"See, that's the key to the whole story." Doug explained. "If that volume had not been lost, and if your granddaddy had owned up to what really happened, a lot fewer people would have had a lot less to explain. And there wouldn't be near as many rumors about how the gold was stolen, or where it's supposed to be buried, or in fact if it even existed. Everybody from President Davis down to the cook got accused of arranging to have the treasure hidden, and every crossroads town within two hundred miles of their escape route has some legend about where they really buried the gold."

I thought about the bookends. The truth is I had totally forgotten the objects with all that had been going on. I told him we'd need to talk again. He left, but not before inviting me to the next meeting of the Sons of Confederate Veterans. I thanked him and said that I was trying to keep a low profile, but that I'd consider it.

Finding the black painted bookend where Eula Mae had placed it on the shelf in the library (propping up a red Morocco-bound set of *Stoddard's Standard Works*), I scraped at the surface with a key. The thick black encrustation flaked away to reveal golden-yellow metal glinting in the afternoon sunlight. In the garage, I found a can of paint thinner. Taking it into the kitchen, I dumped it into one of Aunt Lillie's meat loaf pans. I dropped the bookend in the pan. Three hours later, I was staring at what could only be a gold ingot weighing roughly 4 pounds and bearing the Great Seal of the Confederate States of America.

ON MONDAY AT 7:30 A.M., Eula Mae rang the front door bell and headed off to clean up the house and do the laundry as she had for the past 20 years. Half an hour later, I was drinking coffee in the kitchen when Nick pulled in the back yard and bounded up the tall wooden steps.

"Survive the weekend okay?" Nick seemed in high spirits. "I think it's time we probated Lillie's will, made a quick inventory of the house and checked on the contents of her bank deposit box."

I wondered if he knew what was in it.

"Sure," I said. I had decided to say nothing about the gold ingot. I hadn't found any more in my searches of the house, but presumed that there had been at least two. The mate to the "bookend" I had was apparently the murder weapon.

"Fine, then. Let's do this. I'll get the paper work done at the probate judge's office and meet you at one at the Citizens Bank. We can go through the lockbox, and then spend maybe an hour here doing a rough inventory of the furniture and things. For practical purposes you're now the sole heir, and we really just want to be able to show the IRS that we did our fiduciary duty." I was agreeable.

At 1:10 p.m. we were standing in the vault of the Citizens Bank of Adams County. Nick had presented the proper court orders, and the bank had produced a large pass key for their side of the double lock. In the absence of Lillie's lockbox key – we'd been unable to find it – they had also produced an industrial drill and were drilling away at her side of the lock. A $75 lock replacement charge was made toward the estate.

It was a large box, about 24 inches wide and 36 inches high, embedded in a wall of other large boxes. "Folks around here like to store the family sterling in these big boxes," the bank manager explained. After a few minutes of drilling, the handle was turned and the door opened easily.

I don't know what I expected. Mounds of gold bars, maybe, or cash. Instead there was a neat stack about a foot high of worn, bound journals, the famous diaries of Captain Rutherford. I casually picked up the stack and thumbed through them, searching for the last volume.

The last entry of the last volume was headed "Richmond, February 24, 1865." There was a box of jewelry, a few obviously valuable pieces, but not a lot of it. There were folders of deeds, insurance policies, contracts, etc., all the detritus of a life of 86 years, but no gold. A small sealed envelope lying in the very back of the box caught my eye. On the front in Aunt Lillie's bold script were the words: *"To my nephews Matthew Rutherford V, and/or Lance Rutherford. Personal and Confidential"* The latter phrase was underlined. Nick was distracted with his inventory of the contracts and deeds. He didn't see me slip the envelope into my pocket.

We made formal arrangements for me to take over Aunt Lillie's checking accounts. We left the bank and drove by Nick's office to pick up his secretary and a digital camera. The three of us quickly toured the house, snapping photos in each room while Morgan dictated to his secretary a list of the major items to accompany the photos. He didn't seem particularly interested in any details such as the contents of drawers and cabinets.

In the library, he said only, "I see you and Eula Mae got this place cleaned up right well." Nothing more was mentioned about Lance, or the murder, or me as the prime suspect.

Nick and his secretary left. Eula Mae was dusting upstairs. I went into the front parlor, shutting the sliding doors. I took the letter out of my pocket and stared at it for a moment.

I wasn't quite sure why I hadn't told Nick about it. He had been nothing but good to me, and I had in fact asked for his help with my being a suspect in Lance's death. Deep down, there was something – a lack of trust, or what? And then I remembered. After my father's accident, my dog didn't come home. He had shot my dog.

CHAPTER
Eleven

THE LETTER WAS A SIMPLE, SHORT DOCUMENT. Written in ink on fine, cream-colored, laid stationary, it consisted of two paragraphs.

My Dearest Nephews,

Your reading this indicates that my inevitable death has occurred. You will have one of two reactions, joy or puzzlement. I hope I will have talked with you both. I urge you to make wise use of your good fortune, and not to betray the trust and responsibility that has been placed upon you.

If you have no idea to what I refer, then I have passed away unexpectedly and without fulfilling my long desired obligation to you and our community. I wish you a good life and hope that my estate makes it a more comfortable one for you and your families.

With Love,

Lillie

I had no idea what she was talking about. She had apparently spoken with Lance, and I suspected that the subject of that conversation had gotten him killed.

I thought for a few minutes and called my mother from Lillie's study. "You did go and see Aunt Lillie in the hospital before she died, right?" It was a silly question. My mother never forgets a birthday or anniversary. She writes thank-you notes for the most mundane of occasions and would have been the first to arrive at the most distant relative's bedside in time of sickness.

"Of course, Jack and Maggie took me up to the hospital Wednesday, and I went back every day for a few minutes to check on Lillie. We are – or were – her only family, Matt."

"Did she say she wanted to talk with Lance and me, or the both of us?"

"Yes, as a matter of fact she was rather adamant about it. She made Jack promise to call Lance right away, and I told her you were planning on coming home in the next few days. I didn't think to mention it to you when we talked, but she did keep saying she needed to go over some things with you two. I think it had to do with her estate. I suspect she was worried about the Rutherford diaries, and all her books and papers and so forth."

"Were you there when Lance came by Saturday?"

"No," she paused.

"Matt, what are you looking for? Did you talk with Nick about the police wanting to make you a suspect?"

"Of course I did. I didn't have anything to do with Lance's death – you know that. The cops want to make it all very simple. I think there's something more." I said good-bye and hung up without giving her a chance to ask more questions.

Eula Mae appeared at the door. "I'm all finished. You gon' need me for anything else t'day?"

A light flashed in my head. "Eula Mae. Were you by any chance at the hospital on Saturday when my cousin Lance came to visit?"

"I sure was. I sat with Miss Lillie for a right long spell Saturday. That's my day off, see, and she had done said she was gonna pay me for Thursday when I didn't work. I figured she might need some help with eating or going to the bathroom or something so I just came and stayed there most of the day."

"Were you there when my cousin Lance visited?"

"Oh, yes. And Mr. and Mrs. Bateman, and Preacher Williams, and Mrs. Newsom – I bet there was 20 folks in and out while I was there."

"What did Aunt Lillie say to Lance?"

"Well, now, I don't rightfully know. He came in, and they said hellos for a minute or so, and then she sent me down to the gift shop to get her a hairbrush. When I got back, he was still there, but by then Mr. and Mrs. Barton had come in, and Lawyer Morgan was there. Then the nurse comes in and says there are too many visitors and they all left. I sat there till about 2:30, and I hear she passed real suddenly about 5 o'clock. It's so sad. She'd been doing so much better."

"Did Mr. Morgan talk to Lance?"

"I didn't see them talking, but they did leave about the same time."

"And you're sure you don't have any idea what they talked about?"

She looked a bit put out. "No, sir, I don't. Matter of fact is she still couldn't talk real plain. She'd get her words mixed up and say one thing when she meant another. Or sometimes she couldn't think of the right word. In fact, when I got back with the hairbrush, I saw that she already had one there. I guess she meant to say toothbrush or something ..."

I wrote Eula Mae a check from my aunt's checkbook, signing my name as executor. I told her I'd see her Thursday.

THE NEXT MORNING CHIEF MATHIS CALLED and asked, politely this time, if I could come down to the station for a few minutes. He said I need not bring my lawyer "if you've done got yourself one."

He was polite and a little apologetic. "Matt, maybe we jumped the gun a bit by focusing on you as a possible suspect in your cousin's killing. I've gotten all the preliminary labs back now, and your clothes have no sign at all of any blood on them. The GBI folks tell us that whoever killed Lance should have been splattered pretty well with blood, and since we got at your clothes and shoes before you had a chance to wash them, that moves you down the list. You may have had a theoretic motive and opportunity, but without more evidence you're off the hook." I felt the sun break through the clouds.

"And this." He held up a faxed sheet. "This is the toxicology report on Lance's body. That boy was full of dope. The crime lab found high levels of marijuana, some methamphetamine, and some Ecstasy. When we went over his gear out at Jack and Maggie's farm place last week, we found a good bit of marijuana and paraphernalia. The police in Columbia raided his apartment over the weekend and found some good evidence that your cousin was supporting himself by dealing drugs."

I sat silently.

The Chief continued, "We now figure he had someone with him. They must have gotten half-stoned, broken into the house looking for something to steal and fence, got in a fight and Lance ends up getting killed. That theory ties up most of the loose ends, like for example, the fact that we found Lance's car still parked at the cabin. Now I'm not saying we won't be having some more questions for you, but right now, we're taking the investigation in another direction."

I simply said, "Thanks," and got up to leave.

"Matt," Mathis called my name as I reached the door. "I'm sorry."

I nodded and started to continue out the door when I remembered something. "What about my things? Did you send them to Atlanta, or where? Do I get them back or not?"

That was not what I really wanted to know.

"No. They go to the regional crime lab in Macon. I guess we'll have them back in a week or two. You want me to bring them by?"

"Call me and I'll pick them up. Tell me, Mr. Mathis, do you small-town cops send all of your evidence to the state crime lab?"

"Not all of it." He seemed relieved that I was apparently making conversation and not threatening to sue him. "Only things that need sophisticated testing, like blood or fiber samples. Something simple, like say the murder weapon in this case, we keep here in our evidence room. Why do you ask?"

"Just curious." He'd answered my question. I walked out of his office.

CHAPTER

Twelve

AT THIS POINT, I DIDN'T KNOW WHO I COULD TRUST. I needed some help, for sure, but I had no idea where to turn. If whatever happened was something more than a simple squabble between a couple of dope-heads – as Mathis would like to explain it – I needed to be careful. Maybe it's my basic paranoid nature, but there were just too many loose ends for me to be satisfied with such a neat explanation.

Who could I talk to? My mother was out. Uncle Jack had too much on his plate already with Lance's death, the accusation of drug deal-ing, and so on. I wasn't sure about Nick. Doug Smith? Maybe, but I'd have to get to know him better. I supposedly still had some old friends from high school, but I had not seen or heard from many of them in years. In the end, the only person I could really trust at this point was me. And my track record for the better part of the past year was lit-tered with one bad decision after another.

I decided first to gather as many hard facts as I could. I would then try to determine if I was simply being paranoid, or if Lance's killing did in fact have to do with some hidden hoard of gold instead of a few grams of white powder. When I had figured out as much as possible, I would sit down, put it all together and present it to someone objective. Maybe Nick. Maybe Uncle Jack.

If I was looking for clues, Aunt Lillie's study seemed the place to start. I began with the filing cabinets. Three hours and two pots of coffee later, I decided there was nothing more there than the obvious. She had meticulously kept neat records on her research and writing, all filed in a logical manner. She had notes on things that had interested her, and notes on future manuscripts that would never be written. Other than a fairly thick file folder on the last days of the Confederate government and half a dozen scholarly articles on the Confederate treasury, no mention was made of any stolen gold.

The computer was next. My aunt was evidently what the marketers like to call an "early adopter," someone who will embrace a product or technology at the time of its release and account for many of the first sales. She obviously had been computer literate since the late 1980s. There were stacks and stacks of 3.5-inch floppy disks, all clearly labeled with the file name, date and subjects contained thereon. Beginning in the mid-1990s, it looked like she'd switched to 100 Megabyte Zip disks. For the past couple of years, it looked like she'd been recording her work on CDs. I set up the computer to search for a series of keywords and started the laborious process of scanning all of her files. I looked for "gold," "Lance," "Matt," "treasury," "hidden" and a dozen others. I got hit after hit on individual words, but nothing whatsoever to shed any light on the gold ingots bearing the Confederate Seal used as bookends in the library.

It is sometimes strange how little things make all the difference. My mother has a needle phobia. It started when she was a child and stepped on a sewing needle that had accidentally been dropped on the carpet. The needle had lodged in one of the bones of her foot and broken off, necessitating surgery under local anesthesia to remove it. It was apparently quite a painful ordeal, and thereafter she never was barefooted outside of her bed and the bathroom. Even the most mundane 6-foot trip to the bathroom from her bed in the middle of the night necessitated her turning on the light and finding her hard soled slippers based on the possibility, however remote, that there might be a needle lurking in the carpet.

Perhaps needless to say, the necessity of covering one's feet in the house for protection from sewing needle sticks was foisted upon me from early childhood. I didn't think it strange at the time; after all, my mother explained that she was simply being protective of her only child. It was when I started going to sleepovers at friends' houses that I realized that most 8-year-olds don't routinely wear bedroom slippers. By the time I was ten, I was in full rebellion, cramming my obligatory slippers in the bottom of my knapsack when I spent the night with friends, and going barefooted outside whenever I was out of my mother's sight. By the time I left for college, slippers had been deleted from my wardrobe, much to my mother's voiced consternation. And by dint of habit, I usually took off my shoes when I came home and padded around the house barefoot or in socks.

As I was leaving Aunt Lillie's study, my bare foot detected an irregularity near the edge of the oriental carpet in front of the fireplace. There seemed to be a small depression that I felt rather than saw. With some effort, I managed to move the worktable over toward the hall door. The carpet was still held down on both ends by the filing cabinets on one side and the book-laden shelves on the other. I took the files out of two of the cabinets and moved them to allow me to fold back the carpet just enough to get a look at what I felt. I could barely see the edge of what appeared to be an access panel of some sort cut in the wide pine planks of the floor. Evidently it was not new. What I was feeling with my foot was a small loose board that lifted out easily when I pried at the edge with a pair of scissors. Under this was a folding pull handle.

My heart beating rapidly, I unloaded the books from the shelves and managed to tug the shelves back such that I could now fold the carpet back enough to see the entire door. To the casual observer it would not have been obvious. The flooring planks were roughly 10 inches wide, and the one give-away would have been that the ends of three boards lined up about three feet apart, clearly outlining an area roughly 30 by 36 inches. It could have been a spot where the floor had been repaired, but with the small panel removed and the handle exposed, it was undoubtedly a trap door.

I tugged at the handle and the flooring lifted up easily. I found myself staring at what appeared to be the top of a locked metallic strongbox. It was big and old, filling most of the space and clearly designed for security. I tapped on it with the scissors – it appeared to be made of thick steel, with reinforced riveted sides and two folding handles on either side of the top. In the middle was a key hole with an adjacent lever. Both appeared well oiled. I tried the lever but it didn't move.

I studied the lock. It was clearly old, but I presumed in good working order in that someone – my aunt? – kept it clean and oiled. I retrieved the ring of keys that I had found on my first night in the house and tried any that might work. None fit.

At this point I was in no mood to waste time. I glanced at my watch. 9:35 p.m. The local Wal-Mart closed at 10. I placed the rug back in over the trap door and moved the table over the spot. Grabbing one of my aunt's checks from her checkbook, I drove the two miles to the shopping center in less than five minutes. I chose a heavy industrial drill, two sets of carbide bits, a hammer, a large brick chisel and a small pry bar.

The one open register was manned by a sloe-eyed blond in her early 20s dressed in a blue Wal-Mart vest with a large name tag that said, "Brandi." She only fleetingly looked like the other Brandi, but it occurred to me that I had been too long without female company. She eyed me suspiciously. I smiled. "Not planning any late night B and E, are you?" she asked.

"B and E?"

"You know, like breaking and entering. That's what put my boyfriend in jail for 18 months." She smiled this time and looked at me with a long pause. Was she hitting on me?

"Just doing some late night repairs."

"Oh. You new around here? I haven't seen you before."

"Yes, I just moved back to town, and I'm in a bit of a hurry. Do you suppose …?"

"Sorry," she said and rang up the tools. The total was $106.56.

I pulled out my aunt's check and filled it out. She looked at the name and looked at me. "This is not your check. We can't take your check unless it has your name on it."

"Sorry, see my aunt just died and I'm her executor. It's all been arranged with the bank for me to sign."

"You got any ID? Maybe I need to call the manager."

"Look," I said. "I really need to get back to what I was doing. You do take credit cards?"

She looked relieved. It was getting near closing time. "Sure, that's fine." I handed her a MasterCard with my name on it. She studied it. "You're that fellow from California who's staying in the Rutherford place. I've heard about you. Your brother got murdered."

"Cousin."

"Yeah. Cousin. Whatever."

"That's me." The computer rejected the card. I handed her another, a Visa this time. The transaction went through.

She held the receipt and hesitated. "You sure I don't need to check this with the manager?"

"It's not necessary, I assure you. What time do you get off, Brandi?"

She smiled and handed me the receipt to sign. "Well, I'm off in about 15 minutes, if you had something in mind."

"I do, but not tonight. Maybe later."

"Promise?"

"I promise." She handed me the sack and I was out the door.

CHAPTER
Thirteen

BACK AT THE HOUSE, I MOVED THE TABLE, folded back the carpet and opened the trap door. I had spent a summer in high school working as a flunky at a local self-storage facility. One of my jobs was to cut or otherwise open the locks of non-payers for inventory of the rental unit contents prior to a lien sale. It seemed at the time a useless skill to acquire, but who knows when one might need to do a little "B and E"?

The lock was an old-fashioned, warded lock requiring a large, flat key. When inserted in the lock, it swept through a maze of cut-outs to release a catch so the lever could be turned to retract the bolts that held the door shut. Theoretically such locks are less secure from picking than the modern pin-tumbler type, but from the vantage point of an amateur would-be safe cracker, they are a formidable challenge.

I plugged in the drill and studied the situation. Inserting a 3/8-inch carbide bit, I began to drill a series of closely spaced holes about an inch out from the key hole. The 19th century steel yielded quickly to the 21st century tools. In less than 15 minutes, I had completely encircled it. I placed the end of the chisel just inside the ring of holes, and with a few sharp blows from the hammer, the steel between several on one side snapped. I then hammered the chisel into the opening, and using it as a lever, pried open a space big enough to insert the pry bar. With all my weight, I leaned on the end of the bar and the now-serrated ring covering the lock mechanism popped out.

I quickly found the pin that locked the lever in place and pulled it back with a ballpoint pen. The lever moved freely, retracting the bars that secured the top to the chest. I tugged on the handles and it opened easily.

To my surprise, the chest contained a modern, white, Styrofoam ice chest. Opening this, I found several Zip-Loc freezer bags and a pint-sized canister of dehumidifying granules. There were three plastic bags, each firmly sealed and each containing a book of some sort. I took the ice chest out of the steel vault. In the bottom were two more dehumidifying canisters but nothing else. I laid the plastic bags on the big table and opened them one at a time, starting with the smallest.

The first book was bound in gray leather and stamped in tarnished gold on the front, *"Souvenir Volume of the Reunion of Confederate Veterans, Atlanta, Georgia, April 1875."* It was in remarkably good shape for its age and appeared to have spent most of its existence stored in a dry, light-free place. The second and slightly larger volume was also bound in gray leather. It was entitled *Generals of the Confederacy, with Personal and First-Hand Accounts of their Genius and Bravery as Witnessed in the Recent Glorious Struggle.* The frontispiece listed the author as Bradford E. Sanders and the publisher as Broadnax Press of Atlanta. The date, in Roman numerals, indicated that it was published in 1874. It, too, was in pristine condition.

The third and largest volume barely fit inside a two-gallon freezer bag. It was a cloth-bound ledger with a leather spine, much worn and badly stained. On the front I could make out "Cash Journal." I opened the front and read the first line, written in a bold and now-familiar script:

February 25, 1865. Saturday. It would appear that the end of our struggle approaches rapidly.

It was the missing journal of my great-great-grandfather.

I rapidly thumbed through the diary. Eighty-seven of 100 pages had been filled with script. I perused it without reading it. Some entries were written in ink with a firm hand. Others seemed barely legible, written with small cramped letters in pencil lead. I noted some days' notes covered three or four pages while others were only a couple of sentences. The last entry was from late April, so the whole manuscript covered less than two months. In two months, however, Jefferson Davis and the Confederate government had fled south, Richmond had fallen, and Lee had surrendered at Appomattox Courthouse.

I shut the journal and stared for a moment at the cover. Closing the Zip-Loc bag, I gingerly placed it back in the Styrofoam chest. If this document contained what I thought it contained, it could rewrite history. It could shed light on why my cousin was murdered. It might make me rich.

CHAPTER
Fourteen

I TURNED MY ATTENTION to the two leather-bound books. Their carefully preserved condition and their location in the hidden vault with the "missing" volume of my great-great-grandfather's diaries would certainly indicate that someone – presumably my aunt – placed great value on them. Whether or not they were somehow tied to the gold ingots, or somehow related to Lance's murder, was less clear.

I flipped through the books quickly. The first seemed to be an expensive souvenir album of a Confederate Veterans Reunion held in Atlanta 10 years after the war. It clearly had been printed after the event; there were half a dozen photos of groups of middle-aged, bearded men lined up with regimental flags, and what appeared to be transcripts of the speeches given at a couple of banquets. I noted that my great-great-grandfather, who by this time was in the State Legislature, gave a keynote address entitled "The South in the Last Quarter of the Century."

The second volume, while well-bound, was printed on cheaper paper, now yellowed and brittle with age. It contained biographies of a dozen of the better-known Confederate generals, including Lee, Jackson, Wheeler and Breckinridge. I noted that a small slip of paper stuck between the pages marked a spot in the chapter on Breckinridge. Opening to the page, a penciled arrow in the margin pointed at a sentence that started, "With his trusted adjutant, Captain Matthew Rutherford, General Breckinridge answered the call of President Davis in accepting ..." It appeared someone had saved both books because of their connection to my great-great-grandfather. I was putting the books back in protective bags when it occurred to me that these books looked familiar. I had seen them before. In the library. In pieces.

I tugged open the massive pocket doors separating the library from the hall and turned on a lamp. There was still a faint, foul smell of death. The carpet had not been returned from the cleaners. Protected from sunlight, the longleaf pine flooring under where it had been was a lighter shade, except for an irregular, darker spot where Lance's body had lain. The vandalized books were lying in a pile next to the smashed tables on the hearth. There were a total of six volumes in the pile. All seemed to have been damaged in the melee, but only two were ripped apart, copies of the same two I had found in the vault. I gathered the pieces and began to sort it out.

I started with the reunion volume first. Despite being scattered, the pages were numbered so it was no problem to put them back in order. After about 10 minutes, I realized that the book was complete. None of the pages were missing. I reassembled the volume of biographies. Same thing. No missing pages. Yet, the covers of both books had been ripped off, and the individual pages that had been bound together were separated and scattered.

The logical conclusion was that a note or instructions had been bound in the spine of the book, or something. I gathered up the disassembled parts and took them to the kitchen where there was lots of light. I dumped them in two piles on the table, pulled up a chair and began to examine each piece in detail.

First of all, it didn't make sense that two or more people fighting would totally rip apart two books. Certainly in the struggle a number of books were damaged, but these two had been completely torn apart. In the end, they were mixed up with the rest of the damage in the fight that followed, a clue not recognized by the local police. I laid out the pieces of both books and went over them centimeter by centimeter. I saw no evidence that anything had been pasted under the spine, and I could identify no markings or notes on any pages. The book had been sewn in individual sections of sixteen sheets each. They in turn had been sewn together to make the volume. The covers were pasted on, leather on the outside and moiré fabric for the endpapers inside. A separate, leather spine was attached. All the pieces were there. I rechecked the page numbers to be sure I hadn't missed anything.

I was about to give up when I noticed something in the remains of the volume of biographies. There was a scrap of paper stuck to the outside bottom of the fold of the folio that contained pages 65 to 96. It looked like there had been an extra sheet sewn into the binding. When the yellowed and brittle paper was removed, this corner was held by a bit of glue that had dripped when the spine was applied. I quickly checked the other volume but couldn't find anything similar.

I retrieved the two books that I'd found hidden with the missing diary and brought them into the kitchen to look at them in the bright light. Opening the intact volume to page 64, I discovered an unnumbered sheet of nonsense words between pages 64 and 65, and another similar sheet between pages 96 and 97. This was what was missing. I searched through the intact reunion volume leaf by leaf. I found similar pages between pages 16 and 17, and between 32 and 33. If the same book that had been torn apart had similar pages, the pages were missing.

It was now long after midnight. I photocopied the pages of nonsense words, eight sheets in all. I put the trashed books back on the library hearth and the intact books back in their protective bags. Grabbing photocopies and the three books I'd found in the vault, I stuffed them next to me in the bed, laid the shotgun within arm's reach and tried to get some sleep.

CHAPTER

Fifteen

THE FOLLOWING DAY DAWNED BRIGHT, sunny and considerably cooler. An unusual shift of the jet stream had brought some relief from the heat wave that had gripped the South for the past month. Rain was expected later in the week. I heard lawnmowers in the yard and emerged to find half a dozen men dressed in green T-shirts mowing and pruning. The supervisor, a short, dark-skinned man with a Spanish accent, introduced himself as Arturo and said that Aunt Lillie had, as usual, contracted with their landscape firm to maintain the grounds of Rutherford Hall. All was paid in advance; they'd come by every couple of weeks. I said thanks and went back in to make some coffee.

After being certain all the doors were locked, I laid out the three books from the vault on the kitchen table. I needed to read the journal in detail. I needed to figure out the significance and meaning of the nonsense words from the books. The journal would take time; I started with the photocopies from the books.

The first one I'd discovered from the volume of biographies consisted of four pages of letters grouped in random patterns – presumably in words. The words, if that was what they were, varied in length from one to 10 or 12 letters. They had been typeset with even right and left margins. The pages from the reunion volume were different. They also had been typeset with even right and left margins, but unlike the other book, the letters – with an occasional number mixed in – were all capitals and not grouped into what one would assume were words. The regular arrangement resembled a grid of some sort. The top line and bottom lines consisted of arrows pointing downward. The assumption would have to be that all this represented a code of some sort. I did not have the faintest idea as to where to start.

The phone rang. It was Nick. "Thought I'd call and check on you. You finding everything you need?"

"Sure, at least I think so." I told him I was a bit embarrassed to get out in public. I didn't like the kind of notoriety that allows sales clerks at Wal-Mart to connect you to a murder the minute they learn your name.

"Hey, you need to chill a little." Nick was his usual confidant self. "This is a small town, you're a member of a prominent family, and it's a slow gossip week. Hell, if it were football season, you'd be long forgotten by now."

"Still," I replied. "Look, Nick, I think I'll get out of town for a few days. Maybe go to Atlanta. Look up some old friends." In truth, I had nothing in mind.

"How about going to Savannah? Get a room at the Hyatt that looks out on the river. Eat a little restaurant food. Have a drink or two. Lots of college girls down there on River Street in those bars – Hell, I could tell you a story or two," He paused.

An idea occurred to me. "How about antiques? I always like poking around in antique shops."

"Matt, you don't strike me as the type to waste a good Saturday looking at old furniture." Nick was right. He continued, "But if that's what you want, they've got more than you can shake a stick at."

"It's something to do. After all I just inherited a house full of them. Might as well learn something, or see what I can get if I try to sell them."

Nick took a serious tone. "I hope you're not thinking of selling off

Rutherford Hall in bits and pieces. It's really a treasure – and you know that a lot of the furniture is original to the house."

"Don't worry, Nick. I just need a change of pace. Nothing's for sale. I'm not leaving." I was surprised to hear myself say that.

I carefully rearranged the study, so that to the casual observer, it would appear undisturbed. I put the missing journal in its plastic bag and the gold ingot in a small gym bag, packing the two books and clothes for a couple of nights in another. I drove to the bank, safely stored the gym bag with the valuables in the lock box and cashed a check on Aunt Lillie's account for $1,000. I knew I couldn't count on the credit cards.

Three hours later, I was in a river view room at the Savannah Hyatt, sipping on a beer from room service and pouring over the yellow pages under "Antique Dealers." It didn't take me long to find what I wanted. I circled two promising shops specializing in old books, checked the location on the map in the phone book and discovered I could walk to both. I finished my beer, ripped the pages out of the phone book, folded and stuffed them in my jeans, grabbed my partially emptied gym bag and set out for a walk.

Savannah is a beautiful city. It was laid out in the 1730s on a high bluff overlooking the river of the same name. The grid of streets running parallel and perpendicular to the river is regularly interrupted by intimate tree-lined squares whose live oaks shade wrought iron benches and statues of Revolutionary War heroes. The first shop on my list was at the corner of one such square, the proprietors living in the Georgian mansion facing the square, while their bookshop occupied the former carriage house opening on a side street. The small faded sign said "B. Planer, Antiquarian Booksellers."

I opened the door to a small, low-ceilinged foyer. My presence was announced by a jangling bell disturbed by the door. The light was dim, but a firm female voice from a doorway to the right called, "Come on in."

I peered in the room. As my eyes adjusted to the relative darkness,

I could make out a large book-lined room with two large glass display cases in the middle. Behind a counter on the other side sat a thin elegant woman, her black-streaked white hair pulled back in a bun. She wore a blue linen dress and white pearls, and seemed overdressed for the occasion. She acknowledged my presence without smiling.

"Can I help you?"

"You do specialize in old books?" I asked. It was a dumb question.

"Look around you." She paused, sizing me up. "What are you selling?"

"How do you know I'm not buying?"

"I've been in this business too long. Anybody your age who walks in this shop with a bag on their shoulder is selling. Usually some family book. Sometimes inherited. Sometimes stolen." She paused again, staring at my eyes and waiting for my reaction. "I'll venture yours is inherited."

I opened the gym bag and withdrew the two leather-bound volumes that I had found in the vault. I took them out of their plastic bags and carefully laid each on the counter, their covers facing the old woman. "I'm Matt Rutherford." She eyed the books and didn't respond. The bad news must not have reached Savannah. She opened each book carefully, turning the pages one by one.

After five minutes of silence, she said, a bit more cordially, "I was sorry to hear of your aunt's death. Her name was well known in this household." I'd been wrong.

She looked up at me. "So why did you bring these here? Surely a Rutherford has not been reduced to selling the family jewels?"

There was a tinge of sarcasm in her voice.

"No," I lied. I'd been doing a lot of that lately. "We were doing an appraisal of the estate for tax purposes, and we had a question about these two books." I had no idea who we meant.

"They appear to be in good shape, but there appears to have been some misprinting, or a flaw in the binding or something. The appraisers were divided as to how to value them. I was going to be in Savannah anyway, and volunteered to bring them by to let you have a look at them. You were highly recommended." The crumpled yellow pages were burning in my pocket. She smiled for the first time.

"Let me get my husband."

She disappeared down a small hall toward the big house. I looked around the room. It was filled with hundreds of leather-bound volumes in all shapes, sizes and hues. There was a musty smell of dust and old leather. A dehumidifier hummed quietly in the corner. The cases displayed open volumes with neatly typed cards by each, giving title, provenance, significance and price. Very, very expensive volumes, I thought.

Presently Mrs. Planer reappeared, pushing a white-headed man in a wheelchair. His right leg had been amputated above the knee. "Allow me to introduce my husband, Bernard Planer. Bernard, this is Matt Rutherford, Lillie's nephew."

Unlike his wife, Bernard smiled immediately and sincerely. He, too, was formally dressed in a light linen suit with white starched shirt and a meticulously tied silk tie. "Pleased to meet you, Mr. Rutherford. Your dear aunt was a friend for many years. Lately though, I've been in poor health – please forgive me for not standing." He held my hand with a firm grip. "My wife says that you'd like an opinion about your books. That's our business. Do you want a formal appraisal or just a quick opinion? The latter's free."

"Oh, I imagine we'll need a formal opinion at some point, not only of these but quite a few others. Right now we're just sorting out the more difficult items."

His wife reached under the counter and drew out a high-intensity lamp which she set on the counter and focused on his lap. She handed him first the reunion volume. He ran his thin pale fingers over the cover and slowly turned the pages, pausing occasionally to study one thing or another. I noticed a slight involuntary tremor. He stopped momentarily when he came to the page of nonsense letters. "What is this?" he asked to no one in particular.

"Well, that's one of the things we had a question about. We thought ..."

He raised his hand for me to be quiet. He finished with the first volume and examined the second, again pausing at the pages with the grid of letters and numbers. I kept silent.

Several minutes later he said, "Very nice books, Mr. Rutherford. Excellent condition. Remarkable state of preservation. But at the very best they may be worth a couple of hundred dollars each. Hardly unique."

"What about those pages of jumbled letters and words? We were not sure if they'd detract from the value."

Bernard the bookseller smiled and looked at me with a curiously wry grin. "Well, Matt, it looks as if you've discovered, or perhaps I should say rediscovered, the famous Rutherford Cipher."

I swallowed hard.

CHAPTER

Sixteen

"MATT, YOU DON'T MIND IF I CALL YOU by your Christian name, do you? Let's be honest with one another." Bernard looked at me with amused intensity.

"I don't believe for a moment that you arrived in this shop on someone's recommendation, or that you are truly interested in the value of these books. No, I suspect you're curious about the legend of the Rutherford gold and somehow have arrived at the conclusion that these, these 'codes,' or whatever you want to call them, somehow hold the key to finding it. I do hate to disappoint you," he said.

I saw no sense in lying. "Mr. Planer, I apologize, you're right, but let me explain."

"You don't need to apologize or explain. You should be thankful for the whim of fate that caused you to stumble into this humble establishment. I believe that I can save you a lot of time and disappointment. But I don't mean to be rude. How is your family?"

Omitting the exact circumstances, I explained to them that I'd been living in California and had decided to move home about the time of my aunt's death. I briefly mentioned my cousin's death, again deleting the details, and that I was now the sole heir to her estate. I said that she seemed to place some special value on these books because she'd taken such good care of them, and that pricked my interest. I admitted I'd found the establishment of B. Planer, Antiquarian Booksellers in the yellow pages.

"Since I had to be in Savannah anyway on some other business," I lied, "I thought I might find out if these books had any special significance or monetary value. And, yes, I was curious about those pages."

Bernard laughed. There was a rattle in his chest. He coughed. His wife sat impassively. I still did not know her given name.

"Let me tell you the story, and I'll start with the ending first. The quick and short answer is that the object of your curiosity is nothing. A meaningless mélange of letters. But that didn't stop some folks in the early part of the last century for getting rather excited about it. That's how I first met your aunt. A strikingly beautiful women in her day, by the way," he said.

Mrs. Planer scowled.

"It was not long after World War II," he continued, "about 1949 or 1950, if my memory serves me. I was on a buying trip to New York. Our particular field of expertise is books from and about the South, so I was surprised when a younger dealer I'd just met offered to sell me an excellent copy of this book for an outrageous price." He held up the volume of biographies. "Even then it would have been worth only a few dollars, but he wanted a thousand or more, as I recall, and told me it contained the 'famous Rutherford Cipher', of which I'd never heard. He told me some complicated tale of gold stolen in the last days of the Civil War from the Confederate Treasury, and that it had been buried, and that only three men had known where, and so on, and so on. Anyway, he purported that the key to the location was contained in these pages of what he called 'coded text' and that, if found, the hoard would be worth millions. He wouldn't tell me much more, but he did mention Walkerville and Rutherford. Naturally, I didn't buy the book, and more or less forgot about it. Retrospectively, it would seem that he'd been scammed into buying the book and was trying to recoup his losses by unloading on me.

"As fate would have it, about three months later, your lovely aunt walked in the door of our shop looking for an out-of-print volume on the South during Reconstruction, and I made the connection between the name and the town. We talked and found that we shared a number of common interests. We became close friends."

His wife suddenly rose and rushed out of the room. I did not want to ask Bernard to define "close friends."

"She was, of course, quite aware of the legend of how the Rutherford fortune got its start and assured me it was totally false." He paused and looked around to assure himself that we were alone in the room. "I knew her very well. I don't think she would have lied to me about anything. Captain Rutherford was your grandfather with, what, three greats?"

"Two," I replied.

"Anyway, the story goes that your grandfather ended up in Richmond at the end of the war. The legend is that he, another captain from Atlanta named Bradford Sanders, and a third officer, Josef Hermann, a Jewish immigrant originally from Germany but living in Savannah at the start of the conflict, supposedly conspired to divert and bury a fortune in gold bullion. The story has it that the deed was done with the knowledge, if not the blessing, of one or more cabinet members to keep the treasure from falling into the hands of the Federals.

"I don't recall the exact dates, but Captain Hermann died of typhus around 1875. I don't think he had any family — not in this country, at least. Captain Rutherford died sometime around 1910. Bradford Sanders, the author of this book, died a few years later. He had no direct heirs. In the late teens, several copies of the Sanders book surfaced containing these pages of gibberish. I have no idea how the rumor got started or where the name 'Rutherford Cipher' came from, but for a decade or more in the 1920s, some of the best mathematicians in America worked to 'decode' this text. About that time someone came up with a copy of this book with its 'mysterious' text." He held up the reunion volume. "That only added fuel to the fire. Finally, around 1930, a bookseller in New Orleans solved the problem, much to everyone's disappointment. There was no gold. These books contain printer's errors, Matt. Nothing more, nothing less. Simply printer's errors." He smiled. His attention seemed to drift off for a moment. Was he thinking of Lillie?

CHAPTER

Seventeen

MRS. PLANER REAPPEARED IN THE ROOM and took her place behind her husband. Her eyes were red and her makeup slightly smeared.

The old bookseller continued. "I think I can best illustrate the solution to the Rutherford Cipher with a little show-and-tell. How much do you know about printing and bookbinding, Matt?"

"I spent five years in California in the information technology business. Words exist only as 0s and 1s. Need I say more?"

"Such a waste. Allow me a bit of pedantry. Esther, let's show young Rutherford our workshop."

So her name was Esther.

Silently, Esther wheeled her husband down the narrow, dimly lighted hall toward the house. We crossed a courtyard and entered through a paneled door into a small foyer with a polished brass grate on the other side. Pulling open the grate, she rolled the chair into a small elevator and motioned for me to follow. She pressed a large lever to one side and we moved slowly up past the first and second floors. On the third floor, she pulled back the grate and said in a toneless voice. "Welcome to our world, Mr. Rutherford."

The room was huge. It occupied the entire upper story of the elegant, old mansion. Massive windows hung with tattered curtains, looked out on the square. An elevated platform, that must have been a small stage, was at the opposite end of the room. A concave ceiling was covered with a faded trompe l'oeil of clouds surrounding a god-like figure. Diminutive cherubim and seraphim hovered around the edges, peering down to the floor below, a floor covered with boxes and stacks of books. In the center were three long worktables equipped with fluorescent work lights. On the one-time stage, half a dozen intricate, antique printing and binding machines stood silently like some Borgian orchestra.

"The former owners – my forebears in this case – entertained well," Bernard explained. "In this day and age we have little use for a ballroom, hence our workspace amidst this faded glory." Rolling his chair to one of the worktables, he motioned me to stand by his side.

"Let me give you a little primer on bookbinding, Matt. I won't bore you with the details of history, but suffice it to say that since the advent of movable type in the mid-fifteenth century, printing technology has steadily advanced. Volumes from the latter third of the 19th century represent a mixed bag. You have some that were printed and bound very much as they were 100 years earlier, and some others using technology not appreciably different from that of a hundred years later.

"Let's take an individual page," Bernard said as he held up a single sheet of paper. "This has two sides, back and front. Theoretically it would require one run through a printing press for each side, clear?"

I nodded.

"That's not very efficient, but if I folded the paper like this, and made the fold the spine of the book, I could have four pages. If I folded it again," which he did, "I could have eight pages, and so on. Hence most old manuscripts were printed on very large sheets of paper which were then creased and cut to produce more pages with the same effort.

"One thing that has remained constant is that most books, both then and now, are made up by joining together groups of these bound pages, called *quires*, into a larger single group which is referred to as a book. The most common size of a quire is sixteen pages, which is made from a large sheet that folded three times. Here's a late 19th century volume that I'm rebinding. Look at this." The individually bound quires were clearly seen.

"Now as you can imagine, with all the folding and manipulation of the sheets, centering of the printed type on the page is most important. In setting up their presses, most printers would have a dummy set of type to run a few test sheets prior to the actual press run of the manuscript. This was to check print margins, alignment, inking and so forth. I think even now a number of popular computer publishing programs use dummy text that you simply click and replace. A long way from cellulose and ink, but the same concept." I nodded. He was right.

"Hence to the books at hand. Sometimes these printed sheets used to check alignment would get accidentally bound into the finished volume, particularly in semi-automated shops like the ones that bound the books you brought in. They may look mysterious, but they're not. They are simply errors in printing and binding that escaped what we would now call quality control. In the end, a good story, but much ado about nothing."

I WANDERED BACK TO THE HOTEL SLOWLY, taking time to read the historic markers, sitting every now and then for a few moments in a shady square to watch the tourists pass by in their horse-drawn carriages. Was Lance killed because of some long-debunked rumor of hidden gold? Or were the stories true and Bernard and the others the ones had been fooled?

The last diary would have to hold the key, but it was more than hundred miles away locked up in a bank vault. I decided I needed a drink.

IT WAS NEARLY 8 P.M. WHEN I ARRIVED back at the Hyatt. I stashed the gym bag with the books in my room and headed for the bar. Happy hour was over, the drinks-before-dinner crowd had gone and the place was empty except for two elderly couples with loud northern accents complaining about the South in general, especially the gnats. I hadn't noticed.

I took a seat at a window table and ordered a double Maker's Mark and water. After half a decade in California, my tastes usually ran to wine, but I was home and stressed. The waitress brought a bowl of salty snacks and asked if I wanted to run a tab. I nodded and she disappeared behind the bar.

I nursed my drink and watched the boats on the river. A noisy crowd of convention-goers wandered in, declared the place "dead" and headed for River Street. Three women in their early 30s breezed in and sat at the table next to mine. I could see from their name tags they were attending a bankers' conference. They ordered gin and tonics and vodka martinis and were on their third round by the time I ordered my second drink. One of the three left, and, after some tittering, the blond nearest me turned and asked, "Are you local?"

"Do I look local – or should I try to act the part?"

"No, I'm sorry. We're just from out of town and this is our first trip to Savannah. The conference was over this evening and we wanted to go out. Thought you might know of a good restaurant, or club, or whatever. Hey, why don't you join us?" Her name tag said "Julie", and she introduced her friend, a striking woman with streaked blond hair as Pam. "We're from Louisville." She pronounced it "Lou-e-ville."

"I take it that's the one in Kentucky. The Louisville here in Georgia is near my hometown, but we pronounce it with the 's.' " They giggled. They were too old to giggle.

"I'm Matt Rutherford from Walkerville."

"Where's that?"

"Near Louisville, if that tells you anything. About two hours from here toward Atlanta."

We talked. A slightly overweight and seriously overdressed banker with neatly coiffed hair came in the bar. They hailed him over and introduced him as Bill, the branch manager for whatever bank they worked for in Kentucky. They had another drink. It was decided we should all go out to dinner. Bill called Elizabeth's on 37th on his cell phone. He spoke for a moment, pressed the mute button and said, "They've got a table for two if we can get there in fifteen minutes, or they can seat us all if we wait until 10:30."

Julie said, "I'm really hungry."

Pam said, "I'm not."

I said, "Why don't you guys go. Pam and I can wander on down to River Street and catch some food in one of the pubs." Julie and Bill left.

As they walked out, Pam said, "She's been after him for a long time. I guess she'll get lucky tonight."

"And you?"

Twenty minutes later we were in her room, entwined on the sofa. A bottle of champagne was half empty and she was tugging at my belt. "Don't you think the bed would be better?" Pam asked.

"Depends what you had in mind."

Two hours later, I was awakened by the sound of a phone. I was still half drunk, but groped in the darkness for the receiver. Pam had picked it up. "Oh, hi, honey." A pause. "Well, I was going to call, but we went out and it was late. I just came back to the room and crashed. They've really been working us to death down here." Another pause. "Good. Sounds great. I'll see you tomorrow afternoon, then." A pause. "Love you, too."

It occurred to me that I hadn't asked her last name.

CHAPTER
Eighteen

I HAD INTENDED TO SPEND A COUPLE OF DAYS in Savannah. I thought I needed it, or deserved it. The events of the day before had me obsessed, and besides, I was nursing a well-deserved hangover.

Pam had kicked me out of her room sometime around 5 a.m., making excuses about "maybe it would be a little hard to explain if someone saw you here" and the like. Not that that stopped her from taking advantage of my willing body one last time before I left – or was it the other way around?

I stumbled up to my room and crashed, only to be awakened by the persistent knocking of the maid several hours later. Sunlight was streaming in the window. I groped for the clock on the bedside table. 10:04 a.m. My head was throbbing. My mouth felt like I'd been licking dust. I ordered a pot of coffee, a bowl of fruit and Alka-Seltzer from room service before dragging myself into the shower.

An hour later, I was feeling well enough to function. I checked out in the lobby, paying cash, and called for my car. As I was waiting on the valet attendant, an airport mini-van pulled up and a mixed group of a dozen or so travelers that had been waiting in the lobby piled in. Pam and Julie were among them. Pam saw me and waved. She started to come over and speak but thought about it, hesitated and got on the bus without looking back. My head pounded. I didn't care.

The quickest way home was by Interstate 16, an undistinguished stretch of divided highway connecting the port city of Savannah to the central Georgia city of Macon. The claim to fame for I-16 is its monotony as it stretches through endlessly repeating vistas of open flat fields interspersed with planted pines whose straight green rows disappear into wooded darkness. The infrequent exits lead to narrow, paved two-lane roads that wend their way toward dying and forgotten towns with names like Soperton or Stillmore. Occasionally the lanes wander apart, trapping some interesting bit of terrain between them. Just beyond Milepost 97, I caught a fleeting glance of the sunlight reflecting from a lake hidden amongst tall oaks and pines in the wide median. Stuck on the edge of the mowed shoulders every few miles are white crosses, some adorned with names or dates or fading plastic flowers commemorating another driver lulled to sleep by the repetitious sameness of the road.

I was too hung over and too stoked with coffee to fall asleep. I had to figure out what was going on. Clearly the missing journal must hold the answers – had I been too distracted by the books, or was I only seeing part of the picture? An hour and a half after leaving Savannah, I took the Walkerville exit and pulled into Lillie's driveway 45 minutes later. It was just past 2 p.m. I was feeling better and beginning to get hungry.

I heard the vacuum running as I opened the door. I had forgotten it was Thursday. Eula Mae was hard at work, singing quietly to herself while she cleaned the downstairs hall. She stared at me as I came in the back door. "Mr. Matt." She paused. "You looks a little peaky. You OK?"

"I'll live, Eula Mae, thanks. I think I had a bit much to drink last night," I said.

I walked in Lillie's study and plopped down in her desk chair.

"Oh, I know just the thing. Let me get you fixed. My man, Ernest – rest his soul – was kinda bad to drink, and I know just the thing to do you up." She disappeared in the kitchen and returned a few minutes later with a glass of warm liquid. It smelled like beef broth and tasted salty.

"What is this?"

"It's Mama Eula's Re-jew-vin-ater." She strung out the syllables. "Guaranteed to cure what ails you."

"What's it got in it?"

"Just you drink it," she insisted.

An hour later I was feeling fine. She never did tell me what it contained.

I sat in the chair, the computer in front of me, sipping on the elixir. I noticed that the keyboard had been moved from where I thought I'd left it. Had I stacked the diskettes like that? Something attracted me to the window. The curtains were slightly ajar, but I was sure that I'd closed them carefully when I had broken into the strongbox hidden under the floor. I noticed there were still some crumpled papers in the trashcan.

I called Eula Mae who was now dusting in the parlor. "Eula, have you cleaned this room today?"

"Not yet. I kinda liked to clean that room when Miss Lillie was here. She was so 'culier about her stuff, you know. But if you wants me to, I can get to it now while you're ..."

"Have you been in here at all today?"

She looked at me strangely. "No, Mr. Matt. Why you ask?"

"Because I think someone has." I walked over to the window and pulled back the curtain. It was unlocked, but I didn't remember checking to see if it had been locked when I left. I turned back to Eula Mae. "When you came in this morning, was the alarm set?"

"Yes, sir, and I used that code you gave me to cut it off."

"Was there a flashing red light, or anything on the little read-out that said 'Alarm Memory'?"

"No, sir!" I decided the hangover must have confused me. I knew I could trust Eula Mae, but I checked anyway. Only she and I had codes to the system. I entered the master code in the keypad. The memory showed that I had set the alarm with my code the morning before, and she had disarmed it with her code this morning. No alarms, no other entries or exits. I went back in the study and examined the window. Nothing. I pushed it up and peered out at the shrubbery below. Barely visible in the soft earth about a foot out from the foundation were two linear marks where it appeared the soil had been disturbed. Leaving Eula Mae perplexed, I rushed outside to get a closer look.

The ground was firm and dry. It hadn't rained in more than two weeks, but I thought the marks looked fresh. There were two small furrows perpendicular to the house, roughly 18 inches apart, an inch deep and each about four inches in length.

I studied the marks as Eula Mae peered out the window with a curious look. Then it occurred to me – the ladder in the tack room. I retrieved it from the old stables. The legs fit the marks precisely. The height was perfect, with the top resting on the window sill under Eula Mae's puzzled gaze. "You thinking we done had another break-in? Lordy, I hope not! The last one's the one that got Mr. Lance kilt."

I CHECKED THROUGH THE HOUSE QUICKLY but carefully. Nothing appeared to be missing. As far as I could tell, all of Aunt Lillie's files were intact, and no disks or CDs were obviously missing. I didn't call the police. We weren't exactly on good terms to begin with, and I didn't want any more investigation than necessary at this point. And, too, what was I going to tell them? That some things might have been moved around or that the curtains didn't look exactly like I'd left them? What I couldn't figure out is how someone could manage to get into the house without setting off the alarm.

I found the card of Mike, the technician who had fixed the alarm system the day after Lillie's funeral. He remembered me – the $20 tip must have helped – and said he'd be right over.

We were standing in the study. Mike had examined the system and pronounced it working and free from signs of tampering. I'd shown him the window and the marks in the earth behind the shrubbery. He agreed that someone *might have tried* to get in, but doubted if they'd succeeded. "But wait," I asked. "What makes you say that you think they attempted to get in but didn't?"

"The motion detectors didn't go off. Maybe they peeked out in the hall and saw them."

"Whoa, hold on!" I was confused. "You say peeked out in the hall, but how could they?"

"Well, it seems from what you've told me maybe they got in this room, but you said nothing's missing, and if the burglar leaves without stealing something, that means the alarm system worked, doesn't it?" He grinned, as if he'd once again proven his worth.

"But how could they get in this room without setting off the system? What is that?" I pointed at a white disc-shaped object affixed to the ceiling. A small red LED light in its middle blinked every couple of seconds. "Isn't *that* part of the alarm system?"

"Yes, but that's a combination heat and smoke detector combined with a glass-break sensor. It's got a wireless link to the main alarm panel in the kitchen panty. See, the sound of breaking glass has a very characteristic frequency which this unit picks up."

"You mean that's *not* a motion detector? And what about the window alarms?"

Mike looked at me as if he were trying to explain nuclear physics to a kindergarten student.

"Look, this is an old house. It's sitting on 16-inch hewn joists. The walls have six-inch heart pine studs covered with lathing and plaster. You just can't be running low voltage wires everywhere. So what we do is this. We set up what's called a wireless network, with multiple sensing devices reporting back to the central alarm panel. Much easier and much more efficient. Hell, you'd spend more repairing the damage of hard-wiring this house than you'd spend for the whole alarm system," Mike said.

"What about the window alarms?"

"Well, you don't really need them in most cases. First of all, people should keep their windows locked," he paused, and pointed a finger at me, "which means that if somebody wants in they have to break in. The sound of a breaking window will set off the alarm. It's really pretty much standard in older houses like this."

"But don't you have wireless window alarms?"

"Sure, but do you realize how big this house is? Hell, as many windows as you've got it would cost ..."

"Do it."

"Huh?"

"I said do it. I want alarms on every window. I want a motion sensor in every downstairs room. And Mike," I paused, "I want them now."

Mike looked at me as if I were a paranoid fool. He glanced at his watch. "Well, it's kinda late. I guess if I got started in the morning ..." I laid $200 on the desk.

"Of course, if I got started tonight I could probably be finished by bedtime." He scooped up the bills and headed for his truck.

The truth be told, I had no real idea as to whether or not there'd been another break-in. Common sense told me there hadn't. My only evidence was my hung-over perception that some things had been moved around the desk and that the curtain might have been disturbed. The ladder marks under the window – if that's what they were – could have occurred anytime. It hadn't rained since Lance's murder. Perhaps he, or whoever was with him, had tried the window before breaking in the door. The area was protected to a degree by the eaves of the house so it was conceivable that the marks had been there for much longer. Was it all happenstance, or more? Was I becoming one of those crazies who hears secret radio transmissions intercepted by the fillings in his teeth? I decided to stick to wine.

Mike finished his installation by 11 p.m. and pronounced Rutherford Hall "the goddamnest safest house in town." Safe or not, I went to bed with my father's loaded shotgun within easy reach.

CHAPTER

Nineteen

AT 8:58 A.M. FRIDAY I WAS STANDING in front of the main door of the Citizens Bank of Adams County. The two old books that either held the key to a fortune in hidden gold or were marred by some pretty egregious printer's errors were safely nestled in the gym bag slung over my shoulder. As the clock on the courthouse tolled nine, the bank's vice-president flipped on the lights in the lobby and unlocked the doors to let in the waiting throng of one eager customer. He greeted me warmly by name and asked if he could be of any assistance. I told him that I'd been straightening up at Lillie's and had found some valuable jewelry that I thought should be in the bank's vault rather than at the house. He agreed, officiously nodding his head and smiling a bit too broadly.

I supposed that for a small-town bank I was now classed as a big depositor who warranted special treatment. He led me into the vault and turned his key in the bank's side of the double lock, then left me alone to sort out my valuables.

Making sure I was unobserved, I placed the two books in the box and put the missing journal volume back in my bag. I spent five minutes needlessly leafing through a few deeds before closing and locking the box, signing the register, and cashing another check for $1,000.

Eula Mae was off and I'd have Rutherford Hall to myself. I planned to go home and try to decipher my great-great-grandfather's handwriting. Half an hour later, I was seated at a table in Lillie's study, the book in front of me, a yellow legal pad and pen to my right, and a mug of strong coffee to my left. The answer to all my questions had to lie in these pages. I opened it and began to read.

February 26, 1865. Saturday. It would appear that the end of our struggle approaches rapidly. Gen. B., being the practical man that he is, has issued orders that the Government must prepare for the day when Richmond will be abandoned. There is little doubt of this now …

The entry was a long one. The final paragraph caught my eye.

Gen. B. is not usually a secretive man, but tonight he said he was on a special mission and asked me to go with him. We waited until well past 9, and then he insisted that I remove my cap and cover my uniform with his manteau, such that we'd look like two gentlemen returning from a late evening and not be recognized. We walked to the residence of Sec. Trenholm. It's a magnificent place in this time of privation. A finely dressed Negro servant greeted us. While the Gen. and the Sec. conferred in the parlour with closed doors, I was treated by his staff to as fine a meal as I've had in this city. I supped on ham, some poultry (pheasant?), winter greens and fresh bread, together with a generous cup of French brandy. The Sec.'s reputation as a man of unlimited wealth seems true. After two or more hours, the Gen. emerged and, with thanks all around, we departed. He did not volunteer the nature of this meeting, nor why I should accompany him.

Several things were immediately evident to me. The first was that I had no basic working knowledge of the Confederate government. I presumed that "Gen. B." referred to Breckinridge, but I was not familiar with "Sec. Trenholm." The other thing that should have been obvious was that my grandfather was keeping a personal journal, not trying to explain or document what, in retrospect, would be a memorable moment in history. Unlike the neatly annotated textbook edition of *The War Diaries of Capt. Matthew Rutherford,* this was raw source material. It was like attending an opera in Italian without a program guide. You can guess at the story line, but you're never quite sure that you've grasped it completely. Clearly, I needed either a quick education or help from someone familiar with the events and the players. But who could I trust? I decided to read on and try to make some sense of things. I needed to have a better feel for what was going on. I needed to know why this particular diary was never published and why its very existence denied. I continued reading.

> *February 27, 1865. Sunday. The Sabbath usually being my day of rest, I was surprised when the Gen. sent word early that I was to remain nearby, as he'd likely want to speak with me later. As I write this now near midnight, I must admit that I am still not sure what is happening. Around dusk, Gen. Lee and several officers arrived. Generals L. and B., after conferring amongst themselves, then met with Pres. Davis at his residence. The news and more important the expectation of future news looks bleak. Gen. B., who may or may not share things with me depending on his mood, observed that our efforts should be directed toward an honourable peace, and that our thoughts must be for the future — ours and our children's. I was then told privately to meet him at Sec. Trenholm's residence at 10, and to arrive on foot and unobserved. I did not object – it would not have been my nature – but in verity I was hoping for a repast similar to*

that of last night. Truth be told, I would have settled for the scraps. Once again the Gen. and the Sec. talked quietly in the parlour, but this time the Gen. emerged and asked me to join them for a cigar and brandy. This was most unusual, not to mention against protocol, for my superior officer and a member of the Cabinet to ask me to join them as a man among men for tobacco and a drink. Both were quite common, however, and we got on well. Presently the Sec. says that the Gen. speaks highly of me, and my bravery and initiative at the New Market battle. He then makes as if he's making idle conversation, but I feel that he was probing my mettle, for what I know not. After half an hour or so, the Gen. says it's late, and we bade the house farewell. I was instructed to journey home by a different route and make no mention of the evening to anyone. The Gen. looked me square in the eye and said, "Rutherford you are a man I can trust." I could not decide if it was a question or a statement, but I took it as the former and said, "to death, sir."

February 27, 1865. Monday. This morning, I was summoned by the Gen. and told that I was being assigned to different duty. My reaction at first was that I had misspoken the evening before — perhaps the brandy had softened my wits while hardening my tongue. He assured me though that I was one of the officers for whom he held the highest esteem and that this assignment was for our future and our children's, which is what he had said the day before without explaining it. He told me that the one prize that the Federals would like to possess if or when they take Richmond is the bullion and specie in the treasury. He revealed that Sec. Trenholm and he had been discussing this, and that the Sec. was as impressed with me as the Gen. was, and that I was the fit and proper choice to help them implement saving this

*treasure from the Yankee invaders who have so devastated
our lands. He reminded me of my father's letter accounting
the dog, Sherman's pillaging and destruction of our own
meager homestead and asked if I wanted to reward such
men with ill gotten riches. I told him of course no, and that
I was his faithful captain ready for his assignment. I was
told then to choose two other officers whose trust and friend-
ship for me was strong, and who could be trusted with a
vital task for our nation and our people. I was to give him
the names, he would make arrangements, and on the morrow, we are to report to the Treasury offices and take our
orders directly from Sec. Trenholm. I am to admonish all as
to the importance and secrecy of our work, but am to personally keep him informed in light of what he calls "our
brotherhood of trust." This is all very strange, and I — a
farm boy from Georgia — am not accustomed to being treated as an equal and confidant by a superior officer and a
man who once served as vice-president of the United States.
I have no specifics, but I fear that I am not being told all.*

There was no note for February 28. The journal resumed on March 1.

*March 1, 1865. Wednesday. I now realize why I have been
assigned to the Treasury. The Gen. always called me a practical and can-do fellow, and the problem in this beleaguered
city is the simple necessity of finding packing boxes and
crates. I question the importance of our duties, but I am a soldier and I follow orders. As the Gen. instructed me, I have
chosen Capts. Sanders and Hermann. They are both from
Georgia and I have known them for some months. Sanders is
a cracker from Atlanta and was in charge of a number of
Richmond warehouses for the Quartermaster Corps. He is
well connected and can scrounge with the best of them. In*

addition to trusting him, he is a practical fellow, with much common sense. Hermann was born in Prussia and ended up in Savannah, how I know not. He has been here in Richmond assigned to the cipher office of the Signal Corps. He is one of the most remarkably intelligent and educated men I have ever met. Sec. Benjamin, when he was Sec. of War, placed him in his position, which I believe is a plum one, perhaps because they are both members of the Tribe of Israel. He is a rotund and curly-haired fellow, always smiling and always with a cigar. I have told them only in the broadest terms our assignment, but they are both eager as our assignment will assure that should the evacuation of Richmond become necessary, we will be amongst the first out with the treasure.

The following days' notes seemed routine. The three Captains collected boxes and crates while clerks and supervisors at the Confederate Treasury determined what could be destroyed or abandoned and which records must be saved. Trenholm – who by this time I'd recognized was Secretary of the Treasury – was in and out frequently. The note on March 13 caught my eye.

Sec. T. is fearful for the safety of the treasury, and has come to this decision. We are to separate most of the bullion from the gold and silver specie and pack it separately. He says the Treasury records and papers will travel with the gold and silver coin, but in case we are overtaken by Federals or marauders, we should divide the hoard so as to lessen the chances of it all being found and taken at once. He has determined that we should pack two gold ingots, each of which weighs about 8 pounds, wrapped in cotton in the bottom of each crate of papers. That way the weight of the whole is not such as to give away the contents, and a thief bent on stealing gold or silver will go for the crates and barrels of coin. He quoted "The Purloined Letter" by Poe, with which I am not familiar, but Capt. Hermann is and agreed it would be a good ruse, if it came to that. Sec. T. has decided that this should be done in secret by the three of us in order to avoid any rumors of this leaking out. In turn, he says, the guards will be put on the barrels of coin while we three only will "guard the papers." He winked when he said this.

The diary was difficult to read and at times even more difficult to understand. The places and people and events described by my great-great-grandfather were so foreign to anything I knew or understood that I scarcely knew how to interpret them. Much attention was given to the mundane in a city clearly doomed by advancing enemy forces. He chaffed at his assignment, railing that it was one for "privates, not battle-tested officers." On April 1, he recorded that a dispatch from General Lee revealing the Confederate loss at Five Forks meant that the Danville rail line was the only means of retreat. There was no entry for April 2. A brief note dated April 3 said simply, *"Arrived in Danville late afternoon. I have seen the fires of Hell."*

Events had evidently quieted by April 4. In painstaking and color-ful detail, Captain Rutherford described the evacuation of the Confederate government from Richmond. His train, containing the gold from the Treasury plus several hundred thousand more dollars in gold reserves from the Richmond banks, had been among the last to leave. He described a city in flames, with rampant looting and a total breakdown of civilian and military authority. He and Capts. Hermann and Sanders guarded the "papers and records" in one box-car, while midshipmen under the command of a Captain William Parker guarded the "treasure" in several others. He observed,

Sec. Trenholm's plan, however far-fetched it may have seemed to me when it was hatched, appears to be working.

More than a hundred heavily armed men now guard less than half the wealth of a failing cause, while three of us, pistols in holsters, oversee the rest. Capt. Hermann, the chess player and thinker among us, is concerned. He sees this as what he calls a gambit—a new word for me—in which we three are pawns in a larger game whose strategy is obscure. The problem with this, he says, is that in the board game pawns are frequently sacrificed for strategic advantage ...

CHAPTER

Twenty

OVER THE FOLLOWING DAYS, the journal described in detail the day to day life of a rebel government on the run. The news for the most part was not good. On April 6, fearing for the safety of the one hard asset left to the Confederacy, the train carrying the gold and silver and the Treasury "papers and records" departed Danville, Virginia, for parts south. Stopping briefly in Greenville, they arrived in the railway hub of Charlotte, North Carolina, on April 8. The note for that day reflected frustration:

> It is becoming increasingly unclear as to our future, and what role we are destined to play. Hermann, who seems most suspicious of our assignment, never misses an opportunity to talk with travelers, stragglers, paroled officers and soldiers, or anyone who can shed light on the bigger picture. He keeps talking about the end-game — another chess term I am told — and our part in it. Sanders, being a Georgia boy like me and unaccustomed to the European intrigues of the like recounted by our German friend, continues to have faith in our cause and our leaders, especially Gen. B. Even

though we've been together now for more than a month, I am constantly amazed at Josef's knowledge of world history. He speaks of this struggle, this war, this revolution as only one amongst innumerable others that mark the history of human existence. Tonight, he educated us about the ancient Greeks and their wars. He spoke of Sparta and Athens, of Persia and the Delphian League, of victories and defeats, of peoples enslaved and peoples freed. Lost for a moment in his words, our hunger and our fear of the morrow disappeared ...

On April 10, the notes recorded that once again the treasure train moved south, this time toward Chester, South Carolina, where they were to travel westward by wagon and rail to link up with President Davis and the remnants of the Confederate government in its flight toward Florida. Arriving late in the afternoon, the treasure under guard of the Midshipmen and the "papers" under the guard of Capts. Rutherford, Hermann and Sanders were transferred to wagons for the overland journey to Newberry, South Carolina. The plan – according to the diary – was to place everything back onto railcars headed for Abbeville, South Carolina. They arrived in Newberry late on the afternoon of April 15. The record for that day reflected a sense of shocked finality.

April 15, 1865. Saturday. Newberry, S.C. The news today is that of despair. Word has reached us of Gen. Lee's surrender of the Army of Northern Virginia at a place called Appomattox, and that three days ago the city of Mobile fell to the Federals. The Confederacy is clearly no more. When we arrived this afternoon, a telegram signed by Sec. Trenholm and Gen. Breckinridge awaited us. It directed Col. Parker to proceed with his men and the gold to Abbeville, while leaving the Treasury papers under our guard in a warehouse near the depot. No mention was made of further orders, but we are instructed to wait until we are contacted. Parker and his men set out by rail near dusk after helping us unload our charge into a sturdy brick cotton warehouse. We three are considering what we should do ....

The three captains apparently spent the next day waiting for further orders. It was clear from the diary that only they, General Breckinridge and Treasury Secretary Trenholm knew the true contents of the boxes of "papers and records" that they were guarding. The note for April 16 seemed routine.

April 16, 1865. Sunday. Newberry, S.C. This is a quiet little town, thus far spared of the war, but the fear of Yankees and bands of marauding renegades is voiced on the streets. A sad story was told to me by an old woman today. She came to the warehouse where we guard our boxes and asked if we might be of service to a fellow soldier, now dead. She is a widow-woman who takes in boarders. Some months past, a young man from South Carolina wounded in Virginia was passing through this town on his way home. He was unable to fight, having lost his left hand to a Minie ball, and having an infected wound on his left leg. She did not know or could not recall the battle, but both his father and brother were killed there and it was a miracle that he survived, or so she told it. By the time he reached this town, he was too weak to travel, so she took him in until he could recover sufficiently to move on. He told her that he was the last surviving member of his immediate family, his mother having died of malaria in the 1850s and that should he die, his last wish was to be buried on the family farm. His father and brother were both buried in unmarked graves at the battle site. His state worsened over the next weeks after his

New World of which he was a part gave him birth. He had invented a new way of assaulting fate. "Make new!" was to him as it was to Pound much later on an imperious command which completely controlled him.

If he was to enlarge his opportunity he needed room, in verse as in everything else. But there were to be no fundamental changes in the concepts that keep our lives going at an accepted pace and within normal limits. The line was still to be the line, quite in accord with the normal contours of our accepted verse forms. It is not so much that which brought Whitman's verse into question but the freedom with which he laid it on the page. There he had abandoned all sequence and all order. It was as if a tornado had struck.

A new order had hit the world, a relative order, a new measure with which no one was familiar. The thing that no one realized, and this includes Whitman himself, is that the native which they were dealing with was no longer English but a new language akin to the New World to which its nature accorded in subtle ways that they did not recognize. That made all the difference. And not only was it new to America—it was new to the world. There was to be a new measure applied to all things, for there was to be a new order operative in the world. But it has to be insisted on that it was not disorder. Whitman's verses seemed disorderly, but ran according to an unfamiliar and a difficult measure. It was an order which was essential to the new world, not only of the poem, but to the world of chemistry and physics. In this way, the man was more of a prophet than he knew. The full significance of his innovations in the verse patterns has not yet been fully disclosed.

The change in the entire aesthetic of American art as it began to differ not only from British but from all the art of the world up to this time was due to this tremendous change in measure, a relative measure, which he was the first to feel and to embody in his works. What he was leaving behind did not seem to oppress him, but it oppressed the others and rightly so.

It is time now to look at English and American verse at the time Whitman began to write, for only by so doing can we be led to discover what he did and the course that lay before him. He had many formidable rivals to face on his way to success. But his chief opponent was, as he well knew, the great and medieval Shakespeare. And if any confirmation of Shakespeare's sacrosanct position in the language is still sought it is easily to be obtained when anything is breathed mentioning some alteration in the verse forms which he distinguished by using them. He may be imitated as Christopher Fry imitates him, but to vary or depart from him is heresy. Taken from this viewpoint, the clinical sheets of Shakespeare as a writer are never much studied. That he was the greatest word-man that ever existed in the language or out of it is taken for granted but there the inquiry ends.

> Sweetest Shakespeare, Nature's child,
> Warbled his native woodnotes wild.

With Milton came Cromwell and the English Revolution, and Shakespeare was forgotten, together with the secrets of his versification, just as Whitman today is likely to be forgotten and the example of his verses and all that refers to him.

The interest that drove Whitman on is the same one that drove Shakespeare at the end of his life in an attempt to enlarge the scope of written verse, to find more of expression in the forms of the language employed. But the consequences of such experimentation are always drastic and amount in the end to its suppression, which in the person of a supreme genius is not easy.

From what has been said thus far, you can see why it is impossible to imitate Shakespeare; he was part of a historic process which cannot repeat itself. All imitations of the forms of the past are meaningless, empty shells, which have merely the value of decorations. So that, if anything is now to be created, it must be in a new form. Whitman, if he was to do anything of moment, could not, no matter how much he may have bowed down to the master, imitate him. It would not have had any meaning at all. And his responsibility to the new language was such that he had no alternative but to do as it bade him.

Though he may not have known it, with Whitman the whole spirit of the age itself had been brought under attack. It was a blind stab which he could not identify any more than a child. How could he, no matter how acute his instincts were, have foreseen the discoveries in chemistry, in physics, in abnormal psychology, or even the invention of the telephone or the disclosure of our subterranean wealth in petroleum? He knew only, as did those who were disturbed by his free verse, that something had occurred to the normal structure of conventional aesthetic and that he could not accept it any longer. Therefore, he acted.

We have to acknowledge at once in seeking a meaning involving the complex concerns of the world that the philosophic, the aesthetic, and the mechanical are likely to stem in their development from the same root. One may be much in advance of the other in its discoveries, but in the end a great equalizing process is involved so that the discovery of the advance in the structure of the poetic line is equated by an advance in the conception of physical facts all along the line. Man has no choice in these matters; the only question is, will he recognize the changes that are taking place in time to make the proper use of them? And when time itself is conceived of as relative, no matter how abstruse that may sound, the constructions, the right constructions, cannot be accepted with a similar interpretation. It may take time to bring this

We hired four good horses with tack and brought the caisson to the loading dock of the warehouse. By lantern light, we pried open each of the boxes and carefully laid 91 bars of gold in each of the two coffins we'd purchased. Tying them down firmly with rope, we lashed the coffin with the body on top. The warehouse had several dozen bales of cotton. With difficulty, we pushed several next to the crates that now contained only treasury records, and placed a large can of lantern oil on top of the stacks. We tore open one bale, set a candle in the middle of the cotton and lit it, thinking it would give us at least a half hour's start before the conflagration began. We set out at a rapid pace near midnight, led only by the light of the moon. An hour later, from a small rise some miles south of town, we could see the flames and column of dark smoke as the warehouse, the records and evidence of our crime burned in the night.

We traveled for two days without major problem. Many soldiers were now on the road traveling home, and at times we traveled with a group of up to 10 men. Our story was that we were taking the bodies of comrades home for burial and that seemed to stop any more questions. We made camp by a stream late in the afternoon of the second day and had no sooner started our fire when we found ourselves surrounded by a Yankee scouting party. There were about 10 of them on fine, well-fed horses. We were still of course in our uniforms, but Captain Hermann — always prepared — offered an excellent set of forged parole papers for us, stating that we'd been released in Virginia and were making our way home to Georgia. The Union Lieutenant was an arrogant, suspicious fellow from New York, and he had lots to say about our cause, but we held our tongues as we had several rifles pointed at our heads. He poked in our saddle bags and then pointed at the coffins and said, "What's that?"

I told him we were taking the bodies of fallen soldiers home, sir, and he then looks at the tracks made by the caisson and says it's a mighty heavy load. I told him the coffins were lead lined, but he directs a Sergeant to open them. Fortunately he chose the one on top. He pries off the lid with a bayonet and sees the lead inner coffin inside. He looks at the Yankee Lieutenant, as if to say, "They're telling the truth, sir," but the Lieutenant says to cut into it. The Sergeant stabs it with his bayonet. There is a hiss of escaping gas followed by foul smelling fluid that spews out on the Sergeant and the Lieutenant who had come over to see. The Lieutenant gets very angry and his men, who I think hated him as much as we did at that point — started to laugh. He orders silence and rides off without another word. We put the top back on the coffin and spent a quiet night thereafter.

The rest of our journey was uneventful. We reached the town and the C---- farmstead, but not before we'd stopped and each of us put 10 gold bars in our saddle bags. The remaining 152 bars were left equally divided in each coffin. The Negro overseer and the cousin who had been left in charge of the farm were glad to see us. We told them that these were the bodies of S----, his brother and father, and while they were saddened to see them, they were given comfort that the family had returned to its final resting place. We personally dug the graves and placed the coffins in them ourselves so as not to have to explain the weight to anyone. The preacher arrived and we held a brief service before the Negro hands filled in the graves. We told those present of the heroism of the C---- family and how we planned to return later and erect a proper monument to their memory.

Our crime committed, we three parted ways. Capt. Hermann headed south toward Savannah while Capt. Sanders accepted my invitation to be my guest for a few

days at what remained of our farm.
Thus, I end this journal. It was started with the greatest
of hopes and ends with what may be the greatest of crimes.
May God have mercy on my soul.

I sat and stared at the yellowed paper. One hundred fifty-two gold bars. Eight pounds each. One thousand two hundred-sixteen pounds of gold. I flipped on Lillie's computer and clicked on the Internet browser. Several minutes later, I had what I needed. Roughly 14.6 Troy ounces to the pound. That came to 17,754 ounces of gold. The current gold price was roughly $350 per Troy ounce. Over six million dollars in gold, which I could probably triple, given its historic value. My life had taken on new meaning.

That night I was awakened from a deep sleep by a nightmare. I was with someone; I didn't know who. We'd found the gold buried in a small cemetery deep in a forest shadowed by gnarled oaks draped with flowing grey Spanish moss. The sky became dark – a storm was on the horizon. Lightning flashed as we dug ever deeper into the soft brown earth. Finally we struck something solid and scooped away the soil to reveal a perfectly preserved pine coffin. On its surface, in script that seemed to emit a faint glow, were the letters "S.C." The other person – I couldn't see his face – was using his shovel to try to pry open the lid. At first it wouldn't move. Then, suddenly, it sprang open to reveal something horrible.

I sat up in bed, instantly awake and in a cold sweat.

CHAPTER

Twenty-Two

I SPENT SATURDAY MORNING PACING around Rutherford Hall and thinking. What should I do? For the first time in my previously well-ordered life, I had no obligations. I had time, I had money, I had a place to live. I had no concrete plans for my future.

Should I go for it? Try to find where the gold had been buried? Maybe shed some light on Lance's murder? Or should I forget it, take my time, relax for a while, maybe think about where I'd want to spend the rest of my life once I got out of this dead-end town?

Once, when I was in college at Duke, I took a course entitled "The Philosophy of Science." A quote from the Pensées of the 17th century French mathematician Blaise Pascal was burned in the back of my mind: *"If you win, you win everything. If you lose, you lose nothing."*

Pascal was writing about the impossibility of certainty in proving the existence of God, but the principle applied. What did I have to gain? Millions of dollars in gold whose rightful owners were long dead. What did I have to lose? Nothing. For practical purposes, I'd already lost everything that I had at one time thought important to me. I decided at that very moment to go for it. Later — much later — I realized I should have remembered the time.

SATISFIED WITH MY DECISION, I fixed myself a sandwich for lunch and was just finishing when the phone rang. It was Doug, calling in his capacity as Commander of the local chapter of the Sons of Confederate Veterans.

"Matt, how are you? Hadn't talked with you in a few days and thought I'd check in," Doug said.

"Pretty good, I guess." I was still preoccupied with the gold and not in a mood to be especially friendly. I figured he wanted something.

"Look, I know you've been sort of laying low with this thing about your cousin's death and all, but how about being my guest at a little get-together tonight? I'd called you earlier in the week, but no one answered."

"I was in Savannah."

"The SCV is having its Annual Family Picnic this evening. We do it the last weekend in August every year – right before the kids go back to school. Your Aunt Lillie used to come. I know it's late to call, but I think you'd enjoy it – give you a chance to meet some people."

"Doug, thanks," I interrupted him. "I really do appreciate your thinking about me, but I don't think I can make it."

"Hey, Matt, come on! What are you going to do? You and your family are a part of this town. You can't sit there and hide in that big house forever. We're the Capt. Matthew Rutherford Camp No. 854 of the Sons of Confederate Veterans. We can't have the great-great-grandson of the man our group is named for avoiding us. It'll be low key, a little food, a little beer, some good guys and their families. You *need* to be there!"

"OK. You've got me, but ...."

"No, buts. Pick you up at 6:30."

The phone went dead.

William Rawlings, Jr.

THE FORTY-THIRD ANNUAL FAMILY DAY PICNIC of the Captain Matthew
Rutherford Camp No. 854 of the Sons of Confederate Veterans was held
– to my great surprise – in the spacious front yard of none other than
Nick, my attorney. Though Nick and my father had been close friends,
my contact with him had been limited and I knew little about him.

I realized that he had evidently done well. His house was set some
quarter mile off the highway just to the north of town. It would probably have been visible from the road if one were looking for it, but in
this part of the South people who build big houses tend to hide them
from the public's view. The entrance was by a paved drive set
between modest brick pillars with a simple bronze plaque stating
"Morgan." The drive dipped through a few acres of giant hardwoods
set in a creek bottom, then rose to open into what must have at one
time been a cattle pasture. In the distance, on a small rise surrounded by old growth pines, was a quintessential southern mansion. Six
massive columns supported a broad front gable that covered a wide
porch with floor to ceiling windows opening onto the front rooms. A
gentle slope of mowed lawn tapered down to a small lake set to one
side, while the drive wended its way to a paved circle in front of the
porch. A fountain bubbled in the middle.

A large striped tent had been set up in the yard. To the right, several young men wearing gray forage caps and T-shirts emblazoned
with the Confederate flag were parking cars. Two long portable grills,
attended by beer drinking men, gave off smoke laced with the tanta-
lizing aroma of barbecued pork, while gaggles of brightly clad women
oversaw children who scampered across the tightly mown grass.
"We've been here since six this morning cooking the pigs. Glad it did-
n't rain," Doug observed. A regal figure, ignoring the August heat and
dressed in a long grey frock coat of a Confederate officer, stood on the
front porch of the house welcoming guests. I recognized him as Nick.
We drove into the circle and waited in the receiving line while the
attendants parked the car.

Nick grinned a broad smile and greeted me warmly. "Matt! It's great you could be here. Doug said you seemed a little reluctant ..."

"Well, I'm not sure my being back in Walkerville has created the sort of positive publicity that I'd like."

Nick slapped me on the back. "Ah, you've got to get over that. This is home. You're one of us. Look around you." He waved his hand toward the crowd of prosperous, middle-class descendants of Confederate soldiers. "These are your people. Come on! Let me introduce you ..."

I actually enjoyed myself. I realized that every public event that I'd been to since returning home was related to death. These were friends, and potential friends. Doug Smith was the consummate insurance agent — part politician and part cheerleader. He led me around introducing me to one group and then the next, each time with some new joke or story. His wife, Nan, seemed truly pleased to meet me. Many people welcomed me back to town. Nothing was said of Lance's murder. We drank beer and ate barbecue. We told jokes and laughed.

There was a short program led by Doug as commander and Nick — who by this time had shed his long coat — as host. Several of the older men asked if I was thinking about getting a job locally, the implication being that they'd help me out. I had half a dozen offers from wives to set me up with dates. For the first time since I'd returned to Walkerville, I thought that maybe, just maybe, this might be a decent place to live. It had been two weeks since my aunt's death.

CHAPTER
Twenty-Three

ON SUNDAY MORNING AUG. 25, 2002, I sat down with a large mug of coffee and the full intention of figuring out what I needed to do. Pascal's Wager aside, I needed to get serious. I needed a practical, actionable plan.

The same college philosophy course came to mind. I remembered the professor saying that all facts, occurrences or situations can be put into one of three categories: those that are known, those that are unknown, and those that are unknowable. The duty of the inquiring mind, he'd said, was to attack the unknown with the goal of placing it in one of the other two categories. "You can act on the known and pray over the unknowable."

I suspected there was someone out there who believed, perhaps with a little uncertainty, that the stolen gold existed and was as yet undiscovered. That person was probably responsible for Lance's murder. Unless I'd imagined the whole thing, that person was also the one who'd burglarized Lillie's study while I was in Savannah. He – I'd assumed it was a he – probably had in his possession the pages torn from the books that old Mr. Planer had referred to as "the Rutherford Cipher." Presumably what he did not have was the key to solving the codes.

Lillie would have given that to Lance. But then Lillie had suffered a stroke and had trouble communicating, and it would appear Lance was on drugs, so maybe he didn't understand. Lance may have been looking for the key when he was killed. Short of the dead rising on Judgment Day, exactly what Lillie said and Lance knew would remain unknowable.

My advantage was that I knew the gold did exist. I knew it had been hidden in a family cemetery somewhere several days ride from Newberry, South Carolina. I knew that my great-great-grandfather's journal had said that the truth about the treasure was to be passed on "by word of mouth," so there would be no other written documents. The secret was not to be revealed until 1965, and then to "the oldest male descendant in each family who has reached the age of 30 years ..."

It hit me! My father! His accident took place in 1980. That would have been shortly after his 30th birthday.

I tracked down my mother at the country club. Like many of the other older widows and divorcées, she had fallen into the habit of attending church on Sunday morning and spending Sunday afternoons playing bridge and drinking Bloody Marys at the club. She appeared slightly tipsy and slightly annoyed to see me.

"What brings you here, Matt?" She was nursing a pewter Georgia cup with a napkin wrapped around it.

"Mom, I know this is a strange question, but before he died, did Daddy say anything about some hidden Confederate gold?"

"Oh, God! Not that story again!" She took a long pull on her drink. "He was all up in the air about something one time — I forget exactly when. But that fantasy's been around for years, Matt. If the Rutherford family ever had any gold, I'd sure like to find it." She was more than tipsy.

"But when, Mom? When was he talking about it? How long before he died? Did he mention Aunt Lillie?"

"Matt, I don't remember and I don't want to remember. We were happy, Matt, and then he left me. Your father left me. He died. He left me alone, Matt, all by myself for all these years. Ask somebody else.

Ask Nick. I just want to get back to my game, OK?" She pecked me on the cheek and went back into the club room, her gait ever so slightly unsteady.

I reached Nick at home. He sounded glad to hear from me. "Yeah, get yourself on out here and help me clean this place up." I arrived at his house 20 minutes later. A large white van sat on the lawn and half a dozen men were dismantling the tent while others picked up trash and discarded bottles.

Nick was sitting in a white-painted rocker on his front veranda, sipping a beer and surveying the scene. "Want a beer? You can help me supervise."

We drank beer and exchanged the usual pleasantries. I thanked him for having me out the night before, and told him I enjoyed myself.

"Sort of gave me a new perspective on Walkerville. I guess I've never lived here as an adult," I said.

"It's a good little community, Matt. You should settle down for a while. God knows your aunt made it possible. What brings you out to visit anyway? You could have handled the thank-you note over the phone."

Good lawyer, I thought. Always perceptive, always suspicious.

"Nick, I know this is a strange question, but did my father ever mention the story about the stolen Confederate gold?"

Nick laughed. "That rumor just won't die. Of course he mentioned it. We heard about it when we were just kids. Hell, I remember when we were in high school we bought some old Korean War army surplus mine detectors and spent weeks going over every inch of the Rutherford Hall property. We found nails and horseshoes and broken iron pots, but no gold. Your granddaddy was alive at the time. I remember him running us off after we must've dug 100 holes."

"No, I'm talking about later. Right around the time he died."

Nick looked at me strangely. "Matt, by that time we were grown and had, as they say, put away childish things. Your father was busy practicing law and raising a family. When he died, I lost my best friend." He was silent for a moment, staring out at the men on the lawn who now had the tent laid out and were folding it into a bulky package. He turned to me, his voice cracking. "Don't do what I did, Matt. Get yourself a wife, a family. Get someone to love you. I've spent most of my life chasing the almighty dollar. Forget trying to find some hidden golden hoard. You may end up a wealthy man, but it will only bring you down." His eyes were watery and he looked away. It occurred to me that I didn't know him well.

Nick recovered his composure. We talked for few more minutes before I left. I thought he'd answered my question, but I wasn't sure. For the time being, I'd move that topic to a pile halfway between the unknown and the unknowable.

CHAPTER
Twenty-Four

AFTER BROODING ABOUT THE SUBJECT OVERNIGHT, I came to the perfectly obvious conclusion that to find the gold, I had to unravel the Rutherford Cipher. While there could be multiple copies of it floating around out there, at this point, I knew of only two people who might have a serious, active interest in solving it: me and the person who killed Lance. Even then, I wasn't totally sure that Lance's murder was related to the gold. Maybe the police were right; maybe it was a drug-related killing. There was no real evidence as to *why* he was killed. One more question to join all the others in the "unknown" pile.

The advantage I had was technology. What may have been an insoluble problem in the early 20th century would surely be child's play with modern computing techniques. I'd spent my entire working career in high tech and I had lots of connections. I dragged out my address book – I hate PDAs – and at 11 a.m., 8 a.m. California time, I started calling.

After the first dozen phone calls, a pattern began to emerge. Like me, many of my formerly well-placed contacts were now unemployed or working at interim jobs while trying to get back into the game. Three of the first six people who were still in the industry all had the same suggestion. Call Luke James. That was the last thing I wanted to do.

When Linguafont Technologies had been bought out, he was the only one who walked away with any serious money. The rest of us – the team that had helped take him to the top – got little or nothing. He'd been my friend since college and he'd screwed me. The gold would change everything though, and Luke's assistance in recovering it would have the taste of sweet revenge.

Getting his number was no problem. Luke James was now rich and very high profile. I wondered what the former pocket-protected, mismatched socks multimillionaire was up to now. I dialed the number that a couple of contacts had given me. A languid voice answered the phone on the first ring with three letters, "JVC."

My first reaction was that I'd misdialed but I said, "Good morning. I'm Matthew Rutherford and I'd like to speak with Luke James. Is this the correct number?"

There was a pause, then, "This is one of Mr. James' numbers. How can I be of assistance to you?"

"I'd like to speak with him, if he's available. We've been friends for ..."

"Mr. James has many acquaintances," the voice interrupted. "How is it that you know him?"

"We worked together at Linguafont Technologies. I was...."

"I'm sorry, Mr. Rather."

"Rutherford."

"Forgive me, Mr. *Rutherford*, we've established a special Web site for ex-Linguafont employees with information about outplacement, severance benefits and ..."

"Look," I interrupted her this time, "it's not about any Linguafont business. It's personal. We're friends from college."

"Oh, in that case, I suggest you visit our web site, *Jamesventurecapital.com*. Just click on the 'Contact Us' link and I'm certain that ..."

"Madam, what is your name?"

"Vanessa."

"Vanessa. Listen to me. Luke James and I were friends in college. I'm calling him on personal business. Just tell him I'm on the phone, and I promise you he'll take my call."

"Mr. Rather – sorry, Rutherford, Mr. James has been very successful in business. We get at least a dozen calls a week from salesmen, investment managers, stockbrokers and the like who allege to be Mr. James' friend, his cousin, his former roommate – you name it. And do you know what they want? Access. They all want access to his money. So, if you ..."

"Vanessa, one thing. His socks don't match."

There was a pause. "I'll put you through."

Two minutes later, Luke's familiar voice greeted me. "Matt! How you been, man? What you been up to? Are you running your own company yet?"

Always the same Luke.

"Not yet. I've been on a little vacation back home in Georgia. Taking care of some family business."

"Are you still there? Where is it ... Walkerville? I've got a team in Atlanta right now listening to some pitches from the Georgia Tech crowd. They'll be coming back later this week. Why don't I send the Gulfstream to pick you up? Come out and spend a few days on the boat. We'll take it down the coast, drink a little wine..."

"Thanks, Luke, but I called for a favor. I need some information."

"Sure, name it. I'll help you if I can." His voice was ever so slightly cooler.

"I've got a little project going here, and I need the name of someone who is really good with codes and encryption technology."

"Ah, that's my man, Matt! Always going at it." His voice had resumed its previous friendly tone. "Funny you should ask, we just heard a fantastic presentation for bridge funding from a small startup in Palo Alto. They originally developed some killer apps for mobile encryption algorithms – hoped to sell them to the government. But that fell through and they wanted us to support them while they modified their software for business applications. They had a really good pitch, but we turned them down. I'm pretty sure they're going under. You might pick up some of their people."

"Can you recommend anyone – or better yet give me some names and phone numbers?"

"The girl who made the pitch, what's her name...?" I could hear papers shuffling in the background. "Here it is. Lisa Li. Sharp, Matt, really sharp. Chinese-American. PhD in number theory and cryptography. I suspect she's going to be looking for a job soon. And, Matt, let me tell you. She's a real looker." Luke never did have any style.

We talked for a few minutes more. I got contact information for Lisa Li and three other possible candidates. Luke invited me out at least four more times, each of which I refused. Before I hung up, I promised him I'd visit on my next trip to the West Coast.

He still hadn't figured it out.

Talking with Luke had made me a bit inquisitive. Certainly he seemed to be doing well – it would be hard not to with the money he'd made from the sale of Linguafont Technologies. Out of pure curiosity, I logged onto the James Venture Capital Web site. It was a slick and professional job. They evidently had lots to invest. I clicked on "Principles" on the side bar and was greeted with a page showing head and shoulder photos of Luke as Chairman of the Board, plus three others I didn't recognize who were listed as being the CEO, CFO and CIO. Under Luke's photo I clicked on "Mr. James' Schedule" which led me to a listing of various Bay Area charitable events, fund raisers and the like. A small photo next to the Friends of Catalina Island Banquet listing caught my eye. The caption said, "JVC Chairman Luke James was the sponsor of the FCI Charity Event held July 27, 2002, in San Francisco." I enlarged the photo. There was Luke in all his splendor, grinning in tux and black tie. Standing next to him, smiling for the camera with her arm entwined in his, was my former live-in girlfriend, Brandi.

CHAPTER
Twenty-Five

LISA LI WAS EMPLOYED BY A COMPANY named Code-Text, Inc. The name alone was enough to sink any chances it might have had in the open market. The number I'd been given was answered by an efficient-sounding receptionist with an ever-so-slight foreign accent. She said Ms. Li was out of the office and offered to connect me to her voice mail. I left a brief message stating that I'd been given her name by a group to whom she'd made a presentation, and that I'd like to talk with her about some business. I didn't know how private her messages were so I made no mention of trying to recruit her for a job. I repeated Lillie's number and told her to leave a message if I didn't answer.

I had better luck reaching the next two names on the list Luke had given me. One was an ex-Linguafont employee I'd never met who now was living in Sonoma and working for a winery. He was polite but not interested in leaving California, even for a few days.

The next candidate was a middle-aged woman who had been in the industry since the 1980s. She had just landed a good job with Microsoft in San Francisco and was off the market.

The third candidate seemed to be a good possibility. He was a master's level triple-E with experience in encryption technology, into gaming theory and in need of a job. He said that he'd been laid off earlier in the year in a wave of downsizing at the information storage technology firm where he'd worked as one of the head programmers. We talked for half an hour and he agreed to e-mail me his resume and references. That arrived promptly and I started making calls to his two former employers. He was described as brilliant, but the verbal refs were, at best, hesitant.

It took three more phone calls to old contacts to find out that the real reason he'd lost his last two jobs was a little problem with cocaine. I e-mailed him and told him, that after some thought, he did not appear to be the best fit for this particular project.

That left Lisa. I was about to make a run to the grocery store when she called. She apologized, explaining that she was in New York for a job interview and that she'd gotten my message when she checked her voice mail. It was no real secret that Code-Text, Inc. was going under. About half the original 36 employees had left; the remaining technical staff, including Lisa, were catching up loose ends while furiously searching for other work in a dismal job environment. She said she hadn't been paid in six weeks and that she was living on her credit cards. I told her the story sounded very, very familiar. Reading between the lines, she was desperate for a job.

We talked for an hour until her cell phone battery began to give out, then I called her back at her hotel in Manhattan. She was 26, but her voice sounded younger with a lilting southern California accent. She'd graduated from Cal-Tech in Pasadena with a doctorate in applied mathematics. Luke had been a little mixed up, she explained; her *thesis* had been on the application of number theory to cryptographic solutions. The more we talked, the more evident it became that she had real possibilities.

Lisa knew that I was interviewing her for a job, but I was deliberately vague with specifics. I told her I was looking for someone with a background in cryptographic analysis, and that most of the work would be done in Georgia on a specific project.

"Atlanta?" she asked.

"Outside of Atlanta. In a fairly rural area."

"I don't know. I've seen all those movies about small Southern towns, and ..."

I interrupted her. "It pays very well."

"How well?" She was interested.

"Your old salary, plus 25 percent, plus expenses. A six-figure bonus if you complete the job in three months or less."

"Low six-figure or high six-figure?"

In truth I hadn't really thought about it. But if she did the job I could afford to be generous. "Make it $100,000. Twenty percent down when you decipher a certain code and the rest when something that has been lost is recovered."

There was silence on the other end of the line. Then, "Is this legal?"

"Totally."

Another pause, longer this time. "I think I'm in. I want to know the details. We need to talk in person. And," she hesitated, "I hate to say this, but I'd probably have said yes even if you'd said no."

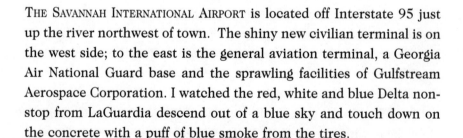

THE SAVANNAH INTERNATIONAL AIRPORT is located off Interstate 95 just up the river northwest of town. The shiny new civilian terminal is on the west side; to the east is the general aviation terminal, a Georgia Air National Guard base and the sprawling facilities of Gulfstream Aerospace Corporation. I watched the red, white and blue Delta non-stop from LaGuardia descend out of a blue sky and touch down on the concrete with a puff of blue smoke from the tires.

I waited for Lisa outside of the baggage claim area. She said she'd be wearing white. I said I'd be wearing a red Polo shirt.

It was Thursday. I'd spent Tuesday and Wednesday straightening up around Rutherford Hall. I'd talked Eula Mae into putting in an extra day's work to fix up one of the front upstairs guest rooms for company. She undertook the job eagerly when I told her that I had a young lady who might be visiting for a few days.

"Lord, I'm glad to hear that," she opined. "Good-looking young man like you who ain't got no women around him – makes you worry sometimes with all them strange things I hears go on in California."

I assured her it was strictly business, and besides there was no decent public lodging available in town. She thought about that for a while and went on with her dusting and sweeping. By the time she finished, the room positively glowed with the fresh ruffled bedspread a sharp counterpoint to the soft glow of the polished walnut furniture. "I'll have you some fresh flowers in here when you get home Friday with that young lady." She winked.

The plan was this. Lisa finished her round of interviews in New York on Wednesday. I arranged for her to pick up a prepaid airline ticket for a Thursday morning flight to Savannah. We'd spend that afternoon and evening talking and that night in the city. If things didn't work out, I'd pay her way back to Atlanta and on to San Francisco on Friday. If she seemed to be the person for the job, we'd head to Walkerville for a couple of days to plan strategy. I'd booked two junior suites at the Westin Savannah. My local bank-issued credit card had finally arrived and I could do such things.

I imagined that I knew what Lisa would look like. Luke had described her as "a real looker," whatever that meant, but he was infamous for his lack of taste. She supposedly was of Asian heritage, but I had no idea what that meant either. I did have a good idea that the average female doctorate in applied mathematics would rate about a two on a scale of one to 10. I was prepared for a short stocky Chinese lady with a baggy dress and sturdy, sensible lace-up shoes.

I found the carousel where the Delta flight number and "Arr. NYC-LaGuardia" were displayed in bright red letters. Leaning against the wall, I watched the passengers descend the escalator and mill around in the baggage claim area. There was the usual mix of business men in suits and ties, families on vacation, and a gaggle of pierced and tattooed students from the Savannah College of Art and Design returning for the fall semester. Finally, I spotted her. She was short, about 5'4" and definitely stocky. She'd told me she was 26, but could have passed for 40. Her white blouse was stained under her arms with rings of sweat from the Savannah heat and humidity, and she was carrying what appeared to be a laptop case over one shoulder and a bulky purse over the other. She heaved a heavy suitcase off the carousel and began to look around as if she were expecting someone.

Smiling, I walked over and stuck out my hand. "I'm Matt Rutherford." She stared at me blankly, and just at that moment, spied an older oriental gentleman to whom she rushed with open arms, babbling away in what I assumed was Mandarin Chinese.

A voice behind me said, laughing, "You'd better be glad I'm not easily offended."

I turned to see one of the most beautiful women I have ever seen in my life.

CHAPTER

Twenty-Six

I'D CHOSEN THE WESTIN BECAUSE IT WAS QUIET, elegant and not the Hyatt across the river which had been the scene of my bourbon fueled interlude with Pam the preceding week.

I handed my keys to the parking valet at the entrance and the bellman whisked our bags away. I registered while Lisa wandered out to stare at the city and River Street in the distance on the other side of the Savannah. "It's beautiful," she said simply. "Growing up in California, you never imagine ..." She didn't finish.

She was beautiful. Tall, with long hair the color of sable, she moved with the litheness of a cat. Her prominent cheekbones, thin, perfect nose and large breasts indicated a mixed racial heritage. We took the water taxi to River Street, then a yellow cab to a small tearoom on Broughton Street where I knew we could get a light lunch and spend the afternoon in uninterrupted conversation. We both ordered salads. She drank iced tea and I ordered hot yerba mate.

We talked idly for half an hour, checking each other out. She knew all about the Linguafont debacle and wanted to know about my previous job there. She said she thought we'd been shafted by Luke, but that was business.

I asked about her family. Her father was from Taiwan and had come to the United States in the late 1960s to study at Stanford. Her mother was a drugged-out, red-headed ex-hippie from Iowa who had fallen in love and married him during an unusually long period of sobriety. She'd melted back into the San Francisco drug underground when their child was just an infant. Her father had soon remarried a native, born American of Chinese descent. Lisa had a normal and uneventful childhood growing up in Los Angeles when he moved south to accept a professorship at UCLA.

"We never traveled much," she said. "I think my whole world has revolved around the West Coast." She paused. "But this city – it's beautiful! Is the rest of the South like this?"

"I think so," I lied. My goal had always been to get out of this place. The waitress removed our plates and I changed the subject. "Let's get down to some work," I said.

I fished in my briefcase and placed a manila folder on the table between us.

"Lisa, first of all, I want everything we say here to be confidential. If we get that far, what I will eventually tell you may be one of the most far-fetched tales you've ever heard, but to my knowledge, it's true. I'm going to broadly outline the problem and have you tell me first if you think you can tackle it. If you can, and you understand the terms of the agreement I'm going to propose, we'll spend the next couple of days in Walkerville going over the details. But let me get to first things first."

She looked at me with suspicion.

"I need you to solve a coded message – actually two coded messages. The information contained in these documents pertains to something that has been lost for more than 100 years, and if ..."

She began to laugh. "Matt, what is this?! I'm a mathematics PhD, not some psychic medium. If you've gotten me down here for some wild scheme ..."

"Lisa, just hear me out. I'm serious, and I can prove that to you, but the information that I possess is sensitive." I didn't tell her that its possession might have led to my cousin's murder. "All in good time, OK?"

"OK," she replied. She was quiet. I could tell she was turning over the potential $100,000 bonus in her head.

I took out the photocopies of the sheets containing the nonsense letters I had found in the two books locked in the vault with the missing journal. I laid them in front of her, spreading them out on the white, linen tablecloth. She reached over and pulled the flickering candle close to illuminate the text. Her bright eyes darted from one sheet to the next.

After a moment, she said, "What is the relationship between these two documents?"

"I have no idea, but I think they both hold clues to the same thing," I answered.

She was silent again while she poured over the text, tracing each line with her long finger, occasionally pausing to compare one section to another. Satisfied, she shuffled them together in a single stack and carefully placed them back in the folder. "So, tell me again exactly what you want me to."

"I want you to tell me what these coded words mean," I said.

"I'm to assume the answer will be in English?"

"I believe that to be the case. German is a possibility, but not likely."

"I took four years of German in college. No problem." She was silent.

"So what do you think?" I tried not to sound eager.

"Now, let me get this straight. You're offering me my old salary, plus 25 percent – that's roughly 10 grand a month, right?"

"Right."

"And you're offering me a bonus of $100,00 if I can solve the problem in three months or less, right?"

"Right. $20,000 when you come up with the solution, and the rest when I recover what's been lost. "

"And this is all legal?"

"So far as I know, yes," I said.

"And I'm getting a written contract, three month's minimum with the salary and bonus spelled out in black and white."

"Yes."

She sat mutely and stared at the flicking candle.

"So what do you think?"

"I think there's a possibility that you're either lying, a damned fool, or crazy, but a greater likelihood is that all three are true." She stared at me without blinking.

"I may be a fool, and maybe a little crazy, but I'm not lying."

"First month's salary in advance?"

"Done."

She smiled and stuck out her hand. "I'm on. It'll be the easiest money I ever made."

She paused and looked around. "Do they serve wine here? I'm from California."

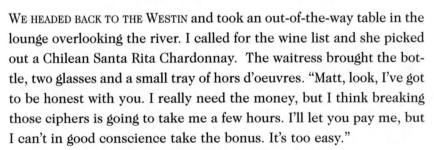

WE HEADED BACK TO THE WESTIN and took an out-of-the-way table in the lounge overlooking the river. I called for the wine list and she picked out a Chilean Santa Rita Chardonnay. The waitress brought the bottle, two glasses and a small tray of hors d'oeuvres. "Matt, look, I've got to be honest with you. I really need the money, but I think breaking those ciphers is going to take me a few hours. I'll let you pay me, but I can't in good conscience take the bonus. It's too easy."

"Lisa, you don't know. Those codes ..."

"Hey, if we're going to be working together, let's get our terms straight. The word is 'cipher,' not 'code.' I'm pretty sure the second one that seems to be divided into words is a polyalphabetic substitution cipher. The other, I'm not so sure about. I'll need to get them both in some sort of electronic database and see about the best way to attack them. I hate to say it, but this pretty much boils down to a graduate level weekend homework assignment. And you've still not told me what you hope to do with the information once we break them."

"Lisa, I think I'm correct in saying that some of the best minds in the country have had a go at solving them at one time or another. I'm certain they got nowhere."

"Wait a minute, this isn't about that hoard of gold that was supposedly buried in, where was it, Pennsylvania?"

"No, not that, I promise you. And if we find what I'm looking for, I promise you'll get the bonus, no matter how quickly you figure things out."

She sipped her wine and gazed at a large container ship moving slowly up the river. Raising her eyebrows and pursing her lips, she said, "It's your money."

CHAPTER

Twenty-Seven

I TYPED UP A BRIEF EMPLOYMENT CONTRACT on her laptop while we sat in the lounge, taking special care to add a strict confidentiality clause. We reviewed it, agreed on the terms, burned it on a CD and had the waitress take it to the business center to be printed while we worked on the Chardonnay. She returned 15 minutes later with two crisp copies and a $22 charge to my room. We signed, the waitress witnessed, and we finished the bottle of wine.

I had planned a more formal dinner at one of the better restaurants in town. With the deal settled and immediate business behind us, Lisa wanted to see the city. Starting out with the sun low in the western sky, we took in the riverfront promenade, then had some cheap house wine at a crowded bar on River Street. We strolled for an hour, moving from one tree-lined square to the next, staring in shop windows and marveling at the architecture. We ended up in the City Market complex just after dusk, cobbling together an eclectic supper washed down with sangria in a small tapas place. Lisa clearly had a brilliant and curious mind, wanting to know the smallest of details about the seemingly most mundane of subjects. We talked about Savannah and the South. I tried to satisfy her curiosity about the history of the area. She was fascinated to hear a Southerner's perspective on the Civil War. Not a word was said about the Rutherford Cipher, or the project.

We left Savannah early Friday morning. I started out on Interstate 16, but Lisa, after a brief study of a worn Georgia map she'd found in the glove compartment, insisted we take the back roads. She was excited. "I love the names of these little towns! There're women: Ellabel and Edna and Undine and Aline. And men: Aaron and Hubert and Emit and Ivanhoe. And then you can't help but wonder what they were thinking when they named three little places in — what's this? Bulloch County – Clito and Piddleville and Hopeulikeit." She laughed. We took our time, turning a two-hour trip into four, with stops to examine country stores, languid rivers that drifted seaward between cypress-lined banks, and vast flat fields of cotton or soybeans awaiting the fall harvest.

Eula Mae was waiting at the back door in a starched white uniform when we arrived at Rutherford Hall. A faint aroma of cooking hung in the air. Lisa was not sure how to react and frankly, neither was I. "I sure am glad to meet you Ms. Li. Mr. Matt has done told me so much about …"

Lisa looked at me quizzically. "Eula Mae, cool it. Ms. Li is here on business, OK? We met yesterday for the first time."

Eula Mae grinned back. "Whatever you wants to tell me or not tell me is fine, Mr. Matt. I just wants this young lady to feel right at home here. Now, let me show you your room, and then I done fixed y'all a big dinner." Grabbing her bag, she motioned Lisa to follow and headed for the stairs.

We satisfied Eula Mae by picking at her huge meal of fried chicken, cornbread, butterbeans, field peas and fresh tomatoes all laid out in portions that would have fed a small platoon. Washing it down with sweet iced tea, Lisa said wryly, "Now I'm beginning to understand why all those guys named Bubba have such big guts." She smiled and served herself more of the fresh bounty of late August.

While Eula Mae cleaned up and Lisa retreated to her room to

change clothes and freshen up, I made a quick run to the bank and retrieved the two volumes containing the Rutherford Cipher from the safe deposit box. We sat down in Lillie's study to go over what I had.

I handed her the two volumes and she flipped through them slowly, pausing when she came to the pages with the nonsense text. "I've been told that this text is referred to as the Rutherford Cipher, and that there've been attempts to decipher it in the past."

"Never heard of it." She didn't look up.

After a few minutes, Lisa said, "Let's see what we've got here to work with." She spent the next ten minutes reviewing the specs for Lillie's computer, pouring over the program files, and checking out the peripherals, especially the scanner. "How old did you say your aunt was when she died?"

"Eighty-six."

"She had great technology for someone that age. You said she had a computer and a scanner – I thought I'd be dealing with an Osborne or Apple II. Yeah, I think we can work with this." She thought a bit and then said, "Here's my plan. I'm going to take your photocopies of the cipher and scan them into a database using the OCR program that works with the scanner, then ..."

"Whoa, hold on. You're losing me in the first sentence. Just give me the gist of it. My degrees are in English and anthropology, remember."

"OK, bottom line: I'm going to take a quick look at what we've got, see if I can't solve the problem this evening, collect my three month's pay and bonus, and head back to L.A. tomorrow."

"Confident, aren't you?"

"I'm good at what I do. I need the money, and it was you who set the terms. You *will* have your checkbook handy when the time comes?"

"A deal is a deal." I had a sinking feeling she might just do it, making her right on two counts out of three. I hadn't been lying, but I was beginning to feel like a bit of a crazy fool. A fool and his money...

LISA SPENT THE AFTERNOON IN THE STUDY. I poked my head in every 30 minutes or so to check on her. She stayed hunched over the computer, occasionally scribbling notes on a yellow legal pad. Eula Mae offered coffee before she left for the day; she accepted but took no breaks from her work. As the grandfather clock in the hall was striking six, she emerged, looking dejected. "Remember what I said about your being a lying, crazy fool?"

"Yes, ..." I said.

"Well, I got it wrong. You were *not* lying, and I'm beginning to think that I'm the crazy fool."

"What have you come up with?"

"I'm not sure, Matt. I *really am* good at codes and ciphers, but this one – if it is just one – throws me.

"When I first saw this yesterday in Savannah, I was thinking, hey, simple Vigenère cipher, at least for one of the parts. Today, when I found out that you retrieved them from books printed in the 1870s, I thought, 'Wow! Piece of cake. Simple frequency analysis and I'm outta here.' But now, well, I'm not so sure. Let me ask you a question. Are you *absolutely sure* this text contains some sort of encrypted information?"

The sinking feeling returned. "I believe so. If you want me to be perfectly honest, I've been told – based on some second-hand information – that it does not." I explained to her in broad outlines what the old bookseller had told me.

"Printer's error! Damn!" She paused for a moment. "But, Matt, that begs a question. If someone, who by all rights should know that this is not a cipher, told you that fact, and assuming he had no interest one way or the other in lying to you, why in God's name would you promise me tens of thousands of dollars to try to solve what may be an insoluble problem?"

I didn't reply. I was trying to think what to say. She watched my eyes carefully.

"You have other information. That is the only logical conclusion."

I hesitated. "Yes."

William Rawlings, Jr.

"Are you going to share it?" She stood with her arms on her hips, eyes burning.

"If I have to."

CHAPTER
Twenty-Eight

I TOLD HER EVERYTHING, or almost everything. I mentioned that my cousin had died, but I didn't bother to tell her that he'd been murdered less than three weeks earlier in the library directly beneath her bedroom. I didn't tell her that I was on the suspect list, albeit not still at the top. I did explain to her about the famous *War Diaries of Captain Matthew Rutherford*, and how I had "accidentally" discovered the missing diary while straightening up after Lillie's death.

We were sitting at the kitchen table, munching on Domino's pizza and drinking iced tea from a huge pitcher Eula Mae had left in the fridge. "So you actually have the diary that states in no uncertain terms that your great-great-grandfather and some other officers stole gold bullion from the Confederate Treasury in 1865?"

"That's right," I said while nodding.

She picked at a piece of pepperoni on one of the remaining slices in the grease-stained box. It came loose with a long string of cheese which she held above her head and lowered slowly into her mouth. "You know that I checked you out before I came down here?"

"No, I didn't."

"I guess you've been wondering just how crazy or desperate I am.

Think about it: You call me up out of the blue, offer me more money than I normally make in two years for what may be a three-month job, and then invite me down to some strange city for an 'interview.' Sounds to me like the plot of a slasher movie. But you got good refs. People said you were a decent guy. Fair, honest, hard-working, fun. A friend of mine even knows your ex, Brandi. Even she didn't have anything bad to say about you. In fact, she sort of said she missed seeing you."

I laughed. "You amaze me, Lisa."

Cramming the last slice of pizza in her mouth, she mumbled, "You ain't seen nothing yet!"

LISA SPENT THE NEXT HOUR TELLING ME in detail what she'd found. The pages of garbled letters from the two books appeared to be fundamentally different. For the sake of clarity, she called them Cipher 1 and Cipher 2. Cipher 1 was from the reunion volume. It consisted of a series of regularly spaced letters in rows and columns with arrows at the head and foot pointing in the same direction. Cipher 2 was from the biography volume and was quite dissimilar from Cipher 1.

On the surface it would appear the text was divided into words of varying lengths, but no pattern was immediately evident. Taking her yellow legal pad, she sketched as she talked, moving at once from a pizza munching 20-something to the consummate professor giving remedial lessons to a slow pupil.

"My first thought was that Cipher 2 would be a fairly simple matter," Lisa explained. "The fact that it was divided into what appeared to be words, and the fact that it dated from the 1870s should have made it child's play. It wasn't that simple when I got into it, though. It appeared to be what's called a polyalphabetic, or Vigenère substitution cipher. The basic techniques have been around for 500 years or more, and up until the early twentieth century, they were considered totally secure.

"Let me give you an example. First of all, in a substitution cipher one letter has been substituted for another, clear?"

I nodded.

"You have to assume that the substitution is done in some regular fashion so that the pattern of changes is the same for all letters. The English alphabet has 26 letters, beginning with A and ending with Z. Let's make up a new alphabet we'll call 'Alphabet B' that has the first letter shifted to the last position, but everything else remains the same. This alphabet would begin with B, C, D..., and so on, and end with X, Y, Z and A. Are you with me still?"

Again, I nodded.

"Now take the word 'CAT.' If we encrypt it using Alphabet B, we'd find that C, which is the third letter in the regular alphabet becomes D, the third letter in our new alphabet. And A becomes B and T becomes U. Now instead of the regular word 'CAT' in what we refer to as plaintext, we have the encrypted word 'DBU.' Simple, eh?"

"Not really, but I see what you're saying," I said.

"If you sent that word as an encrypted message, the recipient would simply shift the new letters to the left and you'd have 'CAT' again."

Lisa paused and took a gulp of tea. "OK. That's a simple substitution cipher. Well, imagine that since there are 26 letters in the alphabet, you could easily come up with 26 alphabets simply by shifting the first letters to the last. You'd have the regular alphabet beginning with A, a second beginning with B, a third beginning with C, and so on. In a polyalphabetic substitution cipher each letter of the encrypted text is changed based on a different one of the 26 alphabets. You need a 'key word' to ..."

"Hold on, you're losing me now." I was beginning to get a bit confused.

"I think I can show you better with an example. Let's say you want to encrypt your name, 'Rutherford.'"

She wrote on her legal pad

RUTHERFORD

"We'll make up a simple keyword, say 'BAD.'"

"Are you trying to tell me something?" I interrupted. She smiled.

"Now, above the word we want to encrypt — the plaintext as it's called — we write the keyword, like this, repeating it as many times as we need to." She wrote on the pad

BADBADBADB
RUTHERFORD

For the letter R we use Alphabet B, for the letter U we use Alphabet A, for T, Alphabet D, and so on. We shift the letters and now 'Rutherford' becomes 'Suxievgove.' Neat and simple, no?" She laid the pen on the pad and beamed.

"No! And how do you know all this anyway?" I asked.

"My PhD thesis, remember?" She took a sip of tea and continued. "The beauty of all this is that if you use a keyword with three different letters like in this example..." She pointed at the legal pad "...any one letter of the plaintext can be encoded." She paused, doing the math in her head. "Any one of 17,576 ways."

"I'm impressed."

"Sounds complicated, but these techniques have been ..."

"No, I mean by you." She blushed, momentarily at a loss for words.

Regaining her composure, Lisa continued, "Vigenère ciphers were widely used in the Civil War. Up until the early part of the twentieth century, they were considered pretty much unbreakable. Then someone came up with the technique of frequency analysis. It works like this: E is the most commonly used letter in English, followed by T, then A and so on. Short documents are hard, but long documents like these," she pointed at the folder holding the photocopies of the Rutherford Cipher, "should be easy. You start looking at patterns of occurrence, and when, for example, you get two of the most commonly occurring letters repeating themselves in a group with one other letter, you can bet you're dealing with the word 'THE.' That's pretty easy to understand, hey?"

"For those of you with PhD's in math. For the rest of us — no way."

"OK. I'll cut the technical talk, but here is the summary. I haven't really worked on Cipher 1 because I thought Cipher 2 would be easier. I've come up with zip on Cipher 2, which could mean any of several things: One, the keyword is a very long phrase that can't be determined by frequency analysis. Two, it's double or triple encrypted. That is, someone encrypted the text and then did it a second or even third time using a separate key. Three, it's not a cipher at all and simply jumbled letters on a piece of paper."

"What do you think?"

"Honest? Remember you're paying me no matter what."

"Honest."

"I think it's real. I think it has the smell and feel of a cipher, and I want to know what it says. I can't prove it, and what I've done with the computer thus far has not told me much. I think it's there. I've got three months to find it or I'm $100,000 poorer."

I smiled.

"So let's bag it for today. I'm pretty tired. I want to sleep on it and, as one of your Southern heroines said, tomorrow is another day."

CHAPTER

Twenty-Nine

I AWOKE THE NEXT MORNING to find Lisa gone. More precisely, Eula Mae had knocked on my bedroom door with that pronouncement a few moments past 7. "She ain't here, Mr. Matt. She's done taken off."

"Eula Mae, for god's sake, it's 7 o'clock. What are you doing here?"

"Well, seemed to me, since you got company, you should act like the Rutherford you are and be a good host. So I took it upon myself to come over here and fix y'all some decent breakfast 'stead of that yoghurt stuff you eats. I brewed up a big pot of coffee and was bringing some up to Miss Lisa when I found that her door's open and she ain't here."

I thought for a moment. "Eula Mae, how do you know she's not in here with me?"

That possibility evidently hadn't occurred to her. "Oh, my lord! I am so sorry, Mr. Matt. I never ..."

Just at that moment, we heard the front door shut and Lisa bounded up the stairs in bright green shorts and a cut off T-shirt. "Oh, hi, Eula Mae, Matt. I hope I didn't wake you. I like to get in my morning run before the rush hour traffic."

Eula Mae threw up her hands and said, "Well, *that's* one thing you ain't never gon' have to worry about in this here town. The only rush hour here is when they have a sale on fishing worms at Henry's Bait and Tackle."

She retreated back down the stairs, calling over her shoulder, "If you want breakfast, it'll be in the kitchen."

We sat at the kitchen table and were served sausage, grits and scrambled eggs. Lisa whispered so as not to disturb Eula Mae, "If I'm going to be spending any amount of time here, we've got to do some negotiating on the food. I'm more of a salad and sushi type."

"We'll work it out," I smiled.

She had evidently put a lot of thought into the cipher problem overnight. "This is what I think we need to do. I want to spend some time today on the other document, the one I call Cipher 1. Maybe I should have tackled it first, but I was so sure I could solve the other one quickly ..." She paused. "Anyway, I'll spend a few hours trying to get a feel for it this morning. If I'm making progress, I'll keep plugging away at it this afternoon, tonight and whenever. If I can't solve it quickly, we'll take the afternoon off and I'll fly back to San Francisco tomorrow morning. Which ever way things go, I have one special request before I leave."

"Which is?"

"I want a guided tour of Walkerville. All I've ever seen of the rural South was in movies and on TV. *In the Heat of the Night, The Dukes of Hazzard, To Kill a Mockingbird* — you get the idea."

"I am at your service, ma'am," I said.

AT NOON, LISA EMERGED FROM LILLIE'S STUDY. I had left her alone this time while I went out for newspapers and to the hardware store to pick up a list of items that Eula Mae had given me. She seemed disappointed.

"Matt, I'm not getting much of anywhere. I scanned in the letters and have put them through every obvious permutation looking for some sort of pattern. Nothing!"

"Lisa, don't get discouraged so quickly. I told you that these codes have apparently stumped..."

"*Ciphers*. Not codes. The word 'code' implies that the text is changed on the level of words or phrases, like 'The grass is green.' means 'We attack at dawn.' These are *ciphers*, Matt. Each individual letter has had another letter substituted for it. What we've got to do is figure out the pattern."

———————◆●◆———————

WE SPENT THE AFTERNOON RIDING AROUND TOWN. I played tour guide. To someone who'd grown up in Los Angeles, Walkerville seemed like an exotic foreign country. It was Labor Day weekend. The town was deserted with most folks heading out for one last bit of sun at the lake or beach. We toured the copper-roofed Courthouse built in the 1870s to replace the one that General Sherman had burned during his infamous March to the Sea. We visited the county Historical Society museum housed in the antebellum mansion that had been Sherman's headquarters for a few days in November 1864. Lisa was fascinated by the exhibits. She read with rapt attention first-person accounts of the invasion of the Northern army and the suffering that followed its scorched-earth policy.

"This is amazing. It's terrible! In school they don't teach you that all this happened. Do you realize that General Sherman would be prosecuted as an international war criminal, if he'd allowed and encouraged his army to do these sorts of things today?"

"Perhaps, but that was nearly a 140 years ago, and the victors in any struggle have a way of rewriting history to show them in the best light. After all, Sherman is remembered for his famous 'War is Hell' quote. One thing though, it might give you some insight into why my great-great-grandfather felt justified in taking the gold from the Confederate Treasury rather than let it fall into the hands of the Yankees."

"Yankees. That's the first time I've heard you use that word," Lisa said. She was right. I hadn't really thought about it until then.

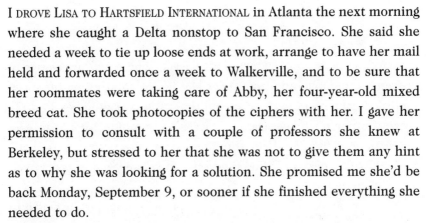

I DROVE LISA TO HARTSFIELD INTERNATIONAL in Atlanta the next morning where she caught a Delta nonstop to San Francisco. She said she needed a week to tie up loose ends at work, arrange to have her mail held and forwarded once a week to Walkerville, and to be sure that her roommates were taking care of Abby, her four-year-old mixed breed cat. She took photocopies of the ciphers with her. I gave her permission to consult with a couple of professors she knew at Berkeley, but stressed to her that she was not to give them any hint as to why she was looking for a solution. She promised me she'd be back Monday, September 9, or sooner if she finished everything she needed to do.

Driving back, I thought about Lisa's reaction to Walkerville. She truly liked it. I had been so eager to leave it.

CHAPTER
Thirty

I ARRIVED BACK IN TOWN SHORTLY AFTER 1 P.M. There was a message on the answering machine from Aunt Maggie insistently inviting me to "a little birthday dinner" for my mother. It was September 1 and I'd forgotten her birthday, again. It wasn't something I could in good conscience refuse, and on thinking about it, realized it probably looked like I'd been avoiding everyone since Lance's murder. I needed to make amends.

There wasn't a lot I could do to work on my search for the gold until Lisa returned, so I resolved to spend the following week mending bridges and catching up on Lillie's affairs. I needed to meet with Nick about the estate; I had collected a stack of bills that needed to be paid, as well as about two dozen letters that needed to be answered.

I was dreading the evening, but things turned out well. I arrived at 6 to find the group – my mother and aunt, plus a dozen friends of their age – in the back yard sitting in folding chairs and sipping cocktails and beer while Uncle Jack tended half chickens roasting slowing on his industrial sized grill. I shook hands all round, tolerated several hugs, grabbed a beer and headed over to "help" Jack. He brought the subject up immediately.

"Matt, I know this thing with Lance's death has been hard on all of us, but I don't want you to think for one minute that we suspect you had anything to do with it. We've known for a long time that Lance had a problem with drugs. We've tried to help him. I guess we just didn't want to admit it, but deep down, I can't say I'm surprised that it came to this. I'd really thought he was going clean up his act. We'd had him in rehab last year – cost us a bundle. He'd sworn he was not using, but when he got home just before Lillie died ..." It may have been the smoke from the grill, but I saw a tear well up in Jack's eye.

"Uncle Jack, you don't have to ..."

"No, let me finish. I just want you to know that we've accepted things. We love you – you're the only Rutherford left now and we're counting on you to look after us in our old age." He tried to smile.

A group of husbands bored with their wives' gossip had wandered over, drinks in hand. Tom Kerwin, who ran the local Ace Hardware, spoke. "Matt, who was that good-looking lady I saw you with yesterday?"

I didn't anticipate that. "Oh, she's a consultant I know from California. We're working on a little project." I tried to sound nonchalant.

"Really? You sure were looking at her like there was something more. 'Course she's a lot to look at." The group chuckled; Tom grinned and sipped his drink.

WHEN I RETUNED HOME, LISA HAD LEFT A MESSAGE on the machine to the effect that she'd made it home safely and would be in touch.

THE NEXT MORNING, DOUG CALLED to invite me to the "Guy's Poker Night" on Wednesday. "If you're going to be here for a while you ought to get to know some people," he explained. "This'll be a good chance." I didn't object.

I spent Monday afternoon in Nick's office. It was Labor Day, but he had called and said he was in a mood to work and we'd have no interruptions. We went over the preliminary figures for the estate in some detail. I had roughly $125,000 cash in several checking accounts, several hundred thousand more in CDs of varying maturity, a very substantial brokerage account that he bemoaned had lost a good bit with the drop in the market, "and of course, the timberland." I hadn't realized it, but I had also inherited about 1,800 acres of planted pines and mixed pine-hardwood forest. "That's what's going to make us have to pay the IRS. I'll see if I can't get a lowball appraisal on it, though. Maybe save us a little bit. I estimate you'll have a basic yearly income of about $150,000, but on average it'll be a lot higher when you factor in the timber sales every five years or so. You now own about three square miles of Georgia forest. Want to take a little tour?"

Nick arrived at Rutherford Hall at 7 on Tuesday morning. Instead of his usual Mercedes, he was driving a well-worn Ford F-250 Supercab pickup. "My hunting truck," he explained.

We ate breakfast at one of the local restaurants. He was in his best form at being one of the guys. He worked the room, shaking hands, slapping backs and subtly drumming up business from amongst the denim clad crowd of farmers, loggers and other early risers. We spent the morning riding over logging roads and familiarizing me with my newly inherited property. It was beautiful. Huge stands of mature timber stretched as far as the eye could see. We saw deer and quail, and surprised a family of foxes as we rounded a curve in a narrow dirt road.

"What are you going to do with all this, Matt?" Nick asked. "It's been in your family for generations."

I started to answer, then said simply, "I don't know."

I SPENT THE REMAINDER OF TUESDAY AFTERNOON and all day Wednesday in Lillie's study paying bills and returning letters. My mother and Aunt Maggie had written the obligated acknowledgements for the flowers, food and memorial contributions sent after Lillie's death. I replied to a number of letters, stating that neither the estate nor the diaries were for sale but that at some point in time we would hope that Lillie's valuable collection of papers and manuscripts would be made available to the public. I had no idea what I was talking about, but it sounded good and would buy me time.

At 8 p.m. Wednesday, I rang the doorbell at Doug's split-level. His home was in an older neighborhood populated either by families on their way down or their way up. Doug definitely fell into the latter group. His wife, Nan, her two children tugging at her skirt, met me at the door immediately and unnecessarily apologizing for "this tiny little house." She ushered me through a door off the hallway that led to a downstairs rec room festooned with Confederate flags. Seven men in their late 20s and early 30s were earnestly engaged in a game of poker around a large round table. The room was blue with cigar smoke and the table crowded with empty and half-full, long-neck beer bottles among the cards and piles of chips.

Doug waved and stood up.

"Guys, I want you to meet my good friend, Matt Rutherford." I was introduced around the table. I had met a couple of the players at the SCV picnic. The others were two lawyers, a family practitioner and two lower-level managers at one of the local manufacturing plants. Doug motioned for me to sit down next to him in a chair and placed a pile of poker chips in front of me.

"This is your stake. We don't play for cash, but we do keep records. Wade over there owes me about 10,000 points which I fully intend to collect one of these days. OK, enough talking. John, it's your deal."

Again, and much to my surprise I enjoyed myself. The guys were intelligent, educated and good poker players. This life, so different from what I had known and thought I wanted in California, was somehow appealing. I went home with 4,500 points owed to me.

By Friday at noon, I had finished paying the bills and had taken care of most of the pressing issues with Lillie's estate. Feeling guilty about not spending more time with my mother, I called and invited her to lunch at one of the local restaurants. When I returned, I had a message from Lisa.

"I'll see you about the middle of the day Monday. I'm catching the red-eye Sunday night and will get to Atlanta about 8. I'll pick up a rental car and drive down — you *are* covering expenses, remember? I've been working on the data all week, and I've talked with some people I know at Berkeley. I'll tell you about it when I get there, but suffice it to say that I've got some good news and some bad news."

The phone clicked off. I wanted to call her back but realized that she hadn't given me her home number.

CHAPTER

Thirty-One

EULA MAE HAD LUNCH WAITING on the dining room table when Lisa drove into the yard. She'd rented a bright blue four-wheel-drive Jeep Wrangler and grinned as she climbed out. "Like it? The color's Patriot Blue. Thought I'd buy one with the little bonus I've got coming. This seemed like a good chance for a test drive."

"You've solved it!?" I was ecstatic.

"Well, not quite." She paused as she opened the back to grab her bags. "But I'm going to."

"You're close then, I presume."

"Ah," she tugged at a large soft-sided suitcase, "Not really."

"Then what?"

"Matt, I'm confident and I'm me. That's what." She deposited the large bag at my feet, turned and headed for the back steps.

We ate lunch, chicken salad and sliced fruit this time, while Lisa filled me in on the latest gossip from the Bay Area high-tech community. The Rutherford Cipher was not mentioned.

The dishes had been cleared and Eula Mae had served coffee when I finally said, "You said you had some good news and some bad news. Want to share?" It was clear that she'd been avoiding the subject.

"OK. Which do you want first?"

"The bad news, I guess. At least we can end on a positive note."

She became serious. "I spent some time last week at UC Berkeley. At Code-Tech, we worked fairly closely with a professor named Jack Feinberg. He was – still is, I guess – on the Board of Directors. I think he had put a good bit of his own cash in the business. His specialty is information management systems, but his hobby and his passion is cryptography. He runs a cryptography Web site, does a lot of high-dollar consulting and is probably one of the top minds in the country in that field. He's divorced and he's *really* been wanting to go out with me. He's a little old for me – in his early 50s – but he's the one person I'd turn to first to help solve this kind of problem.

"So I called him. Told him I had a consulting job, and naturally he offered his free advice over dinner at his club. I put on my best Suzie Wong outfit with the ankle-length split skirt. It was all the poor guy could do to keep his eyes on the road after he picked me up. We actually had a good evening, until I pulled out the photocopies and laid them in front of him. We were sitting in this cozy little booth, he fumbles in his pocket for his reading glasses, studies the papers for about 30 seconds and breaks out laughing.

"I asked him what was so funny, and he said, 'I see you've rediscovered The Rutherford Cipher.' I played dumb while he gave me the whole story – in fact, I think he wrote an article on it one time – about 'cipher hoaxes.' He told me basically what the fellow Planer told you. It looks real, but it's not."

She could see the look of disappointment on my face. "So, he's the ultimate expert?"

"No, he's just *an* expert. And that's the end of the bad news part."

"And what exactly could be good news after that?" I asked.

"From my perspective, I don't think he'll ask me out again, but that's not what you're paying me for. The good news is that I spent a couple of days with a group of really bright kids at the Berkeley Cipher Club. They're an informal group of geeks and nerds, all terribly bright and all into ciphers and computer gaming. I got some good ideas and three CDs full of unique decrypting shareware. Now I just need some time to work on it."

"You're that confident, eh?"

"I'm starting to test drive new cars. I must be," Lisa said with a smile.

I SAW VERY LITTLE OF LISA for the next three days. She arose early, went for a run, and then shut herself up in Lillie's study, emerging only for coffee and food. I took her out for dinner in the evening. She was pleasant, but subdued, still clearly mentally involved in solving the problem at hand. Every so often, I'd hear her on the phone with someone discussing one mathematical algorithm or another. Each time I stuck my head in to offer support, she'd smile and say, "I'm going to figure it out yet."

On Thursday at 2:45 p.m., I heard a whoop followed by Lisa screaming at the top of her lungs, "Bingo!" I rushed in the study to find her sitting with her feet propped on the desk, arms folded across her chest and a huge smile on her face. The laser printer was spewing out sheet after sheet of paper covered with letters and text.

"You've figured it out?"

"Yes and no. I have just realized what I've been doing wrong. Matt, all this time we've been assuming that these two documents are *ciphers* and that they are somehow related. Feinberg was right – some of the best minds in the country have worked on this stuff and nobody, I repeat *nobody*, has come up with anything. So I asked myself, what were they doing wrong? And then it hit me. The experts are accustomed to deciphering messages written by other experts, when meanwhile these documents that we call the Rutherford Cipher were not written by experts. They were written by amateurs who didn't follow the rules!" She paused to let the thought sink in.

She continued, "For the time being I gave up on Cipher 2. I worked with it for hours and I still can't come up with any better set of options than those I gave you when I first looked at it. The text I refer to as Cipher 1 is shorter. It suddenly occurred to me, what if it's not a cipher? What if it's, say, an anagram with scrambled letters that follow some hidden pattern? So I wrote a quick program to ask the computer to start making words out of the letters, using each letter only once and focusing on words of six letters or greater. At first, I got a lot of garbage, and then, as I tweaked things, I began to get words like "paragraph" and "article" and "section." I then went back and asked the program to see if the letters that made up the most commonly found words occurred in any regular pattern. I finally discovered that if I eliminated the arrows at the top and bottom of the page and looked at every 16th letter, this pattern emerged." She handed me single sheet with regularly spaced letters.

W O U Q B B 9 Z 2 T M Y K J **V O L U M E**
A C N T R O 7 3 G X 8 W N U R F **P A G E**
4 R T N V C 9 0 Q P I **P A R A G R A P H**
E V R T X 6 I M Y Q G S D **P R E F A C E**
2 R B Z S R K L 5 O U Y M B G F **B O O K**
D F P A 6 X 4 I H 2 G B Q **C H A P T E R**
N N H 8 O W C X 6 7 X I L E T **V E R S E**
I W Q 8 1 H V P T C U L **P R E A M B L E**
C V N I 0 P E F A Z B G X **A R T I C L E**
S 6 Y I P Q D F M G B 5 I **S E C T I O N**
A T 9 U P L Q S E C 6 **P A R A G R A P H**
3 U Y B V X L R E M 6 T **F O R E W O R D**
R O Y 2 H Z Q X 9 T E L J G B **T I T L E**
Y 7 C V I U X Q O E D 6 U P **S T A N Z A**
L Q A U R 6 O 9 V B Z I K R **E P I L O G**
E R T Y 5 8 I 0 C B J P L F **L E T T E R**

There were a total of 16 lines of 20 letters, every line ending in a word that she had highlighted in boldface type. Each word had a literary significance.

"I finally understand what's going on. Cipher 2 is in fact a Vigenère cipher. It's probably encoded with a very long text key that is taken from some other document, hence the references to 'paragraph' or 'verse.' Now all we've got to do is figure where to look for that." She smiled broadly. "I've had it for ciphers today, Matt. How about a beer and a ride in my jeep with the top down?"

CHAPTER

Thirty-Two

WE WERE SITTING AT THE DINING ROOM TABLE when the hall clock struck noon Friday. For three hours, we had been racking our brains trying to make some sense of the list of words in Cipher 1. Lisa had made the basic decision that the order of the words probably meant something, and that we could assume they were read from the top of the page to the bottom. That being the case, the word list was as follows:

VOLUME
PAGE
PARAGRAPH
PREFACE
BOOK
CHAPTER
VERSE
PREAMBLE
ARTICLE
SECTION
PARAGRAPH
FOREWORD

TITLE
STANZA
EPILOG
LETTER

Each word was at the end of a 20-letter line. The letters, numbers and symbols that preceded them seemed to be random fillers for the space.

As we discussed it, we felt even more strongly that Cipher 1, not really a cipher as Lisa so carefully pointed out, appeared to hold the key to solving Cipher 2. "It could be anything. For example, take these three words here, 'Book', 'Chapter,' and 'Verse.' The obvious reference would be to the Bible, but where to start? There are something like 66 books in the Bible, about 1,200 chapters and more than 30,000 verses."

I looked at her quizzically.

"Don't worry – I looked it up. I'm smart, but not *that* smart." She smiled, brushing back her long black hair.

"It's got to be something obvious. Think about it, Matt. You're writing an encrypted message that you want to stand the test of time. The key has to be something that you know will be around in 100 years. You can't just refer to some letters carved on some old oak tree, or to some popular novel of the day. The missing data has to be in a document whose existence and accessibility can be assured over time. Either a book or what? Have you searched the house thoroughly?"

"Of course, but not with this in mind."

"Well," Lisa rose and headed for the library.

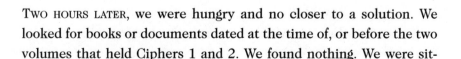

TWO HOURS LATER, we were hungry and no closer to a solution. We looked for books or documents dated at the time of, or before the two volumes that held Ciphers 1 and 2. We found nothing. We were sitting at the kitchen table munching on tuna fish sandwiches washed down with Sprite.

Lisa spoke. "Matt, I want to know if you've told me everything."

"Of course." I didn't know where she was going with that question.

"You told me your cousin had died. You didn't tell me he was murdered in the library, shortly after your aunt's death."

"You're right. I didn't. I thought you might have turned down the project if you knew everything. How did you find out?"

"I didn't at first. I'd picked up a copy of the *Adams Sentinel* at a convenience store that first morning I went jogging. I didn't start reading it until I was on the plane back to San Francisco. There was a little blurb on one of the back pages to the effect that the local police suspected Lance's death was drug related. I made a few phone calls and did a few Internet searches."

"But you didn't say anything. And you came back."

"Yeah." She looked at me for a moment and continued. "I think by that time, I'd gotten to know you. You didn't do it. You're a nice guy, Matt."

This time, I told her everything, leaving nothing out.

Lisa was silent for a moment and then said, "I want to read the diary. You've told me what it says, but I want to see it for myself. There's got to be something there."

The bank was just closing as I slipped in through the front door. Retrieving Captain Rutherford's missing diary from the safe deposit box, I rushed home. Lisa took it, flipped through a few pages and headed for her room. "Think I'll do a little reading. See you in the morning."

AT 4 A.M., I was awakened by noise from downstairs. I'd armed the security system before going to bed and it had not gone off. I cracked

my bedroom door and saw light coming from the hall below. Pulling on shorts and a T-shirt, I quietly crept down the stairs to find Lisa in a long, loose-fitting nightshirt, sitting at the dining room table furiously clipping away with scissors at what appeared to be photocopies of Cipher 1. A tape dispenser was sitting in front of her. Piled on the table was an odd assortment of items that included a rolling pin, a flashlight, the tube from a roll of paper towels that she'd removed and thrown in a pile on the floor, plus a broom handle, a thin iced-tea glass and other assorted cylindrical objects.

"Lisa?" She jumped at the sound of my voice.

"God, you scared me! Matt, I've got it! I've figured it out. Cipher 1 is not a simple anagram, it's a scytale! And these," she said, pointing excitedly at the pile of objects in front of her, "are going to help us find the key!"

I looked at her as if I thought she'd lost her mind. I did, actually. "Lisa, are you OK?"

She kept intently snipping at the photocopies and taping long strips of paper end to end. Without looking up, she said, "I'm great for a woman about to be a $100,000 richer."

I watched her in silence. The only sounds were the regular ticking of the grandfather clock in the downstairs hall, the scissors cutting through paper and the occasional screech of tape being pulled from the roll. Presently she stood up, proudly holding the long narrow strip of paper she'd made by taping the ends of her cuttings together. She grabbed the broom handle with her left hand and, raising her right that held the cascade of letters on paper, proudly said, "Behold the scytale!"

I stood and looked at her. Her beautiful delicate features glowed in the soft light of the brass Eastlake chandelier that hung above the table. Her dark straight hair, slightly unkempt, drifted over her right eye. The nightshirt, normally ending at mid-thigh, had ridden higher as she held her trophies above her head. Under other circumstances, I thought to myself, but instead said, "Lisa, what the hell is a scytale?"

CHAPTER
Thirty-Three

"THE INFORMATION WE NEEDED was in the diary all along," Lisa said. We were sitting at the kitchen table. It was 5 a.m., and we were both still dressed – or semi-dressed – in what we'd been wearing when I came down the stairs an hour earlier. "With all due respect to your grandfather and Colonel Sanders ..."

"Captain Sanders."

"Sorry, Captain Sanders. Anyway, Jacob Hermann was clearly the brains of the operation. Your grandfather, probably unknowingly, gave us some insight into Captain Hermann's mind. Think about it: He worked in the Signal Office so he had to be familiar with codes – in fact, he probably wrote a lot of them. He was educated and familiar with Greek and Roman history. And he mentioned a story by Edgar Allen Poe, 'The Purloined Letter.' There's another Poe short story, 'The Gold Bug,' where the location of some hidden pirate treasure is discovered by solving a fairly simple substitution cipher."

"But how did you realize that Cipher 1 was a scytale?"

"Well, I read the diary through three times before I fell asleep. I think I was trying to get inside the mind of our Captain Hermann. In the night, something – a dream, I don't know – woke me up. I don't really remember all the details, but in the dream, I think I was a Greek commander wanting to send a coded message across enemy lines. I used a scytale! It's so simple and one of the oldest known forms of military codes. The encoder and decoder are simply wooden staffs – or any cylindrical objects – of equal diameter. You have one and the recipient of the message has the other. You wrap a long strip of parchment or skin or whatever around one of the staffs so that it covers it but doesn't overlap, then write your message so that each letter is on one turn of the strip. You then unwind it, fill in the spaces with random letters, tie it around a messenger's waist as a belt, and send him on his way. The recipient gets the strip and 'decodes' the message by wrapping it around his staff of equal size. Voilà, the message is reproduced.

"So now we've got to find that object, and what I was doing with all this junk," she pointed at the flashlight, rolling pin, etc., that we had now moved into the kitchen, "was trying to get a feel for the size of the thing we're looking for."

"And?" I asked.

"I figure about two inches in diameter and at least five inches long."

Grinning, I said, "Well, I've got something a good bit ..."

"Don't even *think* about going there!" Lisa said with mock disgust, her eyes twinkling.

WE GOT DRESSED AND DECIDED TO GO OUT FOR BREAKFAST. Lisa's presence in the same country restaurant where Nick and I had eaten earlier in the week created a stir. Half a dozen men I scarcely knew came over to introduce themselves and welcome me back to town, the real reason being that they wanted to get a close look at Lisa.

Stoked with strong coffee, we returned to Rutherford Hall and decided to start the search again in the library. Despite the fact that we'd cleaned everything and repaired the damage, I still could clearly see Lance's swollen body lying in the middle of a pool of dried blood. Lisa was examining the handles on the fire tools and said, "I wonder why the killer didn't hit your cousin with a poker. That's the way it always happens in the movies."

The murder weapon! Of course. The answer was that Lance could have had it in his hand when he was attacked. His assailant could have taken it away from him. If Lance were holding it, then... "Lisa, I think you just said the magic words."

The bank was closed Saturday, but its president answered his cell phone on the 12th hole of the golf course. He agreed to meet me at noon. Again, I bought my gym bag stuffed with old clothes and made sure that he couldn't see me as I removed the gold ingot from the safe deposit box and slipped it in the bag.

Returning to Rutherford Hall, I gingerly laid the bar on the kitchen table. I didn't know if it was a duplicate of the one the police were holding, but I assumed it was. We examined it carefully. It was not round, but rather trapezoidal in cross section. It was roughly two inches thick by seven inches long and weighed, according to Lillie's kitchen scale, a shade under eight pounds. The ingot looked as if it had been cast in a mould, then stamped near the middle of one side with the Great Seal of the Confederacy. To the left of the seal, the letters "CSA" were stamped vertically, and on the right, in three lines were stamped 'MDLXIII', 'Assay 0.991,' and '#453.' On the opposite side of the bar, two sharply inscribed parallel lines were located roughly an inch and a half from each end.

"What do you think?" I asked Lisa.

"We'll soon find out." Holding one end of the taped paper strips against the ingot, she wound the strip tightly around it. The letters aligned perfectly revealing the 16 words neatly encircling the gold bar. My pulse began to race.

She unwound the strip and studied the bar, then the letters, and then the bar again. This time, she held the start of the strip exactly on the edge of the scribed line on the reverse side of the ingot and began to wind it tightly. The three letters "CSA" on the strip lined up perfectly with the same three letters stamped in the bar. She continued to wind, ending with the last turn exactly touching the scribed line at the other end of the bar. On the front, the three lines on the right side that had given the year, assay and control number now read 'Article II, Section 1, Paragraph 3'. "We've done it!" she whispered. "Matt, we've done it!"

The key had to be found in only one document. The letters "CSA" for Confederate States of America and the references to Articles, Section and Paragraph meant that we launched an immediate Internet search for the text of the Confederate Constitution. We found it on a Yale Law School Web site. Article II, Section 1, Paragraph 3 read:

> *The electors shall meet in their respective States and vote by ballot for President and Vice President, one of whom, at least, shall not be an inhabitant of the same State with them-selves; they shall name in their ballots the person voted for as President, and in distinct ballots the person voted for as Vice President, and they shall make distinct lists of all per-sons voted for as President, and of all persons voted for as Vice President, and of the number of votes for each, which lists they shall sign and certify, and transmit, sealed, to the seat of the Government of the Confederate States, directed to the President of the Senate; the President of the Senate shall, in the presence of the Senate and House of Representatives, open all the certificates, and the votes shall then be counted; the person having the greatest number of votes for President shall be the President, if such number be a majority of the whole number of electors appointed; and if no person have such majority, then from the persons having the highest numbers, not exceeding three, on the list of those voted for as*

President, the House of Representatives shall choose immedi-
ately, by ballot, the President. But in choosing the President
the votes shall be taken by States, the representation from
each State having one vote; a quorum for this purpose shall
consist of a member or members from two-thirds of the
States, and a majority of all the States shall be necessary to
a choice. And if the House of Representatives shall not choose
a President, whenever the right of choice shall devolve upon
them, before the 4th day of March next following, then the
Vice President shall act as President, as in case of the death,
or other constitutional disability of the President.

"It's perfect! Lots of stilted legalese that no one would ever in a thousand years find without the ingot. And it's long enough to make a Vigenère cipher virtually unbreakable. With a key like this you could try literally trillions of solutions and you still wouldn't stumble on the right one. No wonder all the experts thought it was a hoax."

"But, Lisa, I don't understand. *What* exactly is the keyword?" I asked.

"The whole damned thing, Matt. The whole damned thing!" With a few key strokes, she cut and pasted the computer text into a text editing program. Quickly eliminating spaces and punctuation, Lisa pasted the modified text into one of the shareware programs she'd gotten from the Berkeley Cipher Club. She said, "Here goes," and pressed the "Enter" key.

The screen went blank. We looked at each other. Then I noted out of the corner of my eye that the data feed light on the laser printer was blinking. The first sheet emerged at a seeming snail's pace. With sweating palms, I turned it over to read,

Weburiedthegoldinthecountyofbarnwellinthestateof
southCarolinainthefamilycemeteryofamannamed-
solomoncartwell...

Lisa screamed and hugged me. "God, Matt! We did it! We did it!" I could smell the scent of vanilla in her hair and felt her breasts as they pressed against my chest.

For that one instant in time, the world stood still.

CHAPTER
Thirty-Four

"JUST WHERE THE HELL IS BARNWELL, South Carolina?" Lisa was munching on a cookie and studying the corrected printout. Without much difficulty, she had inserted punctuation and spaces between the words to make the decrypted text more readable. It was a long and detailed description of where the gold had been buried.

We buried the gold in the County of Barnwell in the State of South Carolina in the family cemetery of a man named Solomon Cartwell. The two graves containing the gold are those of Solomon's brother and father, Nathan Cartwell and Emanuel Cartwell. Their bodies were lost in battle. The cemetery is located about a mile from the main river road on a high bluff overlooking Four Mile Branch on the southeast side of the waterway. To reach it journey south and east on this road about three miles from the lower ford over Upper Three Runs Creek. This runs into the Savannah River near a place known as Point Comfort. There are small creeks, but Four Mile Branch is the first bold stream to be crossed. There are several mills here and a good ford over the stream. Some short distance past the ford a small track leads toward the river. The ground to the south and east of the stream has been cleared for farming, but the land to the north is low and swampy. The last farmstead to be reached before the land falls into the large swamp that is beside the river is the Cartwell place. There is a substantial house, several barns, and a number of houses for the negroes. A quarter mile beyond the house the cemetery is on the edge of a large pasture in a grove of large live oak trees. Just beyond the land falls steeply to the Four Mile Branch. On April eighth, eighteen seventy we held a memorial for our fallen comrades and laid marble tombstones over their three graves. The Cartwell relatives were grateful and swore to maintain this site in their family. A younger cousin Jodie Cartwell is now in charge. We leave it to our children's children in the distant future to determine how to recover this bounty from what we have consecrated as hallowed ground.

"And just how are we supposed to figure out what 'the main river road' is, or how far 'a short distance' should be?" Lisa appeared frustrated. "All this work …"

"Hey, we've done the hard part. Now all we've got to do is launch our new careers as grave robbers. Remember, you've earned the first 20 percent – the rest comes when we recover the gold."

"Look, Matt," Lisa was perturbed. "I signed on to help you solve a technical problem. I'm not into things that are going to get me thrown in jail. *Especially* if they involve digging up graves."

"No, you're right. I can do this on my own from here on out – I think." I paused. "You're right." I repeated myself. "We just agreed that I'd pay you part when you cracked the cipher and the rest when I recover the gold. So I guess you're out of here. Just as soon as I get you a check."

"Yeah, I guess so." She spoke softly.

"OK. Well, I really do appreciate all you've done." I didn't know what more to say. "So, let me go find my checkbook." I headed toward the study feeling drained. I sat down at Lillie's desk, opened the checkbook and wrote two checks, one for the remainder of Lisa's three month's promised pay and the other for $20,000, the down payment on her promised bonus.

I took my time, signing the checks with my most formal signature before carefully folding them and placing them in an envelope. I was killing time. I didn't want her to leave. I looked up to see Lisa standing at the door.

"Matt, I've been thinking." She bit her lip. "You know, I really don't have much to do back in California. Do you suppose maybe I could hang around for a few days? Maybe help out a bit."

I walked over and kissed her, firmly and for a long time.

WE WERE BOTH HUNCHED OVER THE COMPUTER. My Google query for "Barnwell" produced dozens of useful Web sites. We were logged onto barnwellweb.com and clicking on the various links. I was seated at the keyboard. Lisa stood looking over my shoulder, her hand on my back. "Looks like a thriving little town," she observed. "County population just above 20,000. City population 5,635. They've got a county museum, a local weekly – the whole thing! And more cute little towns with people names – Hilda, and Kline and Elko. When do we leave, Matt?"

The thought hadn't occurred to me, but clearly we couldn't figure out the location of what had been the Cartwell farm more than 130 years ago sitting in front of a computer. "I don't know. We need some good maps for a start."

"How about the ones online?" Lisa asked.

"Tell you what let's do. You work here on finding out what you can while I make a quick run to the county library to see if I can find some old maps of South Carolina. They've got a pretty good historic book and manuscript collection. If I remember correctly from a high school project I worked on, there are some 19th century atlases."

"Sounds great," she said. I grabbed a legal pad and headed for the library.

The Lazard Memorial Library was unusual for a town of Walkerville's size. It was huge, ornate, and well funded. All this was due to the past generosity of the Lazard family whose last surviving member, a physician named Troup Lazard, had been killed in a spectacular plane crash precipitated by an equally spectacular scandal involving drugs, money and murder. The Lazard name, chiseled in the marble above the door, lived on despite all, as did the generous endowment that had originally built the building and purchased the books.

I arrived with an hour to spare before the late Saturday afternoon closing time. The librarian, a pleasant but severe woman in a simple brown skirt and white blouse, ushered me into the Historic Books room. The air conditioner kept the temperature in the low 60s. The muted, indirect lighting gave me the sense of walking into a cave. "We protect the books by controlling the temperature and humidity," she explained. "And of course you know that direct lighting can fade and destroy leather bindings." I nodded my head as if I cared, and asked her to help me find what I was looking for.

After half an hour, we had come up with a leather-bound history of South Carolina published in 1880, plus half a dozen maps from various books and atlases showing the Barnwell area and the nearby Savannah River. I skimmed the history book. There was no mention of the Cartwell family in the Index of Family Names. The maps proved more useful, especially an 1825 one from a thick volume entitled *Mill's Atlas*. I identified the Savannah River and the tributaries referred to in the cipher, Upper Three Runs and Four Mile Branch. After a few words of protest, she allowed me to photocopy and enlarge the map of Barnwell County, watching me intensely to be sure I handled the books with the care and respect their age demanded. Replacing the books carefully in their designated spots, she carried the copies to the desk and counted them again before pounding quietly on the adding machine and announcing that I owed 85 cents. I gave her $20 and told her to keep the change. She blushed and was saying something about children's literature as I left.

I arrived back at Rutherford Hall to find Lisa in the kitchen stirring a pot on the stove. She saw my surprised look and said, "I can cook, too." She pointed to a stack of printouts on the kitchen table. "We leave tomorrow morning. Pack your bag for a couple of nights." On the top of the pile was a reservation confirmation from the Historic Mills Plantation near Barnwell. I picked it up. She'd printed it in color on the inkjet printer. There was a photo of a white-columned Greek revival home seen through a long allée of moss-draped, live oaks. Below her name I read "Sanford Suite, Two persons, Queen bed, non-smoking."

CHAPTER

Thirty-Five

WE LEFT FOR BARNWELL EARLY THE NEXT MORNING. Lisa said nothing of her plans other than to note that, "I got us a room in what sounds like a pretty good place." She had seen me reading the reservation confirmation. The pot she'd been stirring on the stove turned out to be what she described initially as a "Chinese version of hot gazpacho"— and later admitted that she'd made it up from whatever vegetables she could find in the fridge. It was wonderful. Adding toasted bread and a half a bottle of pinot grigio, we made a great meal of it.

Afterward, we spent a few minutes going over the maps that I had copied and half an hour or so reviewing things she'd downloaded from the Internet. She then disappeared off toward the local mall, shopping list in hand. "For the trip," she explained. "I may be a while, so don't wait up for me. I'll see you first thing in the morning." By 10, Lisa hadn't returned. I went to bed disappointed. I heard her come in about 11 a.m.

We ate a light breakfast, loaded up her bright blue Jeep and hit the road. She drove, I navigated. Since we'd be arriving at midday Sunday, we decided to spend the afternoon checking out the town of Barnwell and then start our search in earnest when the courthouse opened Monday morning. Based on what Lisa had found on the Web, we thought we'd start at the clerk of court's office researching old deed records and hoping to find a plat. If that didn't work, we'd try the county library or the museum. I had the idea of trying to look up any news articles that might have been written about the memorial ceremony held in 1870 referred to in the decrypted cipher. Lisa opined that we could start by searching the local doctors' offices. "That's about the age of the magazines in *my* doc's waiting room. Maybe they kept a few local papers."

We drove east along back roads. It was a beautiful September day, with only a rare wispy cloud floating in a vast expanse of blue sky. The roadsides were dotted with the yellow wildflowers of late summer. There was a hint of fall color in the leaves of the tupelo and sweet gum that lined the streams along the road. We passed through the tiny farming towns of Wadley and Millen. The gently rolling land of Adams County gave way to straight-rowed fields of cotton, seas of dark green speckled with the yellow-white of flowers that would later produce fuzzy bolls of white fiber. Near Sylvania, the landscape began to change as red clay became sandy loam. Pine forests were now interspersed with stands of scrub oak. The highway crossed large swamps, thick with moss-draped cypress. We stopped and put the top down. Lisa bundled her long hair into a ponytail and smiled silently as the sun glinted off her Wayfarers.

We crossed the Savannah River and arrived shortly in Allendale, a name I remembered from high school as the place to go when you were 18 with a pregnant girlfriend and needed a quick no-questions-asked marriage by the local justice of the peace. The land here was sandy, and it appeared the main industry was farming. Turning north on U.S. Highway 278, we arrived in Barnwell shortly after noon. Lisa produced a map of the city that she'd printed off the Internet. We switched places and I drove while she navigated.

Barnwell appeared to be a typical rural southern town, steeped in local history and shuffling through a shabby middle age toward an uncertain future. The sign at the edge of town proclaimed that a visitor would be welcomed if he or she were a Lion, a Rotarian or a member of Kiwanis International. Lisa directed me to turn off the main highway and follow a street that led downtown. Stately old homes lined the drive. Some were well maintained; others down at the heels. Massive oaks cast dappled shadows on the quiet Sunday streets. Consulting her map, she said, "We should be coming up on the library." It came into view on our right, housed in a large, white, older home converted for that purpose. "That must be the County Museum," Lisa pointed at the former carriage house behind the library.

We arrived at the city square, such as it was. Whatever charm it may have had at one time had disappeared with the years. The architecture was generally modern, and unimpressive to say the least. "Maybe they had a fire?" I observed. Around a half-acre-sized bit of haphazardly mowed grass were a few overgrown flower beds and a motley collection of low market stores, a Masonic Hall with a beauty parlor downstairs, a pharmacy, a karate studio and assorted government offices. The one architectural gem was the Courthouse. Lisa read from her printouts. "The Barnwell County Courthouse was completed in 1879 and was constructed to replace a previous structure burned in February 1865 by Sherman's Army. Damn, that guy was everywhere down here. I presume that means we're out of luck for any property records before then."

"You never know what you'll find," I replied. We spent the next hour cruising around, taking in the sights and being stared at by the Sunday-after-church crowd who were evidently unaccustomed to tourists in shiny blue Jeeps.

THE HISTORIC MILLS PLANTATION BED & BREAKFAST was located some fifteen miles out from Barnwell near the whistle stops of Norway and

Denmark, "and just north of Govan, Olar and Ulmer, which must mean there are at least a few Scandinavians around here," Lisa observed. The original plantation dated from the late 1700s. The main house, now the B & B, was built in the heyday of cotton in the early 1850s. Somehow it had avoided Sherman's torch and had been owned by the same family for more than a century. We turned off the main highway onto a well-maintained dirt road, following Lisa's carefully copied instructions. The road led through dense forest, then transected a large field lined on either side by a white-painted fence. Horses grazed on one side, cattle on the other. A small sign at a gate said simply "Mills Plantation" with an arrow pointing down a gravel drive that disappeared into the woods in the distance. We turned in and momentarily were rewarded with a spectacular view of the house at the end of a long straight drive.

We parked in front next to half a dozen other cars with tags from Arizona, New York and California. A long-haired young woman, who could not have been much older than Lisa and I, emerged to greet us. "Welcome to Mills Plantation. I'm Jackie Mills. You must be the Lis?"

Lisa spoke before I had a chance to reply. "That's right, I'm Lisa, and this is Matt."

The proprietress extended her hand. "I'm please to meet you, Lisa, Matt." She called over her shoulder to a teenager who had appeared at the door. "Grayland, help Mr. and Mrs. Li with their bags, while I show them their room."

I gave a dirty look to Lisa, who smiled broadly. "Jackie, please call me Matt. I'm really not used to being called 'Mr. Li.'"

"Oh, sure. We're really quite informal here. You'll be with us two nights, I believe? I do hope you'll like your room. It's the best in the house, actually. The only reason it was available was that I had a cancellation just before your wife called to make reservations." We climbed a broad set of stairs from the foyer and entered a huge bedroom suite dominated by an ornately-carved, four-poster rice bed. Lisa walked over and fingered the carvings on one of the massive posts.

"The bed's actually older than this house," Jackie said. "It was carved by slaves on this very plantation in the 1830s. Probably bring a fortune at Sotheby's."

She walked over and drew open the curtains. Beyond the oaks, we could see another large field and a line of trees in the distance. "Over there," she pointed, "is the North Fork of the Edisto River. You should see it. I hope you'll join us for some riding tomorrow."

"Or tonight," Lisa murmured under her breath, winking at me.

Grayland, who was introduced as Jackie's younger brother, arrived with our bags. I spoke. "I think we're in good shape, Jackie. We probably need to get some of this road dust off of us."

"Of course. Well, dinner's at 7:30, and we start serving cocktails in the parlor downstairs at 6. Come down and meet the other guests."

"Of course," Lisa mimicked. "But do you suppose we could get a little ice first?" Jackie nodded and Grayland scampered out the door, returning momentarily with a large silver ice bucket.

Jackie handed us the keys and they left. Lisa was rummaging in her bag. "What is the ice for?" I asked.

She turned around, triumphantly holding up a bottle of Dom Perignon. "Do you have any idea how far I had to drive last night to get this?" She placed it in the bucket, working it down into the ice. Drying her hands, she approached me slowly and deliberately. Standing only inches away, Lisa placed her left hand over my heart and leisurely began to unbutton my shirt with her right. "I think we need to take a long shower while it cools."

CHAPTER

Thirty-Six

WE MISSED COCKTAILS. Were it not for Grayland's soft rapping on our door at 7:15, we probably would have missed dinner, too. Lisa – the real Lisa, beautifully unadorned with clothes and lying beside me on the deep feather mattress – had narrowed my world to the confines of our antique bed. If it had been possible to stop time in that single moment while preserving all the thoughts, emotions, touches and smells that flowed over and through me, I would have done so.

Despite Jackie's claim of informality, dinner at Mills Plantation was a rather elegant affair. The huge mahogany table in the dining room seated 14. Jackie sat at one end; we were introduced to her husband, Peter, who sat at the other. Two seats had been reserved for us. The others were occupied by an assortment of guests, ranging from a couple obviously on their honeymoon to an older man and his wife whose laugh resembled the braying of a jackass. Dinner, all five courses and three wines, was served on fine gold-rimmed china and crystal by two black maids dressed in grey uniforms. The conversation was lively and intelligent.

We declined the offer of after-dinner port in the parlor, pleading fatigue. Peter, who appeared to be a thoroughly pleasant host, said *sotto voce* to Jackie, "I thought you said we just had one honeymoon couple staying with us." Lisa winked, took my hand and led me toward the stairs.

ON MONDAY MORNING AT 9 A.M., we were parked in front of the Barnwell County Courthouse. Long and narrow with a two-level columned portico, in some ways it resembled a church. Two curving cast-iron sets of steps led to the second level of the building that apparently housed the courtroom. The clerk's office and the repository for the county property records were located on the first floor at the end of a wide central hall with marble wainscoting. A young, efficient looking, black woman was sitting behind a desk, reading a romance novel. "Can I help you?" she asked.

"I hope so. We're trying to trace where some of our ancestors are buried. We'd like to find the cemetery so we can visit their graves." The clerk looked at Lisa quizzically, thinking no doubt that there were few Chinese buried in Barnwell County, South Carolina.

"They're my relatives," I explained quickly. "My great-great-grandfather. We were hoping that we might be able to find a plat to the old family farm. He's supposedly buried in a cemetery near the house site."

"Now that I might be able to help you with. I'll just need a little information so we can know where to start." She came out from behind her desk and extended her hand. "I'm Quetzal Jones, and you're Mr...?"

"Cartwell. Matthew Cartwell. And this is my friend, Ms. Li." Lisa rolled her eyes.

"Pleased to meet you both." We walked back to a series of small connected rooms, each lined with huge, bound ledgers slotted into sturdy steel racks. "First, we'll need a name and an approximate date to start looking."

"I'm sure that some of the records date from before the Civil War. I understand that the courthouse here got burned by Sherman's men."

"You're in luck there. The men of the town were able to save most of the courthouse records, so we've deeds and plats going back to the late eighteenth century."

"That's wonderful. We're looking for a plat of a farm near the Savannah River owned by my great-great-grandfather Emanuel Cartwell. He was killed in battle in 1865, and I know that a cousin, Jodie Cartwell, was in charge of the farm in 1870. I believe the property was near a large stream called Four Mile Branch."

"Our records here are filed by name and date, not location. Why don't we start here?" She hefted out a huge volume labeled Grantor-Grantee Index 1865-1888. "OK, now this book contains the names of all persons who sold or otherwise transferred property in those years, as well as the names of all persons who received property. This is taken from deed records." She flipped through the yellowed pages, each filled with flowing nineteenth century script. Running her finger over the "C's" she said, "No Cartwell's here. Let's try the next one."

She replaced the volume and took down the *Grantor-Grantee Index 1889-1902*. Again she turned to the Cs. After a moment, she said, "Did you say the cousin's name was Jodie?"

I nodded.

"Then I think I've got it. Here is a deed from 'The Estate of Jodie Cartwell" to someone named Bibb. Looks like he died in — what's this? — 1890, and his heirs must have sold the farm. Now you said you wanted just the plat? Or did you want the deed, too?"

"I think just the plat. I'm really not sure where the farm was located. I know it was in Barnwell County, and I thought if I got the plat reference we could start our search from there."

Quetzal said, "Fine." The plat reference here is Book T, page 45."
She walked over to another section and ran her fingers across the volumes. "Let's see... Q, R, S, here it is, Book T." Laying it on the table

in the middle of the room, she flipped to page 45. A yellowed, hand-drawn plat lay in front of her. "Do you think this is what you're looking for?" She turned the book around so we could see it.

The plat was crudely drawn, but probably the standard for the late 19th century. Across the top was written in flowing cursive, "Plat of Survey for the Heirs and Estate of Jodie Cartwell of Barnwell County, South Carolina." To my amazement, the plat was remarkably detailed. River Road as referred to in the cipher was clearly labeled, as was Four Mile Branch, plus houses, barns, fields and swamps. On the edge of one field behind the site labeled "Main House" was a square with a Christian cross in the middle and a legend that said "Cartwell Family Cemetery."

I grinned. Lisa grinned. I said, "Ms. Jones, I think you've found it."

"Glad I could help," she replied. "I guess you'll want a copy or two."

"Absolutely!" I was ecstatic. "Now, tell me. What's the best way to track down the exact location of this property in the county? We really want to ride out and see the graves."

"Well, normally I'd send you to the tax assessor's office. They have the best county maps. But you know, roads change and get rerouted, even place names change sometime. This plat is more than 100 years old. If I were you I'd start at the county library. They have a whole room over there devoted to genealogy studies, plus a good collection of old local maps, and the county museum is right next door. I suspect that between the two, they can put you in the right direction quicker. You can always go by the assessor's office if they can't help you at the library or the museum."

We thanked the clerk profusely, paid for our copies and headed for the county library we'd seen the day before. The top on the Jeep was still down, the sky was clear, we were well on our way to finding a fortune in hidden gold, and I was as close to being in love as I'd been in some time.

We parked on the street in front of the library and almost ran down the walkway and up the front steps. The librarian looked up from behind her desk and smiled. I introduced myself and said that we were trying to track down the location of my great-great-grandfather's grave. She said she thought that could be done fairly easily and led us to their genealogy collection which filled an entire small room. "First of all, let me see the plat you have there, and give me just a minute to see if I can't locate it for you on a more modern map."

I handed her the plat, which she studied for a minute, then went over to a shelf lined with South Carolina History books and a dozen or more books of state and regional maps. She consulted one text, then rechecked the plat, then opened a filing cabinet and unfolded a copy of an early 20th-century map of Barnwell County. Next to it, she laid a copy of a modern county map issued by the South Carolina Department of Transportation.

Pointing to the older map she said, "It's pretty clear that your great-great-granddaddy's grave should be right about here. This old plat is remarkably detailed, and under other circumstances you shouldn't have any trouble at all finding it."

I was puzzled. Lisa spoke, "What do you mean by 'under other circumstances'?"

"This." She pointed at the current Department of Transportation Map. In what had been an area of roads, towns, streams and landmarks on the older map was now a blank white space labeled "Savannah River Plant" and below that "U.S. Department of Energy."

"Just what," Lisa asked, "is the Savannah River Plant?"

The librarian gave her a puzzled look, and then smiled. "You really don't know, do you?" she laughed. "The Savannah River Plant just happens to be one of the most heavily guarded nuclear fuel and weapons production facilities in the United States, and your great-great-granddaddy is buried right about here." Her finger pointed at the blank space on the map.

CHAPTER
Thirty-Seven

WE RODE BACK TO MILLS PLANTATION IN SILENCE. The sky was just as clear, Lisa was just as beautiful, but as for me – I felt as if the world had just collapsed on my head. All that Lisa said was, "We were so close."

We both tried to be cheerful, and we both gave up. Jackie Mills was on her knees in one of the front flower beds as we arrived at the B&B. "Lisa. Matt. How was your morning?" She saw the looks on our faces.

"Hey, come on kids. It can't be that bad."

"If you only knew," Lisa started.

Jackie frowned. "It's probably none of my business, but every couple has their ups and downs – even on honeymoons. You two just need to enjoy each other."

Lisa gave a little chuckle. "Oh, no, it's not Matt. He's the most wonderful thing in my life right now." She wrapped her arm inside mine and leaned her head on my shoulder for an instant. "It's just a business project that we were both very involved in. It's taken an unexpected turn for the worse."

Jackie brightened. "Well, why don't you just put that to one side for the moment? You're here in this wonderful spot; we've got a couple of thousand acres of beautiful South Carolina Lowcountry at your disposal. Enjoy yourselves. Things will work out. They always do." She paused. "How about some horseback riding? I can fix you a nice picnic lunch, saddle a couple of gentle rides and point you in the direction of the river. You both know how to ride, right?" We both said that we did and agreed that might be what we needed.

An hour and a half later, we were seated on a blanket in a stand of live oaks on a bluff overlooking the river. Our horses were tethered next to a creek nearby, having feasted on apples sent by Jackie. For *our* part, we were feasting on chicken salad prepared with ground mustard and tarragon, haricots vertes in spicy vinaigrette, and a loaf of crusty French bread. A bottle of good California Chardonnay was mostly empty. The wine had relaxed us. Lisa spoke. "Matt, this doesn't have to be the end of it. We can still figure out some way to get to the gold."

"Are you kidding? The librarian said that place is crawling with security guards, especially after what happened with the World Trade Center last year."

"But it's huge. You know they can't patrol every inch of it all the time. And it wouldn't be like we were terrorists out to steal plutonium or something. No, I'll bet that the cemetery is still there, hidden in the woods and totally forgotten and ignored by everyone."

"Maybe. But how would we even start? We have absolutely no idea about what's inside that area, and absolutely no legitimate way to get in and check it out. For a start, we'd need help, and I'm not sure that I want to bring anyone else in on this."

"Well, I don't know, but there are some other considerations."

"Such as? I asked.

"The rest of my bonus. The deal was that I don't get it until the gold is recovered. Looks like you may have to make it up to me in other ways." She crawled across the blanket and kissed me. The sunlight glinted off her hair as we made love, she on top, with the oak canopy and the blue sky above her.

I hadn't heard a rooster crow since my childhood in Walkerville. I was awakened the next morning by that sound accompanied by the red light of first dawn filtering through the curtains. I stared at the ceiling, suddenly wide awake and thinking. Lisa was curled up in a nest of down pillows, breathing softly. I touched her shoulder and she stirred, rolling over with her eyes still shut and a smile on her face. She murmured, "Don't wake me up. I don't want this dream to end. Right now I'm in the middle of it and I'm naked in this glorious bed with the most handsome man I've ever met, and he's putting his hand on my shoulder, and..." She opened her eyes. "Oh, hi. It's you. I'm not dreaming."

"Lisa, I've been thinking. You're right. We've got to try to recover the gold. We've gone too far to give up now. It's Pascal's Wager again, we have nothing to lose and everything to gain."

She snuggled next to me, and asked, "Who is Pascal?"

OUR TRIP BACK TO WALKERVILLE WAS UNEVENTFUL. We thanked the owners and promised to come back. Jackie observed that we seemed to be feeling better now and we agreed with her that things have a way of working themselves out.

We arrived at Rutherford Hall shortly before 3 p.m.

I should have realized that there was a problem when I saw Eula Mae sitting on the back steps. It was Tuesday afternoon. She worked Mondays and Thursdays. She had a distressed look on her face. "Oh, Mr. Matt. I shore am glad to see you back here."

"Eula Mae, what are you doing here? What's happened?"

"Looks like somebody tried to break in again. The alarm musta scared them off. The police came and Mr. Morgan and your momma came, and they asked me if I'd stay here until you got back. They couldn't get you to answer on your cell phone." Quite deliberately, I had not turned it on since we left Sunday. Lisa looked alarmed.

"I'm sorry. We've been over in South Carolina for a couple of days. When did this happen?"

"Sometime early this morning. Mr. Morgan called me about 6 a.m., but I thinks the police was here about two or three hours before that. Somebody put a ladder up to the study window. They cut out a pane with a glass cutter and then reached in and opened the lock. Mr. Morgan says that new alarm system you put in went off. I say it musta scared them because the police got here real quick and the person musta run 'cause he left the ladder still propped up against the side of the house. Mr. Morgan, he looked around and he say he didn't think they got in. He axed me to stay here today, and if you didn't get back by this evening, he was gonna come over here and sleep with his pistol in case they comes back."

I rushed in the house, Lisa close behind me and Eula Mae trudging up the stairs at her top speed. The study appeared undisturbed except for a window pane half cut out just above the sash lock. Before we left I had hidden the gold bar in the bottom drawer of a chest in my bedroom. It was still there, undisturbed. Nothing else seemed amiss. It appeared that the intruder had been scared away by the alarm.

Lisa said, "How did they know no one was home? Your car was still in the yard. We left some lights on."

"I don't know." I didn't say what I was thinking.

She did.

"Matt, I think we're being watched."

CHAPTER
Thirty-Eight

I REACHED NICK AT HIS OFFICE. "Just where the hell you been, Matt?" he inquired with some annoyance. "Your mama and the police rousted me out of bed this morning at 3:30."

I explained that I had been out of town – nothing more. He said the security alarm had gone off sometime around 3 a.m. The police had responded and discovered the ladder propped under the study window. When no one answered their repeated knocks, they called my mother who told them that she thought I was away for a few days. She, in turn, called Nick and they all converged on Rutherford Hall. Only in a small town, I thought.

Nick continued, "Let me come on over there and let's go over things. I'll see if I can't get Chief Mathis to come with me. With what happened to Lance, and now this, maybe we need to rethink things."

Lisa unpacked the Jeep while I checked the house again to be certain that nothing had been disturbed. I heard her and Eula Mae laughing about something in the kitchen just as I saw Nick's Mercedes drive in the yard. Chief Roger Mathis was in the passenger seat. I greeted them at the back door. Mathis spoke, half grinning, "Looks like the crime rate has about doubled since you got back to

Walkerville, Matt."

I shook his hand, but didn't smile. Nick spoke. "Cool it, Roger. This is serious business. I don't know exactly where you stand in your investigation of the Rutherford boy's killing, but a second break-in here...."

"Third," I interrupted. They looked at me with surprise. I told them about my suspicions after I returned from Savannah, and why I had upgraded the alarm system.

"We need to talk," Mathis said, and we moved into the dining room and sat down for a conference.

Fifteen minutes later, I was not feeling any better about the Walkerville police or about the investigation of Lance's murder. Mathis explained that the police were still going on the theory that his killing was a random act, probably drug related. "Eventually" they'd get a break he said, "probably when somebody gets busted and rats out the killer in exchange for getting the charges dropped. I've seen it happen too many times."

"But Roger," Nick asked, "how do you account for at least one and probably two subsequent attempts to get in the house? That doesn't seem to tie in. You can't really believe a killer would risk it."

"Druggies!" Mathis was dismissive. "Hell, Nick, I've been a cop a long time. These dopers will do anything for their next fix. Big old house full of antiques and silver sitting here – it's a regular magnet for every crackhead in a six-county area. And look at the bright side. Your client here," he nodded at me, "becomes less of a suspect every day."

Nick shrugged, looking vaguely disgusted. I looked up to see Lisa standing in the doorway. I stood up. "Nick, Chief Mathis, this is my friend, Lisa Li." Both men turned and rose.

Mathis extended his hand, "Pleased to meet you."

Nick stared a moment and said, "Lisa Li." She was a stunningly beautiful woman. I could read his mind. "Middle name Annabel?"

"Pardon?" Lisa frowned.

Nick quoted,

It was many and many a year ago
In a kingdom by the sea,
That a maiden there lived whom you may know
By the name of Annabel Lee;
And this maiden she lived with no other thought
Than to love and be loved by me.
"Different spelling," Lisa said, unsmiling.
Later she said to me, simply, "I don't like that man."

———————◆●◆———————

EULA MAE HAD LEFT. I taped a piece of cardboard over the missing window pane in the study. Taking no chances, I found some long screws in the garage and anchored the study windows shut. Lisa and I sat in the kitchen talking. We'd gone over the options again, and once more agreed that if were going to have any chance at all of recovering the gold, we'd need help. "But who?" Lisa asked.

"I don't know. I guess neither of us have any real close friends, at least not nearby. And what we propose to do isn't exactly legal. We've got to find someone we can trust. I don't want to risk even *mentioning* the idea to someone who may decide to turn us in."

A thought occurred to me. "Lisa, I know what you said, but I think I'd like to talk with Nick ."

She looked up sharply. "Matt, I'm not sure I trust him."

"For God's sake, you just met him for the first time today, and you didn't exchange 10 words. How can you not trust him when you don't even know him? Look, he was a close friend of my father and he's still the trustee for the estate. I've known him for years. And equally importantly, he's a lawyer – my family's lawyer. They dance around the edges of legality every day. So why not Nick?"

"I looked into his eyes, Matt, and I'm not sure I liked what I saw."

I called Nick anyway. We had discussed it at length. Despite any misgivings she might have, Lisa had finally conceded that he was – by exclusion – about the only person that we could safely turn to. He agreed to meet us in his office the following morning.

We arrived at 9 a.m. with the missing journal, the gold bar, the printouts of the decrypted cipher and our photocopied plat and maps packed securely in my gym bag. Nick ushered us into the conference room, shut the door and asked, "What's the big secret, Matt? You know, after you called last night I about decided that you two were going to come in here to announce you were getting married or something like that." Nick smiled. Lisa smiled, still cautious.

"No, Nick. Not now anyway. It's something very different. First of all, what we are about to tell you is in utmost confidence. I don't know where this might lead, but if the issue ever comes up in the future, you may need to deny we ever had this conversation."

Nick's eyes narrowed and wrinkles appeared on his brow. "I can do that for you, Matt."

"Nick, you know we talked about the rumors of the stolen Confederate gold, and you said you thought they were just that – rumors?"

"Right."

"You were wrong. The gold exists, and we know where it's buried." I reached in my bag and laid in front of him the gold ingot and the missing journal.

Nick's eyes widened. He stared at the ingot for a moment and then said quietly, "Holy shit."

CHAPTER

Thirty-Nine

WE TALKED FOR TWO HOURS. We went over every detail including my discovery of the missing journal, my trip to Savannah, how Lisa had broken the cipher, and our expedition to South Carolina. Nick listened and was non-committal. "You know you're talking about a fortune in gold? Not to mention its historic value. And with that said, I can think of about two dozen laws you'd be breaking to recover it. Of course, that's beside the fact the federal government would probably have a pretty good legal claim to it if they ever discovered you had it, and *especially* if they found out where you got it. Lisa, Matt, be honest with me, do you really want to risk it all to try to find the gold?"

We both nodded.

"Then what do you want me to do? I can't sit here and advise you to break a whole textbook full of state and federal laws." He crossed his arms, tilted back his chair and waited for a reply.

"We can't do it by ourselves, Nick."

Nick was silent for a moment, thinking. He pursed his lips and stared at the ceiling. "OK. Let me think about it. Meet me back here tomorrow morning at 9 and I'll have an answer for you."

Lisa and I spent the afternoon shopping in Augusta and the

evening in search of a restaurant with passable shichimi. The gold was not mentioned.

TWENTY-FOUR HOURS LATER, we were back in Nick's office. He was animated, upbeat even. Once more, we sat at his conference table. He seemed to be composing his words carefully before he spoke. "I think there are times in your life when you have to make decisions. I've spent most of the past 24 hours thinking about what you said. I've been thinking about two things. First, the legality, or in this case the illegality, of it all and second, whether or not we could actually pull it off. You know, I'm 53 years old. I've made plenty of money and I don't have any significant debts. I'm divorced, no children, no real family to speak of. In fact, Matt, I guess the Rutherfords are about as close to me as any blood relatives. I suppose I could just coast on into old age, doing what I'm doing day after day 'till they come and haul me off to the old folk's home. Common sense tells me I should advise you to either tell the government where the gold is buried and be shut of it, or else burn the journal, melt down the gold ingot to make a necklace for Lisa, and forget it."

Nick paused, again gathering his thoughts. "But I'm not going to say that. I know deep down there's some more life left in me – one last big thing. One last adventure before I'm too old to do it. I've got a plan I think will work. The bottom line is this: I want to go for it. I'm willing to take the risk, and if we fail, I'm ready to take the fall." He hesitated a moment and said, "Let me make you an offer. I'll take a third of anything we recover. In exchange, if we fail, I'll say it was all my idea and that I talked you two into it. You're young. You've got a long life in front of you. I just want to be able to spend the rest of mine on some beach in Costa Rica, sipping rum and watching the chicas." He paused and looked me in the eye. "So what do you think? You want a partner?"

I looked at Lisa. I could not read her eyes. She nodded her head ever so slightly. I turned to Nick and stuck out my hand, "You're on."

We talked for another hour. Nick outlined his plan in broad terms. He said that we needed one more person to make it work, but that he'd pay that person out of his share. Based on what we'd told him and his study of the maps and plat we'd provided, he thought there were multiple possibilities. "Thing is, we'll need some reasonable excuse for being there. We can pose as bird watchers or deer hunters or whatever, and if we get caught, hopefully the worst that will happen is that we'll be charged with trespassing on government property. There are a ton of details, and I've got to find the right person to work with us."

"You have somebody in mind?" Lisa asked.

"One person. I've got to see if he's willing to do it. I'll talk with him tonight."

"And then?" I asked.

"If he goes for it, we start our planning in earnest."

I TOOK LISA TO LUNCH at a small barbecue restaurant that served a good selection of soup and sandwiches. She'd seemed eager as we discussed Nick's plan, but now she was quiet. "Are you all right with things?" I asked.

"Pretty much." She stared at her soup, stirring at a bit of potato with her spoon.

"Wanna talk about it?" She looked up.

"Perceptive, aren't you?" she asked.

"No, but I can sense something's not right."

"Matt, it's none of my…"

"Yes it is. Talk to me."

She looked at me for a moment and then said, "Why did you give Nick a third of the gold?"

I thought before I spoke. "Because, very simply, I don't think we can get it without him — or someone like him. Maybe he's," I paused, trying to think of the right word, "the devil we know." And then it occurred to me that was not what she was asking.

"Lisa, I'm sorry. We wouldn't be sitting here now if you hadn't been able to solve the cipher in the first place."

"I can't say anything. We have an agreement. I signed…"

"Lisa."

"Let me finish! I just wanted to say that maybe I should leave the recovery work up to you and Nick. I came here for a job. I think I've ended up getting involved in more ways than I'd intended. I don't really know how to say this, but I think I really care about you and," she stopped, dabbing at her eye with the napkin.

"Lisa," I didn't know what I wanted to say. "Lisa, we're both adults. I didn't intend to get involved either, but we have, and I guess we both know it. I can't tell you what's going to happen between us, or with the gold, but I can say that I need you as much as I need Nick, but in a very, very different way." I thought for a moment. "How about this? Let me make you a partner, whatever that means. We'll give Nick his share and split whatever's left between us. Maybe that beach in Costa Rica has room for a couple more."

Lisa smiled.

"Want it in writing?"

"No. I'll trust you," she said and stood up, leaned across the table and kissed me.

CHAPTER
Forty

NICK HAD LEFT A MESSAGE on the answering machine that he'd be at Rutherford Hall at 8 p.m. "unless I hear from you otherwise." He said he was bringing someone with him. It was almost dark when I saw him drive into the yard. To my surprise, he was accompanied by Doug Smith, Select State Farm Agent. Nick literally bounded up the back steps, followed by the more deliberate insurance agent who walked uneasily as if he were about to commit a crime. Indeed, perhaps he was. I met them at the back door.

"Matt, you know Doug," Nick said. I nodded, and we shook hands. "We've spent a good while talking, and I've managed to get Doug's firm commitment to help us. I wanted to bring him over, let him have a look at what you've got, and then we're going to sit down and start some serious planning." He put his hand on the agent's shoulder. "I've known this man a long time. We've worked together in the Sons of Confederate Veterans. I know he's bright, he's a hard worker and we can trust him." Doug smiled and looked a little uncomfortable, still dressed in khakis and a short-sleeved blue shirt with a red tie sporting the State Farm logo.

I hope so, I thought to myself. I introduced Lisa. We sat down at the dining room table and I summarized what we knew and where we were to date. Doug said, "You know, I worked with Lillie for years, helping her with her research and all. I always suspected this, but when she died, I figured, whatever secrets there were died with her."

"I guess in a sense they did. There are big pieces of the puzzle missing. I don't know if she told Lance anything before he was killed, or whether or not she'd intended to tell me. But whatever did or didn't happen, we know the story of the gold is real. We know where it is, and now we need to figure out how to get it. I'll be the first to admit, I know nothing whatsoever about the Savannah River Site, or how we should even approach getting inside."

"Well, maybe that's why Nick asked me to help out," Doug replied. "I've hunted ducks over there in the low-country for years, so I've got a pretty good feel for finding my way through swamps. And, too, I can probably get some inside information about security from some buddies of mine who work at the facility." He paused. "But I have just one request first. I *really* want to read the missing journal. My first love is history, and from what you and Nick have told me, this journal could be one of the biggest discoveries in the past century."

I slid the journal across the table to him. Holding it like a sacred text, he disappeared toward the parlor and Aunt Lillie's favorite reading chair. We huddled in the kitchen. Nick found a bottle of bourbon – he knew where my aunt kept it hidden – and poured himself three fingers over ice. Twenty minutes later, he had Lisa rolling in laughter with his stories of practicing law in a small Georgia town. Doug appeared in the doorway, an awed look on his face. "God, this journal, this diary. Do you have any idea what this means?"

We all gave him a blank look.

"This changes history! Don't you see? There's nothing, *nothing* anywhere that even hints about what *really* happened to the gold from the Confederate treasury. It's unbelievable! Secretary of War Breckinridge and Secretary of the Treasury Trenholm were apparently conspiring to steal the gold for themselves, but it looks like your guys – your great-great-grandfather – stole it first. This completely changes history. This document by itself is probably worth millions! It's, it's priceless."

Doug stood in the doorway holding the journal. Nick walked over and took it from him. "It may be. But history be damned. We're going to finish what those fellows started when we dig it up."

For the next hour, we roughed out a plan of attack. Doug would see what he could find out about the Savannah River Site, especially about security, from his SCV contacts in the nearest towns, including Barnwell, Aiken and Augusta. Nick, who had a shallow, draft fishing boat, would scout out security and possible access up Four Mile Branch from the Savannah.

Lisa and I were assigned to gather whatever hard information we could come up with from the Internet and other public sources, especially about the nuclear plant, plus maps and charts. We agreed to discuss this with no one, and to meet again in a week.

The week passed rapidly. I tried to reach Nick a couple of times but his secretary said he'd gone fishing "over near Augusta." I presumed he was carrying out his assignment. Doug also left town, or so his wife told me when I called to ask about a particular map I'd found on the Internet. She said he was at a State Farm meeting in Florida, but I suspected otherwise. Lisa and I discovered the Savannah River Site maintained public-information reading rooms at area libraries. We spent most of a day pouring over documents at the Augusta Public Library without much success. By the next Wednesday, Lisa was putting everything together in a PowerPoint presentation to show to our new partners in crime.

My mother had called Sunday afternoon. "Matt, you've been back in town now for more than a month, and I don't think I've seen you more than half a dozen times."

"I'm sorry. It's just that I've been so busy with Aunt Lillie's estate and all."

We had never been close. That's one reason I'd been living in California.

"Well, I just thought the polite thing to do would be for you to introduce me to the young lady that everybody tells me is staying with you now. I mean, it's embarrassing to go to church and be told that so and so met your son's fiancée, and she's lovely, and don't I feel fortunate as a mother, and then I have to tell them I really haven't met her as yet and ..."

"Mother!" I cut her off. "The *young lady's* name is Lisa Li, and she's here on a business project we're working on. OK?!" I tried to control my voice. "She's not my fiancée. We're collaborating on..."

"Matt." She interrupted. There was a pause. "Just why is it then that Vera Wood told me she saw you two kissing in Dye's Barbecue last Thursday? If I'm going to have half-Chinese grandchildren, I think I have the right ..."

I hung up the phone.

Nick, Doug, Lisa, and I met again Thursday at Rutherford Hall. As I thought, neither Nick nor Doug had actually been where they had told everyone they would be. I drew the blinds in Lillie's study and we pulled chairs up to her work table. Lisa turned the video monitor around and began her presentation. "All right. I guess I'm the designated spokeswoman for what Matt and I have found out this past week." She paused and pointed at a map of Georgia and South Carolina on the screen. "The Savannah River site is big, guys, about 200,000 acres along the Savannah River, part in Aiken and part in Barnwell counties. It started in the early 1950s when the U.S. government confiscated the land for a nuclear-weapon research and production facility. The original site had several small towns, but as nearly as we can figure out, the major buildings were razed when the population was forced to move. During the years, the place has been used for every sort of nuclear program imaginable, but most importantly, for the production of plutonium and tritium for nuclear weapons. In the process, it also has managed to become one of the most highly polluted sites in the eastern United States. Needless to say, they are very tight-lipped about security – especially after Sept.

11, 2001. In the past, you could book tours, but they've stopped that now for security reasons. You can't get in at all without a valid reason and a thorough search of your vehicle."

Lisa picked up the keyboard and pressed the space bar. "Fortunately, the same government, that wants so badly to keep you out of the place, is willing to supply online topographic maps and aerial photos with resolution down to one meter. To wit:" A black and white photo appeared on the monitor screen. "OK. This is a closer view of the Savannah River." Her finger traced along a serpentine line running from the upper left to the lower right of the screen. "Now this is Four Mile Branch." The image zoomed in to show a black string wending its way through a gray forest. "If you overlay a topographic map," she pressed another key, "you see this." Contour lines appeared in red, outlining small islands in the swamp. "Right here on the high ground overlooking the creek is where the cemetery has got to be." A star appeared on the map with the press of a key.

Nick and Doug were clearly impressed. Smith pointed to the screen and asked, "What are these structures here, right across the river on the Georgia side?"

Nick answered, "I've got photos to show of those later. That's Plant Vogtle. It's a nuclear power plant run by Georgia Power."

Doug shook his head. "Hell, we're going to be busting into a nuclear bomb manufacturing site across from a nuclear power plant. We've got to be some kind of crazy!"

CHAPTER
Forty-One

LISA REVIEWED THE REST OF THE DATA we'd collected and handed out copies of the aerial photographs and topographic maps. Nick was watching her like a snake eyeing a bird. I said, "That's what we've been doing for the last week. You guys have any thoughts or questions?" Both Nick and Doug said they did, but we decided to wait until everyone had made their presentations.

Nick was next. "Well, I went fishing last week. I was looking to see if we might try to get to the cemetery from the river, and I think there are some possibilities. I was trying to be practical – if we do get in we've got to get the gold out, and if we approach up Four Mile Branch we're going to need more than one boat. I've fished in the Savannah for years, and usually I put in over near Augusta. Where we want to be is about 25 miles down river from there as the crow flies, more if you measure the actual distance by the river. I called around and found out there is a public boat ramp just down river from Plant Vogtle. It's run by Georgia Power and is open during daylight hours, but they will allow you to park overnight if you get permission in advance. It's pretty isolated and not used much. The good thing is that it is directly across the river from the Savannah River Site, and about two or three miles down river from Four Mile Branch. Here're some photos I took with my digital camera and printed out at the office."

Nick spread a dozen eight-by-ten photos on the table and went over them one by one. "This part of the river is at least 100 yards wide. It's a straight, fast-flowing stream. On the Georgia side," he held up a photo, "the land rises steeply up to a plateau known as Blue Bluff. On the South Carolina side, there's nothing but low-lying swamp that borders the river more than a mile deep before you reach high ground. Just up river, between mile markers 150 and 151, the lower run of Four Mile Branch flows out of the swamp and into the main stream of the river. That's directly in across from this." He pointed to a photo of the massive cooling towers of the nuclear power plant rising in the distance from thick forest. Billowing columns of thick steam could be seen emerging from their tops. They resembled huge pagan temples built to satisfy a god that demanded regular human sacrifice. In the foreground was a high security fence topped with barbed wire and festooned with yellow and red striped signs reading "No Trespassing."

He held up another photo. "This is the entrance to Four Mile Branch. As you can see, it's a large stream and can easily handle a 12-foot or 14-foot shallow draft boat. See this right here?" He pointed to a blowup of the stream entrance. In the background, just above a large yellow sign reading "United States Department of Energy" and "NO TRESPASSING," was a small, olive, drab, cylindrical object some 20 feet off the ground on a pole that blended in with the trees. "That's some type of monitoring device. I presume it's a camera.

"So that's it. I've made copies of these photos for each of you. Bottom line is, it looks like we can get access to the mouth of Four Mile Branch, but we've got to get past their security perimeter."

Doug was last. "I'm kinda embarrassed that I don't have something quite so fancy as the computer maps or the photos to show you, but I think I've collected a pretty good bit of useful information. I was supposedly at a meeting in Orlando last week – at least that's what I told Nan and the girls. Actually, I've been over in Aiken talking with a few buddies of mine and hanging out in a couple of bars where a bunch of the SRS workers go for drinks. I'll spare you the fine points, but basically, I was trying to find out just how heavily guarded the place is. It ain't Fort Knox, but it must be damned close to it. From what they tell me, the government is convinced that the place is at or near the top of the hit list for every known foreign and domestic terrorist group, and they are on constant alert, especially after what happened with the World Trade Center.

"Security is run by Wackenhut Services. They're a big private firm, and most of their key people are ex-military. In addition to what you'd expect with guard houses at the entrances, fences and so on, there are regular patrols with armed guards and attack dogs, plus a lot of what one half-drunk guy called 'passive detectors.'"

Lisa interrupted, "Yeah, Wackenhut had a page on the SRS Web site, but I saw where they took it down right after Sept. 11."

"Well, that's their mentality right now," Smith continued. "It's like we know the attack is coming, but we don't know when."

"So, what are the options – or do we have any?" Nick asked.

"I was getting to that. Let me hit the highlights and tell you what we're up against. Wackenhut employs about nine hundred people for their security team. That may sound like a lot, but think about it. Security is a 24 hour a day job, so you need three shifts. That means, say, that there are a maximum of 300 people per shift. But everybody works only five days a week, so at any given time you've got," he paused to do the numbers in his head, "about 215 potential guards, and when you allow for supervisors and guys calling in sick, I'd guess they can field a maximum of about 200. From what I found out, most of the security goes to protect the main entrances and about half a dozen sites that contain plutonium and the sort of stuff terrorists might target. So that leaves the rest of 'em to patrol a perimeter that's 310 miles long. They've got to be spread mighty thin."

"Interesting," Nick said.

"Let me tell you what I think will work. The key is getting inside and then avoiding detection while we're there. First I had thought about getting our hands on some Wackenhut uniforms and trying to get in through one of the gates. Once we were in, we could probably find the cemetery site and do our work relatively undisturbed. But we'd have to figure some way to get out with hundreds of pounds of gold bullion. Not good.

"I think the best idea came from that same drunk I was talking to in the bar in Aiken. He's originally from Louisiana, and had worked as a prison guard at the state prison at Angola. He said that prison doesn't have many fences, but doesn't have many escapes, either. Apparently it's on a plot of high ground surrounded by miles of swamp full of 'gators. Prisoners that have tried to escape through the swamp are usually never seen or heard from again. They get lost, starve, or worse. I get the impression that the swamp, between the river and the high ground where most of the reactors are, is what the people at the Savannah River Site are relying on to protect them. I was told they have a few cameras operated by infrared motion detectors, but they don't work right half the time. The video signals are not hard-wired but are broadcast back to a central network and fed into the main security monitoring center."

"Doesn't sound promising," I observed. Lisa nodded.

"Wait, there's more. They also have a small military group permanently stationed there for security back up. They're not directly involved in day-to-day operations, but they coordinate with the Wackenhut guards. Problem is, they've got two helicopters equipped with infrared imaging sensors, and in the last couple of months they've gotten some type of remotely operated drone like the kind the military uses in Afghanistan. It has both regular and infrared video cameras. They can launch it on short notice to check out potential intruders in even the most remote areas."

"So, we're screwed," Nick observed.

"No, not really. All this high tech stuff stops working in bad weather. Guy told me that even an average rainstorm will knock out any useful information from the fixed cameras, and if the weather's any worse, they can't launch either the drone or the helicopters. He said that a lot of hunters looking for trophy deer sneak in during bad weather. If they catch them, they usually give them a scare and a slap on the wrist, but nothing more. They don't want to appear lax, but they don't want the hassle of prosecuting every guy they catch with a deer rifle either."

"So can we do it?" I asked the group.

"Based on what we've found out," Doug said, "I think we can. I really like duck hunting, but there are some places, especially swamps, that in the past you just couldn't risk going into. A swamp is a huge trackless place where there are no landmarks and every tree looks the same. You never know how deep water is – it could be two feet, or it could open into a hole or spring 20 feet deep. What's changed all this is hand held GPS."

"What's GPS?" Nick asked.

"I'm sorry," Doug said. "Global Positioning System. It's a navigation system based on a series of twenty-something military satellites that you can use to find your exact position basically anywhere on earth with an accuracy of about 20 or 30 feet in any direction."

"Oh, I knew that," Nick said. Typical lawyer, I thought. Never admit you don't have all the facts.

"Anyway," Doug continued, "for a couple of hundred bucks you can get highly reliable handheld GPS receivers not much larger than a pack of cigarettes. You just program in the coordinates of where you want to go and follow the arrow on the screen. That way if you're in a swamp you don't get lost." He paused. "Now, I've got a question for Lisa. You can determine GPS coordinates for any spot on these maps, right?"

"I think so. The accuracy will probably be a hundred feet or so, but, generally speaking, the answer is yes," Lisa Said.

"OK, how about this? Lisa, you've got maps and a pretty good idea as to where the cemetery is located based on the plat of the Cartwell estate.

Do you think you could plot out a series of waypoints that take us from the river, up Four Mile Branch and to where we think the gold is?

"Yeah, I think I could do that," Lisa replied.

"Nick, based on what you've seen, do you think we could get a couple of boats – mine and yours – through the swamp and up the Branch?"

"Probably. Of course, I don't know what we'll run into once we get into the swamp. It looks like an open waterway on the aerial photos, but they're a decade old and there may be fallen trees and the like. But, yes, I think we can do it."

Doug grinned. "Then if we can get a route to follow by GPS and can get our boats through the swamp and near enough to the cemetery we can do it."

We all stared at him. I finally spoke. "Sounds good, but you're forgetting about one thing. Security."

"Oh, no, I'm not. *You're* forgetting that this is September, and hurricane season isn't over until November."

CHAPTER
Forty-Two

WE STARTED PLANNING IN EARNEST the next afternoon. It was Friday; Doug frequently took the day off, so no suspicions would be aroused. Nick, of course, came and went as he pleased. We met at Nick's pond house located on a secluded six-acre lake in the forest behind his house. If we were going to do this, we were determined to succeed.

We figured the 152 gold bars would weigh about 1,216 pounds, assuming that the one I had was typical of the bunch. If we took two boats, that would mean an extra 608 pounds for each, in addition to the weight of our gear, plus two people on each boat. "It's gonna be awful close," Doug observed.

"We don't have any idea how deep the water will be, and from my experience, I can tell you that we can't use boats much longer than 12 or 14 feet. I don't think we're going to have but one chance to pull this off, so we need to figure a way to get in, get all the gold and get out in one trip."

We decided we needed a test. Nick had several fishing boats. We chose a 14-foot shallow draft aluminum skiff similar to the one Doug used for duck hunting. I came up with the idea of using concrete blocks for weight and seeing how well the boat carried it. Nick and

Doug headed off in the pickup to find some blocks. Lisa and I stayed at the pond house. She'd been unusually quiet.

"Are you still OK with all of this?" I asked.

"I think so. I just worry that we're losing control. Matt, are you *sure* we can trust these guys? I mean, we're about to do something that is probably very illegal. What if something goes very wrong? What if someone gets hurt – or worse?"

I didn't have a good answer. "I don't know. I don't have any idea what will happen. All I know is that is that there is enough gold to make us both very wealthy. Lisa, there's no half way here. Either we do it or we don't. We go through what we've got to go through to get the gold or else we walk away. You know we can't do it by ourselves. And now that we're not the only ones who know about it, we can either take our share or let them have it all."

"You're right," Lisa said and hugged me. I could tell she was still not certain.

Nick and Doug returned with 47 concrete blocks. Doug was laughing. "Yeah, we walked in Walkerville Builders Supply and wanted to know how much a concrete block weighed. We ended up weighing half a dozen, and they averaged out about 26 pounds. So we did a little calculating and said we wanted 47 blocks. Old Jim, who runs the place, looked at us like we were crazy – buying blocks for the weight. Told him we were building a floating dock and needed some blocks for ballast."

We put the fishing boat in the water and tied it to the dock. Nick got in and we handed him 24 blocks which we figured would be roughly the weight of half the gold bars. He distributed them evenly. The boat carried the weight well. "Looks good," he observed.

"OK, now we add some people and gear," Doug said, and handed him a small outboard motor, a tank of gasoline, paddles, an electric trolling motor with its 12 volt battery, and two life preservers. With each new item the boat slowly sank in the water. Finally Doug stepped in and sat on one of the seats. He peered over the side.

"Maybe five inches of freeboard. It won't work. Too much weight."
He looked over the gear, and handed the outboard motor and gas tank
back to me on the dock. The boat rose in the water. "That'll do," he
observed to no one in particular.

"And just how are we going to get up river? Paddle against the current?" Nick asked. We unloaded the boat and adjourned to the cabin
to discuss it.

We talked for two hours. Nick, forever the lawyer, made notes on a
yellow legal pad. It was obvious that we would need to get in and out
in one day. We couldn't risk trying to spend the night inside the
nuclear site. We went back and forth about the weight of the gold. We
figured that if we disturbed the cemetery it would eventually be discovered, our route of entry would be deduced and security would be
reinforced. Again we agreed that we were likely to have just one shot.
We had to get all of the gold out the first time.

Doug was concerned about the sound of our outboard motors.
"That'll be sure to set off an alarm," he said. We decided we'd need
to use the silent electric trolling motors going up the creek.
Depending on our timing and the current coming back, it might be
possible to float out to the main river and then use the outboards to
get back to the landing.

Figuring out how to handle the weight seemed to be the key. "It's
like that old puzzle about the farmer trying to get the animals across
the river," Nick observed. "He's got a chicken, a dog and a fox. The dog
guards the chicken, but the fox will eat it. The dog and the fox will kill
one another and so on. There's got to be some way to do this."

After much back and forth, accompanied by diagrams on Nick's
legal pad, we hatched what seemed to be a workable plan. We'd put
our boats in late one afternoon at the ramp down river from the
mouth of Four Mile Branch. We'd use the outboards to take us upriver from the nuclear power plant site, and camp overnight on the
Georgia side of the river. "It's desolate country in there and the
chances of getting seen are pretty much nil," Nick said. We would

carry an extra battery for the trolling motor in each boat. Early the next morning, we'd ditch the outboards, gas tanks and camping gear, and float downriver to the mouth of the branch. We'd then use our trolling motors to get up the branch to the cemetery. Once there, we could throw the extra trolling motor battery overboard to reduce weight, load the gold and silently motor or float back to the main run of the Savannah. From there it would be a short downstream float back to the landing and boat ramp. We wouldn't even need to unload the gold. We would just back the boat trailers down the ramp, float the boats on to them, tie them down and be on our way.

Lisa, who'd had little to say during the discussions observed, "There's just one thing. These plans don't leave much leeway for screw-ups." I started to speak but didn't. Nick and Doug nodded, but they, too, were silent.

We decided that our next step would be to get out gear together. Lisa and I agreed to make up the maps and laminate them in waterproof plastic. Nick, now the expert on GPS, said he'd order a couple of top-end models online and have them shipped by overnight delivery. Doug said that if we were going to pose as hunters, we'd need to look the part. "We'll need to carry shotguns with duck loads, and have valid hunting licenses with Duck Stamps and camouflage suits so no one will suspect we're anything more than a bunch of hunters. Matt, Lisa, I suppose y'all don't have any hunting gear." Lisa frowned. I shook my head. "OK. I'll meet you guys tomorrow morning at Wal-Mart. We need to make a dry run to be sure everything works. Then we just wait on the weather."

THE LATE SEPTEMBER AFTERNOON SKY was a clear reddish blue as we rode back to Rutherford Hall. Several thousand miles away on a latitude due west of Guinea and about 400 miles southwest of the Cape Verde Islands, an unnamed tropical depression was forming in the Atlantic Ocean.

CHAPTER
Forty-Three

LISA AND I WERE SITTING IN HER JEEP the next morning at 10 when Doug Smith drove up. "You know, Wal-Mart always has the best hunting gear." He sounded eager. We spent an hour picking out camouflage pants and jackets. Lisa disappeared off shopping while Doug and I examined the camping gear. She returned with a small pair of binoculars and a baseball-style cap for each of us. We ended up buying two lightweight tents, waterproof ponchos, a tarpaulin, four sleeping bags, several lightweight folding chairs, four flashlights with extra batteries, and a 100-foot roll of heavy nylon cord.

Lisa said she'd wait outside while Doug and I checked out. As I was unloading our cart at the register, I looked up to see Brandi, the same checkout girl that had sold me the tools I used to open Lillie's strongbox. She flashed me a smile of recognition. "You never did call me."

"Yeah. I've been really busy."

Brandi efficiently waved our purchases over the scanner and carefully placed them in blue plastic bags. "I'm still here, you know. You promised you'd call." I didn't say anything. The register beeped with each item. "That your girlfriend?" Brandi said without looking up. She nodded her head toward the door where Lisa had just left.

"Kinda."

"Chinese?"

"No. She's from California."

"She looks Chinese to me."

Doug and I split the bill, each paying cash. Brandi handed the receipt to me and said, "My number's in the book. Brandi Chastain. Call me."

"Right," I said, relieved to be leaving.

"Porcupine," Doug said as we walked out the door.

"Pardon?" I wasn't sure I understood him.

"Porcupine," he repeated.

"I'm not sure I get it."

"I said she's a porcupine. If she had as many sticking out of her as she's had stuck in her she'd look like a goddamn porcupine."

I was glad I didn't have to explain it to Lisa.

We rode with Doug to the bait and tackle store where Lisa and I both bought non-resident hunting licenses for the season – we were both still carrying California driver's licenses. Doug bought a dozen military surplus MREs and a box of No. 4 twelve-gauge steel shotgun shells. We then waited in line at the post office to purchase two Federal Duck Stamps which we signed and pasted on our hunting licenses. I had told Doug that Lisa and I wouldn't want to carry guns, but he explained that if we ran into any game wardens and there was a gun in the boat, it would be assumed we were hunting. It seemed pretty ironic to me that in the process of planning to commit a crime we were taking careful pains to be in compliance with state and federal hunting laws. I didn't say anything.

I was not sure where Nick was. Doug was still concerned about the possibility of our getting lost in the swamp, so the three of us spent the afternoon hunched over Lillie's computer designing a test run for GPS navigation. We decided that we'd map out a route that took us on a five-mile float down the nearby Opahatchee River. "We can't get lost and it'll tell us just how much off our maps will be compared to our GPS readings. The instruments that Nick had ordered would be more sophisticated, but we decided we'd try the one that Doug used for duck hunting as a test. We printed out three copies which we sealed in two-gallon freezer bags to protect them from water. Doug said he'd meet us at Rutherford Hall the next day after church.

On Sunday morning, we awoke to a cloudy sky for the first time in weeks. The temperature had dropped overnight and there was early morning ground fog that slowly cleared as the morning wore on. We lay in bed until 10 and ate a lazy breakfast while we read the Sunday paper. Promptly at 1 p.m., Doug drove into the yard. An aluminum boat painted drab green was perched on a trailer, attached to his silver grey Jeep Cherokee. He bounded up the back steps. "Ready for an afternoon on the river?"

I really didn't know him that well, but the prospect of recovering the gold seemed to have energized him.

We followed him in my Explorer to a landing with a concrete boat ramp some five miles downstream from where we intended to start our run. Leaving my vehicle there, we then rode with Doug to the upper landing and watched while he expertly backed the trailer down the ramp into the slowly flowing river. Tying the painter to a tree, he slowly winched the skiff into the stream and then pulled it up to detach the tow line. He parked the Cherokee and trailer on the bluff above the ramp and we all climbed into the boat. "You didn't bring a motor?" Lisa asked.

"No, it's a pretty day and the current will get us there in an hour and a half, max. Let's just enjoy nature while we check out these maps of yours." Doug had programmed the coordinates and waypoints into the GPS. It was small — slightly larger than a cell phone with a gray-green screen measuring roughly two by three inches on one end and a series of buttons below. He pressed a button to turn it on and waited while it locked onto the signals of satellites orbiting high above. He consulted the map and then pressed a couple of more buttons. "Hey, right on! This shows that we're not more than 50 feet from where the coordinates show we should be. You know, this just may work!"

It was a tranquil float down the river. The overcast had given way to layered clouds with patches of blue sky above. Moss-covered cypress trees formed a canopy overhead, their buttressed roots spreading out in shallow edges of the river. Doug sat in the back of the boat, eyes glued on the GPS, occasionally paddling to avoid a log or to keep us in the current and away from the banks. I sat on the middle seat, listening to the silence of the swamp, while Lisa lay back on a nest of life preservers and gazed up at the forest canopy. We were silent for most of an hour, drifting lazily around the bows and bends of the slow, flowing stream. Doug consulted his instrument, occasionally jotting notes on a scrap of paper. It was easy to forget that anything existed beyond the moment.

Perhaps an hour had passed when Doug said, "You know, for the most part, we are exactly on course. Even when we're off, it's usually only by a few dozen feet a most. I think we're going to be OK."

The lower landing appeared around a sharp bend in the river and Doug easily paddled the boat to the ramp. I volunteered to watch the boat while he and Lisa took the Explorer to pick up his vehicle. I watched them drive off and sat in silence listening to the jungle-like call of the pileated woodpecker and the distant hooting of an owl. I realized I had made no plans beyond retrieving the gold. I wondered for a moment if I'd lost my sense of direction.

CHAPTER
Forty–Four

THE RINGING OF THE PHONE awakened me at 7:10 a.m. Monday. I reached out for Lisa and remembered that she'd slipped back to her room sometime during the night, explaining that she didn't want to have to make excuses to Eula Mae. It was Nick.

"Morning, Matt! You seen the weather reports?"

I fumbled for the clock. It was still half light outside. "For God's sake, Nick, it's just past 7. I was still asleep."

"Turn on the Weather Channel. There's a tropical storm heading our way that they predict will become a Category 3 or 4 hurricane. Right now it looks like it's going to hit the U.S. coast somewhere between Brunswick and Baltimore early next week. This may be our chance." Lisa appeared at the door and slipped into my bed. I was holding the phone to my right ear; she began to nibble at my left.

"Where is it now?" I was definitely being distracted.

"Somewhere to the east of the Windward Islands in the mid-Atlantic. They think it's going to turn north and head up the east coast. We've got to keep a close eye on it and be ready to leave on 24 hour's notice." Lisa was now stroking my chest and slowly working downward with her hand.

"Nick, er, listen, let me call you back after I'm a little bit more awake, OK?"

"All right, but we all need to stay in touch. I'll touch base with Doug. Call me later."

"Sure, Nick..."

"Oh, one more thing. They've given it a name. It's Tropical Storm Lenore." Lisa reached out and hung up the phone without giving me a chance to reply. Her head disappeared under the sheet.

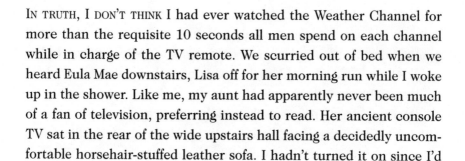

IN TRUTH, I DON'T THINK I had ever watched the Weather Channel for more than the requisite 10 seconds all men spend on each channel while in charge of the TV remote. We scurried out of bed when we heard Eula Mae downstairs, Lisa off for her morning run while I woke up in the shower. Like me, my aunt had apparently never been much of a fan of television, preferring instead to read. Her ancient console TV sat in the rear of the wide upstairs hall facing a decidedly uncomfortable horsehair-stuffed leather sofa. I hadn't turned it on since I'd been in the house.

I couldn't find a remote – the television looked like it predated such perks. It was a color set, however. I turned the dial on the cable box until I found the Weather Channel and settled in to see what they had to say. I heard Lisa come in the back door and speak to Eula Mae. The screen was still listing travel advisories for the Northeast when she bounded up the stairs and flipped a sheath of papers in my direction. "Television!" She said with mock disgust. "So 20th century!" The papers were printouts from an Internet storm tracking site. Tropical Storm Lenore had now been upgraded to Hurricane Lenore and was located about 150 kilometers southeast of Martinique at latitude 13.7 degrees north and longitude 59.6 degrees west. It was described as a Category 2 storm, but was expected to gain strength as it followed a slow north-northeast path that would bring it close to the U.S. mainland by the weekend. A map showed possible landfall in a broad area from Georgia to Delaware. The accompanying text pointed out a stable high pressure system over the southeastern states that might serve to keep the storm off shore and force it more to the north.

Lisa emerged from her room dressed in a T-shirt and shorts and toweling her long wet hair. "What do you think? Is this going to be the weather we're waiting for?"

"I have no idea," I replied.

Later in the morning, I called Doug at his office. "State Farm Insurance, Carole speaking," a professional sounding voice answered. Without identifying myself I asked to speak with Doug. After a brief delay he picked up.

"Hi, this is Doug. How can I help you?

"Doug, this is Matt."

"Hey, man, why didn't you say it was you?"

"I guess I didn't want your employees to think we were up to something. Maybe I'm being paranoid."

"I hadn't thought about that. Did Nick call you about the storm?"

"Yeah. What do you think?"

"Don't know. We'll just have to see. Let's check in by phone every day."

THE STORM WAS MASSIVE AND SLOW MOVING. By midday Wednesday, Lenore had been upgraded to a Category 4 hurricane and appeared to be aimed squarely at a landfall somewhere between Charleston, South Carolina, to the south and Morehead City, North Carolina, to the north. Federal and state emergency management agencies began to tool up for a coastal evacuation. We met at Nick's pond house Wednesday night. Lisa printed out copies of the latest storm forecasts from the Internet and handed them out as we sat around the table. We studied them in silence.

"Looks like the storm will make landfall Monday," Doug said. "If it goes toward the northern end of the projected range we'll have about a day of really foul weather followed by clearing as the wind shifts from the north to the west." No one spoke. Nick rose, walked over to the cabinet and poured a cocktail glass half full of Maker's Mark.

"Drink, anyone?"

We shook our heads.

Finally I said, "We're in it this far. This may be our only chance for months. We might as well move on it."

There seemed to be a sense of relief. I had tipped the scales of doubt from inaction to action. "OK," Doug said. "Final planning time."

Nick produced the two handheld GPS units that had arrived by UPS that afternoon. Doug inspected them and agreed they were state of the art, with built-in land and river maps, lots of memory and an advanced 12-channel parallel receiver.

We decided to leave Sunday. We would meet Saturday at the pond house to pack the gear in the boats. The next morning we would depart separately and in different directions. Nick said he thought it best that we each establish our own alibis so "if anything unexpected happens, they can't tie us together." We agree that sounded reasonable. Doug said he would tell his wife he would be gone for a few days for some early season duck hunting. He did that most years and it would not raise any suspicions with Nan or his office staff. Nick volunteered that he didn't have to tell anybody anything, but that he'd inform his secretary that he'd be in south Georgia on the Altamaha doing some river fishing. I said we'd tell Eula Mae that Lisa and I would be in the North Carolina mountains taking in the Fall leaves.

We got out the map. Doug would meeet Lisa and me at a rural crossroads west of Waynesboro at noon. It would take us an hour to reach the landing, get the boat in the water and secure his Jeep and Lisa's Jeep. We would then head up the Savannah and find a good campsite. He said he'd call and get overnight parking permission from Georgia Power for three vehicles and jotted down our tag numbers on his note pad.

Nick would arrive a couple of hours before sunset so as to be able to link up with us before dark. He pointed out that the area was so isolated there might not be good cell phone coverage. He said he'd pick up a pair of walkie-talkies with a five mile range the next day. Once he got past the nuclear power plant, he'd contact us and we could give him our exact location. Because Nick would be by himself, we decided to pack most of the gear in his boat to avoid overloading Doug's.

We went over the plan one final time. "Are we ready?" Nick asked.

"I think we've tried to think of everything," I said. We agreed to meet Saturday morning to pack the boats.

On the way back to Rutherford Hall, Lisa said, "Matt, you can't think of everything."

CHAPTER

Forty-Five

THURSDAY AND FRIDAY DRIFTED BY in slow motion. We did routine things and made idle conversation. One or the other of us checked the Internet weather report every several hours. By late Friday afternoon Hurricane Lenore was two hundred miles off the Georgia coast and headed squarely for Carolina's Outer Banks. The weather in Walkerville remained cool and clear, thanks to the stationary high pressure cell that hovered over the Southeast. By Saturday morning, we were forecast to have cloudy skies with increased winds and isolated thunderstorms as the warm wet Caribbean air of the storm system thrust itself against the cooler weather inland. The real blow was predicted to hit Sunday near midday. Along the coast, hurricane warning flags were hoisted and evacuations were ordered for low-lying areas.

Both Nick and Doug called Friday afternoon. We agreed that – for our purposes – the weather looked good, and that we'd meet as scheduled the next day to pack the boats.

On Saturday morning, we were once again at the lake cabin. We pulled both boats on their trailers under a large open shelter that Nick used as a pavilion for entertaining when the notion struck him. Today it had become the staging area for an expedition. We spread out the gear such that Smith's boat with three people and Nick's with one would be about equally loaded. Doug produced several folding shovels he'd purchased at an army surplus store. Nick went down a detailed checklist that included insect repellant, toilet paper, and bottled water. Somewhere in the back of my mind there was a vague sense of uncertainty, but I said nothing. I didn't know how Lisa felt, and I was afraid to ask.

Once more we went over the plans for our linking up with Doug, and for Nick to locate us later at our campsite upriver from the nuclear plant. We tested the hand-held radios and found they had an effective range of more than two miles. By lunch time, we finished. Doug said he'd see us at the crossroads the next day. Nick promised to make it to the campsite before dusk. The tents and sleeping bags were in his boat.

Lisa and I spent an aimless afternoon, had a quiet dinner and went to bed by 10 p.m. She held me, but neither of us seemed interested in anything more.

SUNDAY MORNING DAWNED CLEAR AND COOL. Lenore had decided to pause offshore, and now forecasters were less certain of its landfall. I called Nick who said he'd already talked with Doug. We were still on as far as they were concerned. We could always abort the plan at the last minute, but another opportunity might not arise for months, they reasoned. Lisa and I agreed. I called my uncle and told him that Lisa and I were going to the mountains for a few days. I lied and said I'd been unable to reach my mother, but asked him to tell her so she wouldn't be worried about our absence.

We packed a couple of changes of clothes in our gym bags, left a note for Eula Mae, checked the window and door locks, set the alarm system and left in Lisa's Jeep. I had hidden the missing journal, the two books that contained the Rutherford Cipher and the gold ingot on the top shelf of an upstairs linen closet covered with old bath mats and spare towels. The courthouse clock was striking 10 as we pulled out of the driveway.

Wherever Hurricane Lenore might have been at that moment, it was a beautiful day in Adams County. The sky was a pristine blue, and the now-yellowing leaves of the elm trees on the city square fluttered in a cool light breeze. We put the top down and headed east toward our rendezvous point. Once again our route took us past cotton fields, the dark green foliage concealing hints of fuzzy white from early bursting bolls. We passed through Waynesboro with its Romanesque-Victorian courthouse on the corner of Peace and Liberty streets in an otherwise decaying downtown. By the time we reached the crossroads where we were to meet Doug, we could see the massive cooling towers of the nuclear power plant in the distance. The wind had now shifted to the north. Bands of angry looking dark clouds could be seen in the east. We parked and put the top back up. It was 11:50 a.m.

Doug drove up 10 minutes later. He grinned at seeing us. "You're right on time guys. You ready?" It was like we were going on a teenage camping trip, not breaking into a nuclear weapons production facility.

"As we'll ever be, I guess," I replied.

Lisa gave a faint smile and waved. We headed south on River Road, Doug in the lead with us following a discrete distance behind. The road was paved, but little traveled. It skirted around the huge Georgia Power facility that lay between us and the river. When we reached the boat landing, the sky was obscured by slate gray clouds. Gusts of wind whipped through the sycamores and oaks sending bursts of leaves skidding across the paved parking area. An older man in a 1960s vintage GMC pickup was pulling his boat out of the river. "Y'all ain't gonna try to get out in this weather, is ya?" he asked with some seeming concern. He talked with Doug for a few minutes while Lisa and I pulled on our camo outfits over our jeans and shirts. "Well, good luck! And be careful," I heard him say before he drove off.

Doug waved. "He didn't think we knew about the hurricane. I told him we were going duck hunting and he said, "Well, that explains it. Duck hunters are just known for their love of bad weather." He backed the Cherokee down the ramp and winched the boat into the water. I studied the river. It was at least 300 feet wide here. The current appeared to be strong; debris and limbs, thrown in the stream by the storm, rushed by.

The Savannah River Site lay on the other side. Lisa sat on a concrete picnic table in a grove of mature sycamores next to the boat ramp. She took out her small binoculars and studied a large yellow sign nailed to a tree on the opposite bank. I could just make out "No Trespassing" in large letters. "What does it say?" I asked.

"Well, in addition to the 'No Trespassing' and 'United States Department of Energy,' there's a lot of fine print with such fun phrases as 'fines, imprisonment or both' and 'use of deadly force authorized.' "

She looked at me and raised her eyebrows.

"You still OK with this? If we're going to bail, it's now or never."

Doug was busying himself securing the outboard to the boat's transom. Lisa studied him for a moment, not replying. She looked at the Jeep and then, she looked at me. "I've got your back. Just watch mine. OK?"

Doug called, "Let's go."

CHAPTER

Forty-Six

THE SAVANNAH RIVER STRETCHED like a broad highway in front of us. The small outboard struggled against the current and the wind which now had gained force and was blowing out of the north. Bursts of cold rain stung our faces. Doug seemed oblivious to it all, as if this were a routine outing. Lisa and I pulled on our rain ponchos and huddled low in the boat.

We made slow progress upriver. To our right, a monotonous vista of swamp stretched into the distance, marked every hundred yards or so by the yellow signs that threatened summary execution by "Deadly Force Authorized." On the Georgia side to our left, the land was generally a high bluff, punctuated by occasional small streams that now poured freshly fallen rain into the river. Almost immediately opposite the massive cooling towers and only a few hundred yards downstream from what appeared to be the power plant's water discharge port, Doug pointed out the entrance to Four Mile Branch. I could barely make out its sentinel video camera through sheets of rain.

As suddenly as it had begun, the rain stopped and for a few moments blue sky could be seen through broken clouds far above. "Rain bands," Doug yelled over the sound of the motor. "They're pushed ahead of the storm. It's likely to go on all night like this — or longer. I really don't know. If the eye goes further toward the north, we may even get some clearing by tomorrow. If it veers to the south, well, we gonna have to do some hunkering down." He seemed unconcerned.

By 2 p.m., we were far enough past the power plant site to forget any worries about security patrols. Doug checked our location on the map and confirmed it with his GPS. "OK, guys, keep your eyes open for a big creek or stream off to our left," he instructed. Presently, a large open waterway appeared which cut into the river between two low bluffs. "Let's try this one," he said and turned the outboard to steer us toward the bank. Dark tea-colored water flowed out of a wide stream that seemed to disappear into a tunnel of low hanging branches. "I think this is an old run of the river," Doug observed to no one in particular. "Probably leads to an oxbow lake."

We had to bend down in the boat to get under limbs that draped low over the entrance. Once inside, the space opened up, and a calm body of water curving off into the forest could be seen. We slowly followed it until we were about 100 yards from the main flow of the river. "OK. This looks good to me. We can make camp here." Lisa and I looked around. The forest floor was open between huge trees, swept clean of debris and small vegetation by periodic high water.

"Doug, you're sure we'll be OK here?" I asked. "We're not that far above the water. You don't think the river is going to rise with all this rain?"

"Nah," Doug said, and the sky opened up again.

We unloaded our gear in pouring rain. I was cold, wet and unhappy. We managed to erect the tarp and tie it to four trees. Doug unfolded the chairs and directed Lisa to sit down while "us guys find some firewood." We gathered up bundles of what seemed to be soaked driftwood, but within fifteen minutes Doug had a blazing fire and things began to seem less bleak. It was shortly after 3 p.m.

The rain squalls would burst upon us suddenly, accompanied by gusts of high wind, then disappear into periods of drizzle and relative calm. By 5 p.m., I was beginning to worry that Nick had gotten lost. Just at that moment, the walkie-talkie beeped and a familiar voice said, "I sure hope you guys can hear this. I am wet and cold and hungry."

"We got you, Nick. Where are you?"

"Half a mile upstream from the power plant. You got some numbers for me?"

Doug read out our GPS coordinates. After a moment Nick said, "Be there in 20 minutes. Wait on the bank for me with your flashlight."

It was beginning to get dark. By 6 p.m., we were all sitting under the shelter of the tarp next to the warmth of the fire, eating cold MRE and drinking bottled water. The tents were erected with our dry sleeping bags inside.

We talked about nothing in particular for a couple of hours. Nick, as always, was charming, with a seemingly endless supply of tales about people he'd known and criminals he'd defended. We didn't discuss our plans for the next day.

At 8:30 p.m., Doug said he was tired and going to bed. Lisa said she thought she needed some sleep, too. They both headed off to their respective tents. I was too keyed up to sleep. Nick and I sat staring at the fire and watching the orange reflection of the flames flicker against the surrounding forest. The rain continued, waxing and waning in intensity.

"You want a drink?" Nick asked, pulling a plastic flask out of his jacket pocket.

"I may need one, but I'd better not. I don't need a hangover tomorrow."

"You ready?" he asked, taking a long draught from the flask.

"I guess so. I worry that we've missed something or made some bad assumptions. Like that camera guarding the mouth of the creek. Are we sure the weather will knock it out of commission?"

Nick chuckled. "Oh, I took care of that. One shot from 20 yards." He reached in his other jacket pocket and pulled out a small automatic pistol with a long barrel. Next, he withdrew a gunmetal blue cylinder which he screwed on its end, and a modified rifle scope that he clicked on a receiver mounted on the top of the weapon. He held it up. "Ever see one of these?"

I was a little alarmed. "Can't say as I have."

He handed it to me. "Careful, it's loaded. High Standard .22 caliber. Screw on silencer with a scope that's sighted in at 100 feet. It's reputed to be the weapon of choice for CIA assassins."

"Nick, isn't that, like, illegal?"

"And I suppose what we're up to is not?" He had a point. "No," Nick continued, "I didn't exactly go out and buy that. I had a client I was defending one time, a drug dealer. The guy asks me to keep a briefcase for him – said he was worried about somebody stealing it. It was locked and I just put it in my safe without really worrying about it. Well, a couple of days later, he gets shot dead by his girlfriend. I started to turn the briefcase over to his wife, but then I got to thinking about it and decided I better see what's in it first. So I jimmied the locks, and, wow, there's close to $50,000 in hundred dollar bills and this pistol. I just put it back in the safe and left it there. I waited a year and when no one called to ask me about it, I just took it as payment on his bill – which his family never did pay, by the way."

"Don't you have some sort of legal or moral obligation?"

"Are you kidding? Tell the family or the cops I was holding drug money and a silenced pistol for a convicted felon? Hell, they'd have my license in a heartbeat. Matt, listen. The law is not about truth, it's about justice. Never forget that."

He drank from his flask.

I decided to change the subject. "By the way, you never told me what you said to Doug to convince him to sign on for this little adventure we've gotten ourselves into."

Nick laughed again. "Yeah, well, I know that. I was sort of hoping you wouldn't ask. I just told him the cops were wise as to who had been breaking into Rutherford Hall, but in exchange for his assistance on a little project, I could make the evidence disappear." He chuckled and stared at the fire.

"My god, Nick! Are you lying to me? What the hell do you...?"

"Oh, calm down, Matt. We've got things under control. No, I just got to thinking that your break-ins weren't random burglaries. Both times the intruder tried to get into Lillie's study. And the second break-in especially – it was all too precise for your average criminal. The ladder was carefully laid against the side of the house, the glass neatly cut with a tool. I mean, who would know what might be in that room? The list is pretty short, and Doug's name would have to be at the top of it. He's been 'helping' her for several years, but being the suspicious fellow that I am, I have never been entirely sure of his motivations. Sure, he's interested in Confederate history, but it's sort of strange for a healthy young man to spend that much time around an old lady unless he's after something.

"No, after we talked that afternoon I called Doug and said I wanted to meet him at his office after work. I told him the cops had recovered his finger prints from the computer keyboard. You know what his reaction was?"

"I have no idea." I was in shock.

"He said, 'That's impossible. I wore gloves.'" Nick laughed. "What a fool! He was scared shitless, pacing the floor, trying to figure how he's going to talk his way out of things. So I let him stew for a while and then told him that I had the cops in my pocket. I said that I'd let a little money change hands to make sure the evidence disappeared and he'd be off the hook. He grabbed my hand and probably would have kissed me until I said, 'Doug, there's one little favor I need in return.' "

"Nick, don't you realize, he may have killed Lance."

"Nah. Not his style. He wouldn't harm a flea. For years he's been obsessed with the so-called Lost Confederate Gold. It's gotten to be his holy grail. He figured if he got close enough to your aunt, she would eventually tell him what she knew. Looks like she didn't, though. When I told him what you and Lisa had figured out, he would have walked barefooted on hot coals to be a part of it. No, I figure for once Chief Mathis has got it right. Lance may have known about the gold, but whoever killed him sure didn't – otherwise they would have taken the ingot."

I was at a loss for words. Finally I said, "But, Nick, after all that, how do you know you can trust Doug?"

Nick pursed his lips, took a drink and turned to look at me. The yellow light of the fire flickered in his eyes. "Son, in my experience, you can't trust anybody."

CHAPTER
Forty–Seven

DESPITE EVERYTHING, I SLEPT reasonably well. I went to bed, leaving Nick sipping on his whisky and poking at the fire. Lisa had managed to zip the two sleeping bags together to make one huge sack which she'd warmed with her body. She stirred when I stripped off my wet clothes and slipped in beside her, but was soon back fast asleep. The rain continued.

We were awakened the next morning by the tinny sound of a portable radio wailing some country tune and the smell of coffee brewing on the newly rekindled fire. It was still dark. Doug and Nick had evidently been up for some time. Doug shook our tent, "OK, guys, 5 a.m. Time to rise and shine." I was stiff and my mouth felt like cotton. We got dressed and headed off in opposite directions, flashlights in hand, to find the bathroom. When we returned, our two accomplices were sitting by the fire with coffee and high calorie breakfast bars ready for us.

Nick seemed no worse the wear from his drinking the night before. "The big adventure is about to start," he said. "Radio says the storm's going to make landfall near Myrtle Beach. They'd thought it was heading inland toward Charlotte, but now it looks likes it's going to turn north. Weather will probably begin to clear later in the day. Y'all finish your breakfast while Doug and I get the boats ready." Working by flashlight they removed everything unnecessary from the boats. The outboards and their gasoline tanks were placed in the tents. Doug's boat would carry the folding shovels and the remainder of the nylon cord. Nick filled his rucksack with MREs, bottled water, and his flask which he had apparently refilled from an unseen bottle. Doug carried his duck gun, Nick a deer rifle; both carried GPS units pre-programmed with our route. Each boat had a set of paddles, two regulation life preservers, a heavy duty electric trolling motor and 12 volt batteries.

We shoved off at first light. The rain had stopped, but the wind continued. The air began to cool, and a light fog appeared which seemed to carry and amplify every sound. Doug and Lisa took the lead in one boat. I rode with Nick in the other, close behind and in constant sight. We drifted silently down the river, our motors idling quietly at their lowest speeds while the current carried us along. Overnight the water level had risen. Now the main run of the river was littered with the trunks of fallen trees swept along by the current. The bloated body of a dead deer overtook and passed us as if it were on a rush to some ghoulish destination.

After about half an hour, we began to hear the deep throaty hum of the nuclear power plant in the fog off to our right. Doug announced that we soon should be coming up on the water discharge port. It appeared out of the haze, a fog bank in itself, as heated waste water dumped into the river. The two boats drifted through the cloud, disappearing and reappearing from each other's view. Ten minutes later, Doug consulted his GPS and announced, "We're a quarter mile out." Nick looked at his and nodded to me.

By the time we reached the mouth of Four Mile Branch, the fog from the heated water of the power plant was beginning to clear. The wind dropped and a slow drizzle of cold rain began to fall. Without hesitating, Doug quickly steered his boat into the wide mouth of the stream. We followed close behind. I could see the sentry video camera, it's casing smashed by bullets.

"I lied," Nick said. "I shot it four times just to be sure."

Four Mile Branch, in other locations, might be considered a small river. Here it was a relatively clear lane of water that wended its way through a forest of cypress and tupelo. A wrong turn into any of dozens of seemingly alternative waterways that branched off into the flooded swamp would have resulted in our being hopelessly lost. Our GPS kept us on track. Several times, we paused, pulling the boats side by side to consult the aerial photographs with their overlain GPS coordinates. We took one false turn, up what seemed to be a wide waterway, only to find ourselves nearly stranded on fallen logs. We returned to the main waterway without event and were soon back on track. Lisa held the instrument in the front of Doug's boat, silently pointing the direction to steer the boat as she consulted the arrow on the screen.

After two hours of quiet progress deeper into the wilderness, the topology began to change. We were no longer in a flooded swamp, but were now in a deep and narrow stream with low banks covered by river birch. A vast mixed hardwood forest of beech and oak disappeared into the distance around us. I turned around in time to see Nick furtively taking a quick hit from his plastic flask. Our eyes met and he said nothing. The rain had stopped, but the sky remained hidden by low clouds. The land on our right began to rise sharply. "About a quarter mile," Lisa said softly from the bow of the first boat. The stream narrowed, and on one occasion, Doug jumped out into waist deep water to pull away a fallen log.

Just as we thought that we had reached the limits of our ability to navigate, Lisa pointed at a high bluff just ahead rising sharply from the edge of the creek. "Unless I'm wrong, the cemetery should be about a 150 yards back from the top of that bank."

Doug eased his boat up to the bank next to a small tree. Lisa leaped on shore, securing the painter while Nick drew our boat up next to theirs and tied our rope to the same tree. She held out her hand to steady us as we climbed out of the shallow boat. The top of the bluff lay some 50 feet above us. The ground rose at about a 45-degree angle from the stream, making it necessary for the four of us to scramble up using both our hands and feet for support.

We all reached the top simultaneously to find a strange and eerie landscape. We had emerged from the thick woods that lined the stream into a large open field that must have at one time been dense forest. Naked trunks of once-giant trees reached toward low wind-driven gray clouds. The ground was overgrown with thick thigh-high grass, above which an occasional deformed bush pushed its branches up. Tall trees could be seen in the distance on all sides of the open area. "Must have had a fire in here," Nick observed and handed his GPS to Lisa.

We stood still for a moment while Lisa and Doug locked onto satellites and almost in a single voice said, "Over there!" both pointing in the same direction. Discarding our rain ponchos, we set out through the thick wet grass toward what at one time must have been a grove of giant oaks a hundred or more yards away. A single crow flew into the clearing, landing on top of one of the broken trunks. He saw us coming, and giving a cry of alarm, rapidly winged his way off. I could hear the calls of other crows responding in the distance. As we neared the grove, an ornate broken cast iron fence could be seen hidden under a thin layer of vines. My heart raced. I looked at Lisa. Her eyes were wide and she was breathing rapidly.

We came to the fence and circled around to the other side to find a broken gate propped open. There in the center of the grove lay a cemetery. Three white marble monuments gleamed in the light as if they'd been freshly polished. Doug Smith rushed ahead. At the base of each monument was a leaf-encrusted marble slab covering a grave. What appeared to be a five-gallon white plastic bucket was set on the grave in the center. Doug kicked it aside and began frantically brushing away the leaves away with his hands. Carved in the stone was an inscription which he rapidly cleared and read in a trembling voice,

"Emanuel Cartwell, CSA
1822-1865
To Toil Nevermore"

I looked back to see Nick taking another hit from his flask. I looked at Lisa who was smiling from ear to ear. I looked at Doug who did indeed have the look of a man who had found the Holy Grail. At that moment, Nick said, "I think we've found what we've been searching for." He was holding the silenced .22 in his hand.

It was pointed squarely at me.

CHAPTER
Forty-Eight

THE LOOK ON LISA'S FACE was one of terror. She turned to Doug. "Doug."

Doug stood up. "Sorry, Lisa, Matt. This is bigger than all of us." He looked at Nick, "Over by the trees?" Nick nodded and we were marched at gunpoint back to the edge of the bluff where we'd tied up the boats.

I thought they were going to kill us right then and there. Instead, Doug produced two sets of police handcuffs. Locking our arms behind us around two small pine trees, we were left as helpless prisoners sitting on the edge of the clearing while Nick and Doug recovered the shovels from the boat and set out toward the cemetery. We asked, "Why?" and "What are you going to do?" to which they said nothing.

Lisa sobbed quietly. I tried to speak to her, but she said, "Not now." From where we sat we could see both the boats down the bluff and the cemetery in the distance. We could hear two deep thuds as Nick and Doug flipped the marble slabs back to begin digging. The sounds of the spades piercing the sandy soil carried across the field. From our vantage point the two figures soon disappeared below the level of the grass as the hole became deeper. An hour passed. Doug went back to the boat for bottled water. He stopped in front of us, and saying little, opened a bottle which he held while we drank from it.

I said to Lisa, "He wouldn't do that if they were planning to kill us."

Lisa said, "Didn't they give water to Christ on the Cross?"

We didn't talk much. The clouds began to clear and patches of blue sky could be seen above. Lisa said, "You know it's funny what you think about at a time like this." I nodded. "Your birthday is next week. I'd already gotten you a present."

"Lisa, don't ..." We heard a whoop from the direction of the cemetery, followed quickly by a metallic clink.

Doug half bounded across the field toward us and the boats. He held a shiny object in each hand. He started not to pause, but thinking better of it stooped down in front of us and held up two gold ingots, mates to the one that I had found at Lillie's. He was ecstatic.

"We did it! Do you realize we have found one of the greatest treasures of all time! This is amazing! There are dozens and dozens more like these just right over there." Nick called for him to hurry up and he skidded down the bluff and returned to the graves with two empty rucksacks.

During the next hour, they made nearly 20 trips back and forth from the cemetery to the boats, wearing a path in the grass and a muddy rut up and down the bluff. The sky had cleared completely now and warm rays of sunlight began to dry our wet clothing. The sharp light and the rain-washed air defined every detail of the scene before us. Lisa and I tried to talk but found we were as useless at making conversation as we were unable to help ourselves in this situation. We sat in silence, watching our former partners load the gold in the boats.

I heard Doug yell, "That's it." He carried a half-filled rucksack to the boat, while Nick leaned up against one of the dead tree trunks in the cemetery. I could see him taking several long drinks from his flask. Doug returned, and they stood facing one another in heated conversation. He waved his hands in an animated fashion while Nick looked at him impassively, his arms folded across his chest. It was not difficult to imagine what they were arguing about. Finally, Nick shrugged and nodded his head. Doug smiled and stuck out his hand which Nick shook. They spoke a moment more, and then I saw Nick point in the direction of what must have been the hole they'd dug to open the graves. Doug looked in, and Nick pointed again, inching behind him as if to allow him better view of what he saw. As Doug peered in the grave, Nick placed the silenced .22 at the base of his partner's skull and pulled the trigger. Doug jerked and pitched forward into the earth. Nick reached in his pocket and calmly took a drink from his flask. Peering at what I presumed to be Doug's body, he drew his gun again, aimed carefully and fired two more times. He unscrewed the silencer, placed the gun in his pocket, consulted his wristwatch and began a leisurely saunter over toward us.

Nick sat down on the ground facing us. "I guess I should say I'm sorry that's it's come down to this." We stared back at him, stony faced. He fumbled in his pocket for his flask, now two-thirds empty. "You see," he paused as if in thought, "this is the logical end of something I inadvertently got involved in more than 20 years ago. Yeah, Matt, I've known all along about the gold and the so-called Rutherford Cipher. Your father was rightfully the one who should have recovered the gold. It was right after his 30th-birthday, as I recall. He was so excited – in awe, really. Your Aunt Lillie was apparently the keeper of the secret and she'd revealed it to him just the day before. We were duck hunting – you know, sitting there like a couple of guys will do with our shotguns on our laps and taking a few hits of bourbon while we waited on the birds to fly. He'd even brought along a photocopy of the coded message out of those books — wanted to show it to me. We got to talking about all that gold and what we could do with it, and then he starts in about how, before Lillie told him how to solve the code, he'd have to promise to use it 'for the good of the community,' or some such bullshit. So I killed him, made it look like an accident. It was so very, very easy."

I stiffened and tears welled up in my eyes. "You're a bastard! You son of a bitch!" Tears poured down Lisa's cheeks.

"Matt, you have every right to condemn me – God knows I've condemned myself thousands of times. The guilt was overwhelming. I swore if I recovered the gold I'd carry out what had been your Daddy's wishes. I would have used it for good – but you know what?"

I didn't answer.

"I couldn't figure out the damned code. I thought it would be so easy. I spent thousands of dollars – hired the best people I could find and then one day one of them calls me and says, 'Forget it, it's all a hoax.' Tells me the so-called Rutherford Cipher has been floating around for years. And Matt, you know what I thought for a long time there? I thought that maybe your Daddy had made the whole thing up and was just playing a big joke on me when I blew him away with my shotgun."

He took a drag on his flask. "But, hell, I wasn't sure. I thought maybe he told your mother. So I waited a while and started dating her. Tried fucking it out of her, but hey, nothing. So I gave up. Twenty years go past and then you and Miss Li here just waltz into my office one morning and prove to me that I was right all along. Now, Matt, at that point, I had to make a moral decision. I had gotten away clean with what happened to your father. I wasn't really sure if I wanted to start down the same path again. I studied about it and prayed about it and finally realized that I could not commit any greater sins than I had already committed. I was too far down the slippery slope, as they say."

"And what about Lance? Did you kill him, too?" I asked.

"Heavens, no! It was probably drug related, like the cops said. I should admit, however, that I *did* discover his body, apparently not long after the murder happened. I just didn't report it to the police. Poor kid still had his hands clutched around those coded pages he'd torn out of the books — the same ones your Daddy had. It was me who took those, by the way. Anyway, I thought to myself, maybe there is something to this old rumor. I pondered on it for a minute and it occurred to me that maybe I could pin the murder on you. I *am* Lillie's co-executor, and with you out of the way that would give me an uninterrupted chance to search her things. Did you *really* think I'd kill Lance? No, I was working on a way to move you back to the top of the suspect list when you two came to me about the gold."

Nick glanced at his wrist watch. "I need to be shoving off soon, so ..."

"You'll never get away with this, Nick," Lisa spit out. "They'll find my Jeep. You won't be able to explain what happened to Doug."

"Oh, I think to the contrary, my dear. You recall that I arrived at the boat landing after you and Doug left. His car and boat trailer are still parked there. Your little blue toy Jeep is now at the bottom of the river. I put it in neutral and gave it a quick shove down the boat ramp. As for me, I'm allegedly fishing on the Altamaha down in south Georgia. You two are supposed to be in North Carolina anyway. They can spend the next decade searching for you up there. And poor Doug – the fool – went hunting in a hurricane. What do you expect? They'll find his boat floating down the Savannah and assume he fell out. His body will never be found. I do feel bad for him, though. I told him we'd simply convince you by intimidation to split the gold 50-50 with us. To give him credit, your deaths were never in his plans. I guess you two will be joining our late friend over there in that grove of dead trees. A suitable final resting place."

Nick reached into his pocket and drew out the pistol, screwing on the silencer with a deliberate slowness. He looked me straight in the eye, pointed the gun at my forehead and pulled the trigger. There was a click. Nick looked puzzled for a moment, lowered the pistol and pulled back the slide. "Damn! Out of bullets," he said, reaching in his pocket and withdrawing a small box of shells. He ejected the clip and began slipping cartridges in its top. "You would know something silly like this would happen," he said with mock sarcasm. "And I was sure I'd thought of everything."

"Nick," Lisa said, her voice terse and bitter, "You can't think of everything." Out of the corner of my eye, I saw movement in the edge of the forest.

CHAPTER
Forty-Nine

THERE WERE AT LEAST FIVE OF THEM. Full-body camouflage suits with strange-looking hoods and gloves. They must have been approaching on their bellies, working their way toward us under cover of the high grass. They could not have been more than 20 yards away. Lisa stared in their direction with a mixture of terror and fascination.

Nick slipped the last round into the clip, placed the shell box back in his pocket, racked the slide on his pistol and once again raised it to my head. For some reason, he glanced at Lisa. Seeing her gaze fixed on something behind him, he lowered the gun a bit and turned to look. The lead figure, his presence now discovered, leapt up from his crouching position and began to run at full speed toward Morgan. As he did so, the others behind him – I saw now that there were eight in all – rose up as one, each holding a menacing Heckler & Koch 9mm machine pistol pointed in our direction.

Almost in slow motion, Nick sprang up from his crouch, wheeling to aim his pistol. The rapidly approaching figure was now 10 feet away. As he began to lower the gun, his attacker dived toward him in a flying tackle that hit Nick squarely in his midriff. His gun hand flew up involuntarily and the silenced pistol gave a muffled "poof" as it flew from his grip and cart-wheeled away. The two men struggled in a pile on the ground. Nick's resistance rapidly ceased when he looked up and realized he was now surrounded by the remaining figures and was the aim point of seven barrels.

The eight figures moved with precision as if they'd trained for this sort of thing. They wore full-body camouflage suits including hoods with what appeared to be thick plastic viewing points on the front and sides. I could make out enough of their faces to see they were all men in their 20s and 30s. They apparently were in communication through a local radio link; each wore an earpiece attached to a small microphone. The one who tackled Nick appeared to be the leader. By pointing and unheard directions, two of his men disappeared into the forest and returned shortly with a large pair of wire cutters which they used to clip the chain that held our cuffed hands behind the tree.

I started to speak, but the leader held his finger up in a sign to be quiet. Long plastic ties were produced and our hands were bound in front of us. Lisa and I still wore the now severed handcuffs like large bracelets on each wrist. To my surprise, one of the men reached in a small pack and drew out thick cotton hoods which they slipped over our heads as blindfolds. Now bound, sightless and prodded from behind we were marched through what must have been thick forest away from Four Mile Branch and toward the heart of the Savannah River Site. The whole episode had taken less than five minutes. Not a word had been spoken.

We must have walked several hundred yards. Once I heard Lisa say, "Cut it out, you bastard!" but I had no idea what she was talking about. Nick on the other hand, having evidently recovered from the shock of his capture, began loudly demanding that our blindfolds be removed and that we be given, "immediate access to counsel." Half way into the fourth or fifth of his rants I heard a hard "thud" and he fell silent.

Eventually we reached what must have been a road. I could no longer feel or hear leaves under my feet; we now seemed to walking on a sandy open surface. After another 10 minutes, we stopped. I could hear the sound of large diesel engines approaching and the squeal of their breaks as they stopped in front of us. I called out to Lisa, and heard her say from a distance, "I'm here."

Strong arms lifted me up into the back of some sort of truck with bench seats on the side. Others climbed in with me. I could smell the exhaust fumes. For the first time a voice spoke and said, "We're taking you to a receiving facility. Don't try to talk." For the next 15 minutes we drove, first over rough roads, then on a paved highway. Twice we stopped at checkpoints before arriving at our destination.

I was hustled off the truck and led through several sets of doors into a room where a voice instructed me to "sit down and don't move." After perhaps five minutes, I heard the door opening and felt hands tugging at the drawstring that held the hood over my head. The blindfold was removed and I stared around me.

Everything was white. The walls were white, the floor was white and the two figures standing in front of me were also dressed in white suits and hoods similar to the ones our rescuers wore. For some reason I was angry. "Just where the hell am I?"

"You are in a decontamination facility," one of them replied. I could see through her mask that it was a dark-haired woman in her 40s.

"You have likely been exposed to massive amounts of radiation, and our first job is to try to save your life. So, off with your clothes."

With that said, the other figure, a muscular young man, clipped the plastic ties that bound my wrists and produced a key that opened the cuffs. They tossed them in a plastic hamper labeled "Radiation Hazard." Quickly they stripped off my clothes, boots and underwear, even my watch, tossing them all in the hamper and leaving me naked and shivering.

I was half shoved through a door into what appeared to be a shower room. Two more white suited figures awaited me, one with a hose and the other with a large soapy sponge. First I was hosed down like a reluctant family dog undergoing his weekly bath. Next, the figure with the soapy sponge – another woman, I noted – scrubbed down every inch of my skin, from the top of my scalp to the bottom of my feet. This process was repeated three times. Neither spoke. The woman indicated that I should open my mouth which she scrubbed with an oversized toothbrush. I tolerated this – I had no choice – half expecting someone to appear next, brandishing an enema tip. Fortunately, I was spared that indignity.

After more than 20 minutes of washing, I was handed a large thick absorbent paper towel and ushered into the next room where another white suited figure handed me a disposable coverall and a set of disposable slippers. I was instructed to put them on. He pointed to a bench and told me to have a seat and wait. My watch was gone, but it could not have been much more than an hour since our rescue.

Time passed slowly. After about an hour, a burley figure in a radiation suit, yellow this time, came in and instructed me to stand up. Holding an instrument in his left hand, he moved a sensor attached to a cord slowly over my body, staring at the digital readout as he did. He said nothing. He finished and was making notes on a clipboard when I asked, "What did you find?

"Not much. You may have been lucky," he replied. I had no idea what he meant.

Another quarter hour or so passed. The door to the room was opened this time by a serious looking man clad in a grey jumpsuit labeled prominently across the back with the word, "SECURITY."

"What, no protective suit?" I asked.

His expression didn't change. "Follow me," he said.

I was led down a narrow hall. Armed guards were posted on either end. The security man ushered me into a windowless room, furnished only with an exam table, a desk and two chairs, one of which was occupied by a pudgy middle-aged man in coat and tie who was pouring over a thin chart. Mr. Security shoved me down in the chair by the desk and stood an arm's reach away. Mr. Coat and Tie said nothing. He appeared to be studying a table of figures in the chart. Finally he looked up and said, "You are Matthew Rutherford?" I nodded. I had no idea how they'd gotten my name. My wallet — like everything else I was carrying – had gone in the Radiation Hazard hamper.

He continued. "Mr. Rutherford, I'm Doctor Kitchens. You've got a lot going on here as you can well imagine, but our first order here is to try to determine how much radiation exposure you've received. Now what I'm going to do is this. I want to take a brief medical history, and then I'm going to examine you. After that, we're going to collect a blood sample."

"That's fine, but I've got a few questions myself. Where are you keeping ..."

"Hold it, Mr. Rutherford." He cut me off. "Let's get this straight. I said I'm a physician. My sole charge is to assess your current health and perhaps speculate about how much injury you may have suffered as a result of your actions. That's it. Nothing more. I ask the questions, you give the answers."

The security man inched closer. For the next 20 minutes, I was questioned about my health, prodded and poked, and forced to give up six vials of blood. They handed me a urine cup and watched while I collected a specimen.

Having been thoroughly examined, my guard once again bound my wrists with a plastic tie, slipped a hood over my head and led me through a long maze of halls. He indicated that I stand still while he talked with someone to whom he was delivering my care. I could hear typing on a computer keyboard, and the whirring of motors as electrically operated doors clanged open and shut. After some minutes, I was led through a series of doors (we had to wait while they were operated remotely) into a small cell. The guard—a tall, thirtyish black man this time—removed my hood and clipped the ties that bound my wrists. He pointed at a cot and instructed me to sit on it. "You'll be here for a while. Make yourself comfortable." He turned and left. The door clanged shut with a pneumatic hiss.

CHAPTER

Fifty

My cell, for it could only be described as such, measured about 8 feet wide and 12 feet deep. It was actually divided into two parts, a long narrow outer room measuring about 4 feet by 8 feet, and a back room measuring roughly 8 feet by 8 feet. The walls were stainless steel, and the floor concrete covered with some sort of protective epoxy sloping to a drain in the center. Separating the two rooms from one another and the cell from the hall outside were pneumatically operated stainless steel doors that disappeared into the wall when opened.

What few items that might have counted as furnishings were attached to the floor or walls by tamper-proof bolts. In the foyer, as I termed it, a table and stool occupied one end, both securely anchored to the floor. The other end held a flat shelf that could be used as a desk. A spot light from the ceiling was focused on its surface. A legal pad and a soft-tipped felt pen were neatly placed in one corner. In the bedroom, a cot was bolted to one wall, with two shelves at its end holding two towels, a wash cloth, and two of the same coveralls I'd been issued in the decontamination building. On the opposite wall, a combination toilet/urinal extended obscenely from the steel wall. Next to it was a sink with a more highly polished square of steel above serving as a crude mirror. The ceiling proper was probably 9 or 10 feet high but was located above a stainless steel wire mesh that allowed light and air to flow through while keeping the prisoner away from the ductwork and electrical connections.

In both rooms, one wall was dominated by a large mirror of thick glass, no doubt an observation panel for whoever chose to watch me. Small video cameras, two per room, were evident as they peered through the mesh ceiling. I noted that high flow air was pumped into the outer room and seemed to be vented toward the rear of the cell. This was apparently some sort of isolation facility.

I had no idea of the time. My watch was gone, there were no windows, and I could hear nothing in the hall outside. I was lying on the cot when the door to the foyer hissed shut. I could hear the outer door open, and some motion in the front of the cell. After a moment, I heard the outer door close and the interior door opened. A tray heaped with hot food on paper plates, two Styrofoam cups filled with iced tea and a set of plastic utensils sat on the table. I realized I hadn't eaten since we left camp that morning and in a matter of minutes had consumed everything.

I don't know whether or not the food was drugged. I suspect not; perhaps I was just tired. After eating, I lay back on the cot. Sometime later, I awoke to find the lights dimmed but not extinguished, and the tray and remains of my dinner missing. I had heard no one come or go. An hour or so later, the lights came on brightly as the inner door closed again and opened a few minutes later to reveal a tray of bacon, eggs, grits and coffee sitting on the table.

I ate, and now rested and awake, I began to consider our situation. I say "our" because I was worried about Lisa. As far as Nick went, he had confessed to one murder and there were two witnesses who had seen him commit a second. I wanted to scream at him. I wanted to hate him, but I didn't have time. I couldn't understand why we had not been questioned. Surely we were under arrest, but the only contact we'd had with those holding us was a decontamination procedure. Time passed slowly. An hour later, or perhaps it was three hours, a voice from an unseen speaker said, "Mr. Rutherford, we'll be taking you for interrogation in a few minutes. We'd like to advise you that this facility is patrolled by armed guards who have permission to use deadly force. Any failure on your part to cooperate fully would be quite foolish. Do you understand this?"

"I do," I replied.

A few minutes later, the outer door opened and a guard dressed in the same grey jumpsuit ordered me out of the cell. The hood was placed over my head again and I was led a short distance through three doors into a small room. The hood was removed and I could see a table and a single chair facing a mirror on one wall. A microphone was placed in the center of the table. I was told to sit and wait. Time passed. I decided to get up and pace the room, but an unseen voice boomed from a speaker attached to the ceiling, reminding me that I'd been told to sit and wait. I did.

More time passed. The speaker crackled and a voice said, "Your name is Matthew Rutherford, is that correct?"

"Yes, it is," I mumbled.

"Speak into the microphone, Mr. Rutherford. We have several people here and we want to make sure we all can hear one another." There was a pause. "You do understand that you are being held in detention and are subject to being charged with numerous crimes under federal law, including murder and terrorism?"

I felt an involuntary shudder. "If you say so."

"And you understand also that, for any one of several of the offenses with which you may be charged, the maximum penalty is death?"

The shudder came again, this time visible no doubt to my anonymous interrogators behind the one-way mirror.

"I will have to take your word for that."

"We wanted to bring these items to your attention early in this process in hopes that we might count on your cooperation." The voice paused again. "So let's get started. You were born on October

11, 1973, in Walkerville, Georgia. Is that correct?"

The interrogation went on for hours. At least five people questioned me. I volunteered little, but held nothing back when directly questioned. They seemed to already be somewhat familiar with what had happened, and occasionally made references to information that could only have come from Lisa or Nick. I didn't tell them about Nick's confession that he'd killed my father. We took a break. I was given a glass of water, escorted to a restroom and observed while I relieved myself. When I returned to the room a sandwich and a Coke were on the table. I devoured them hungrily.

A few minutes later the questioning started again, this time by a voice I hadn't heard before. "Mr. Rutherford, we've been questioning your comrades and they tell us that you were the mastermind behind this whole scheme. Is that correct?" I didn't like the ominous tone of his voice. I thought the term "comrades" had died with the end of the Cold War.

"No, sir. That is not entirely correct. As I've told you – or maybe it wasn't you, I don't know – we mutually agreed to try to recover a hoard of gold that was stolen from the Confederate Government in 1865."

"That's not what Lisa tells us, Matt." He was using my first name now. "She says you tricked her into this murder plot hatched by you and Mr. Morgan. That the plan was to kill ..."

"You're lying," I said calmly.

"Well, Matt, it doesn't seem out of character for you. Chief Mathis tells us you're the prime suspect in the murder of your first cousin – says you killed him for an inheritance."

I sat quietly for a moment. "I don't know who you are. I can't see you. But you can see me. Look into my eyes. I'm telling you now. I had nothing to do with my cousin's death. Nothing at all."

The speaker was silent. "That's all for today. We understand that you have an appointment with Dr. Kitchens now anyway. We'll talk again tomorrow."

"I want to see Lisa!" I yelled. "Where is she?"

There was no reply.

CHAPTER

Fifty-One

I WAS LED AGAIN, BLINDED, through a maze of corridors. When the hood was removed, I found myself again in the same small exam room with the pudgy doctor who this time was leafing through a stack of laboratory reports that had my name at the top. He was wearing the same suit and tie he'd worn the day before. He seemed friendlier this time. "Hello, Matt. Sleep OK last night?"

"What do you think?"

"Listen, I know you're worried – you have every right to be. But I've got some good news, for *you* at least." I didn't know what he meant by that. "We've been looking at your exposure levels and ..."

"Dammit, you keep saying," I started to rise up in the chair but the guard quickly grabbed my shoulder and slammed me back down. "OK. Sorry," I said. "You keep referring to radiation exposure, but I have no idea what you're talking about."

"You mean they haven't told you?" The doctor had an incredulous look on his face.

"No! They haven't told me a damned thing! Now I demand ..."

The guard's firm grip pushed me down again. "Mr. Prisoner, sir, you don't demand anything in this place. Is that clear?" I sat silently.

Dr. Kitchens stared at me. A vein in the middle of his forehead throbbed and a trickle of sweat ran down his cheek. The room was not hot. He groped in his hind pocket and pulled out a large dingy handkerchief with which he mopped his brow. He stared at me. "They really didn't tell you, did they?"

"No, they didn't." I tried to sound defiant.

"Then I can't say anything – security, you know. But they will have to, eventually. Your blood work looks fine. Now let's get you examined."

———————◆—●—◆———————

MY SECOND NIGHT AND MY SECOND DAY were essentially a repeat of the first. I kept track of time by meals. I spent at least six hours in the same anonymous interrogation room answering the same questions, denying the same allegations, and trying to make some sense of what was going on. I demanded a lawyer. I was told that I was being held for national security reasons and for crimes committed on Federal land and that while I could eventually exercise my right to counsel "that will all happen in due time." I demanded to speak with Lisa, and again, my pleas were ignored.

I did not see Dr. Kitchens again, but was returned to my cell where a large plate of barbecue and Brunswick stew awaited me. While I was eating, I thought I heard something in the hall. I got up and placed my ear to the door, only to be reminded over the speaker by my ever-present guards that the door was locked and would remain so until "we determine it is time to open it." I made an obscene gesture at the video camera and the voice replied, "And to you, too."

Half an hour later, the speaker announced I would be taken for a shower. I was told to gather my towel. The outer door hissed open and I was told to step into the hall. I was not hooded this time and had a chance to examine my prison. Evidently I was in Cell No. One

out of six in this unit. The doors were all the same and marked solely by a number. Somewhere behind one of those other doors both
Nick and Lisa were being held. I wanted to scream. I wanted to beat
on them all and say, "Lisa, are you all right?" but I thought better of
it and walked down the hall to a door marked "shower." The door
opened to reveal a stainless-steel cubicle with a small sink and counter on one end and a shower on the other. On one side of the sink a
comb, toothbrush and plastic razor were wrapped in a sealed plastic
pouch. Shaving creme, toothpaste and a Styrofoam cup were on the
other. "You've got 20 minutes," the guard said. "I'll be standing right
here, and they'll be watching." He pointed to a video camera above
the wire mesh ceiling. The door hissed shut.

I stripped naked, brushed my teeth and shaved – slowly and deliberately. The shower was an open stall with no curtain. Hot and cold
water handles were mounted on the wall. I leaned in to turn on the
water when I spotted three long strands of black hair stuck to the wall
just below the controls. They had been put there deliberately. I
smiled as I pretended to adjust the water. The strands spelled out:

♡UL

On the third day, I was not interrogated. I was taken to see Dr.
Kitchens who examined me for rashes and drew more blood. Under
the watchful eye of the guard, he refused to say any more than he had
before, but did pronounce that I seemed to be doing well.

On the morning of the fourth day, a guard I'd not seen before
opened the door and instructed me to follow him. I was not hooded.
I was led out of the detention facility through a complex of corridors
to a room furnished only with a table and chair. A window opened to
a view of other non-descript buildings. A familiar bag was sitting on
the table. The guard said, "They thought you might be more comfortable in your own clothes." When I had last seen the bag, it was sitting on the floor of the closet in my bedroom at Rutherford Hall.

Inside were several changes of clothes, including shoes and under-wear. My familiar, worn toilet kit was packed on top with my own razor, toothbrush, and comb.

I changed rapidly, throwing the coverall and slippers in the corner and pulling on a pair of jeans and a long-sleeved rugby shirt. I put on socks and slipped my feet into my own worn Docksiders. "How did you get all this?" I asked.

"I don't know, and I don't want to know. This whole thing has moved up the chain of command and we're turning you over to another group. The investigation is been being handled directly out of Washington, and that's all I can say." He watched quietly while I got dressed. "I guess I can say this, though, Mr. Rutherford. You're a lucky man, a very lucky man."

CHAPTER
Fifty-Two

I was now dressed comfortably in my own clothes. The guard, who I noticed was unarmed, led me outside. We stood by the edge of a parking lot while he spoke on his radio, evidently telling someone that I was ready to be picked up. The air was warm, typically so for a day in early October. A faint breeze ruffled the tall pine trees that surrounded the building complex, sending showers of brown needles onto the neatly mown grass. For the first time in several days, I could see the sky. It was a pale shade of blue, with wisps of white clouds scattered about. For a moment, I considered trying to escape, but thought better of it. Neither of us tried to make conversation. We waited in silence.

After a few minutes, a dark green Suburban with tinted windows and government license plates pulled up. The guard opened a rear door and indicated that I should get in. He sort of nodded, and under his breath muttered, "Like I said, a very lucky man."

The driver of the Suburban was a muscular man with close cropped hair. He looked military, but was dressed in a knit shirt and khakis. He acknowledged my presence, made sure the door was shut, and drove off without comment. The fact they were transporting me unshackled and without a guard seemed to indicate I was not considered an escape risk. I had apparently been held at some type of security complex. We passed through two checkpoints and a series of high fences, then drove on a paved road for several miles through gently rolling pine forest. At a sign indicating "Conference Center," we turned into a paved drive that meandered over a stream and up a hill before ending in a parking lot in front of a group of buildings. The driver had kept his eyes on the road, occasionally glancing in his rear view mirror but saying nothing.

The Conference Center consisted of a large central building — apparently a meeting hall with catering facilities — and a series of a dozen or more surrounding individual cabins of sorts, all set in landscaped and manicured grounds. It appeared deserted except for three other dark green Suburbans similar to the one I was riding in, all with government license plates. We stopped in front of one of the cabins. The driver spoke for the first time. "I understand that you'll be staying here for a day or two. I've been told to advise you that the grounds are patrolled and that you should not attempt to leave unless you are given permission to do so. Is that clear?"

I nodded. I couldn't understand what was going on. Two days earlier, I was being threatened with the death penalty, and now I was being moved to what could pass for a corporate vacation retreat. The car door was opened by another nondescriptly dressed guard; I would have described him simply as another muscular young man had I not seen the pistol in a holster tucked in the back of his waistband. The wire from a small earpiece communicator in his left ear snaked down his side to what looked like an oversized beeper clipped on his belt. He grabbed my bag and led me to the steps of one of the cabins.

The guard spoke. "My name is Aaron, Mr. Rutherford. A few colleagues and I will be looking in on you from time to time. You do understand that you're still under detention?"

"I do, but I don't ..."

Aaron smiled somewhat mechanically, "I'm sure that they'll make it all clear to you in time, but for the moment, I think you need to know that you should not try to escape. Clear?"

I nodded.

"Good," he continued, smiling a bit more genuinely this time. He waved his hand to indicate the group of cabins, "These are the local version of VIP guest quarters. Each cabin is actually a suite of two bedrooms, each with a private bath, plus a large informal sitting area, a small conference room and a basic kitchen. I understand they were designed to bring top nuclear scientists together for brainstorming about building better bombs." He paused, turning over his spontaneous alliteration in his head. "Anyway, with the Cold War gone, they don't get the use they once did. So we borrowed them for a few days for you."

"And who is we?" I demanded.

"The government, of course – The United States Government." He didn't seem inclined to say more so I held my tongue.

Aaron continued, "You'll be staying in one of the bedrooms of this bungalow, and just to be certain that you don't go in need of anything, my partner and I will be staying in the other. We'll be available to you 24 hours a day."

Read that as "you'll be under armed guard 24 hours a day." I thought, but said only, "Thank you."

Aaron showed me to my bedroom. It was simple, but well-furnished. I noted the absence of a television or radio. I asked him, "Where are the others, Lisa and Nick? I haven't seen them since we were taken to the decontamination facility. I really need to talk with Lisa. I need to know she's all right."

"I'm not in a position to say anything, Mr. Rutherford. My job is to guard, sorry, be on call should you need any attention. It's my understanding that you have a meeting scheduled with one of my superiors later in the day. I'm sure he'll be able to tell you more."

I took a step in his direction. "Dammit, I have a right..."

Aaron's right hand eased toward his side within quick reach of his weapon. "Mr. Rutherford. You would do well to follow instructions. I suggest that you get settled into your room. Maybe take a cold shower and calm down a bit. Please recall that you are here on our terms, not yours."

I backed off.

I went to the bedroom and shut the door. Through the blinds, I could see thick wire mesh covering the outside of the windows. I lay down on the bed—a comfortable one for a change, and decided to take a nap. I couldn't sleep and stared at the ceiling turning over and over in my mind the events of the past four days. My anger against Nick seethed. I felt horribly guilty for having dragged Lisa, my beautiful Lisa, into all of this. I wondered and worried about radiation exposure. What kind of unholy mess had I gotten us into.

There was a rapping at the door. It was Aaron. "Mr. Rutherford, I've got some things of yours here." I opened the door and walked out into the sitting area. He handed me my watch and wallet. "They've been cleaned thoroughly," he said, as if I should understand what he was talking about.

I glanced through the front window to see another dark Suburban pulling into a parking space in front of the adjacent bungalow. The windows were heavily tinted; I couldn't see inside.

I placed my hand on the door handle and turned to Aaron, "May I?" He shrugged. I opened the door and stood on the small front porch.

Another guard who I had not seen before, again informally dressed with a holstered pistol in his waistband and an ear bud communicator, leaned over to speak to the driver and then walked to the rear of the SUV where he unloaded a blue soft-sided bag. It looked familiar. Walking around to the passenger's side, he opened the rear door. I waited, my heart pounding. Lisa stepped out.

She didn't see me at first. I called, "Lisa!" and she turned toward me. The driver was out of the vehicle now and walking toward the bungalow next door. Her guard was lifting her bag and saying something to her. Without warning, she suddenly bolted toward me.

Almost as one, in a single fluid reflex, her driver, her guard and Aaron drew their pistols and pointed them at her. I leaped off the porch and ran toward her. I could see her guard taking aim and then, realizing what was happening, holster his weapon and motion for the others to do the same. They stood and watched as Lisa flew into my arms.

CHAPTER
Fifty-Three

"OH, GOD, MATT, ARE YOU ALL RIGHT?" Words mixed with pent-up emotions flowed from her lips. "I've been so worried. What's been happening? Do you know anything? They wouldn't tell me if ...?"

"Hey, calm down," I said as if I somehow knew more than she did. "Things are going to be all right now. We're both alive, and that's what counts."

We held one another as the guards watched, silently.

After a moment or two, Aaron approached and said, "Mr. Rutherford, you two have permission to visit together all you'd like, but why don't you let Ms. Li get settled in a bit? We're having food sent in and you can talk over lunch."

Lisa released me from her grip and looked intently at my face. She said again, "I have been so worried. Matt, they told me that you and Nick were trying to blame Doug's death on me and that you'd turned on me and that I didn't have anyone who could help me but if I'd tell them the truth that they'd see if they..." She stopped suddenly as if the pressure that propelled her words had suddenly been cut off. She stared in my eyes. "I didn't believe them for a minute. I told them the truth. I told them that you cared about me and that I cared about you and that you wouldn't say that because it wasn't true."

"I do. And I didn't. And Lisa," I hesitated because I felt a tear welling up in my eye, "I got your message." She hugged me and we said nothing more.

OUR LUNCH WAS SERVED IN THE CONFERENCE ROOM of the command bungalow. The furniture in the sitting area had been moved to one side and a couple of makeshift desks set up on two folding tables. Three laptop computers, a couple of cassette recorders, a laser printer, three telephones and what appeared to be a large pile of interview transcripts littered their tops. A middle-aged man dressed in an open-necked, long-sleeved shirt was seated at one table and engaged in an intense phone conversation as we walked in. Aaron introduced him as "Special Agent Hall." He nodded, unsmiling, and continued to speak softly into the telephone.

Lunch consisted of a stack of assorted sandwiches, potato chips and soft drinks in cans. No utensils, not even plastic. They still didn't quite trust us. We ate on paper plates. Lisa and I sat at one end of the conference table and talked while Aaron and Lisa's guard, who introduced himself as Tom, ate quietly at the other end and pretended not to be listening. Lisa's story was essentially the same as mine. She'd been held next door in Cell 3, and had undergone two very intense days of questioning. She had tried to hide nothing, but her inquisitors, like mine, seemed to assume that we were part of some bigger plot as yet undiscovered. Like me, she'd been subjected to the ministrations of the nebbish Dr. Kitchens. Neither of us had gotten any word of Nick. I turned to our minders and asked, "Where is Nick? He's not here, is he?"

Tom spoke. "I don't think we'll be seeing much of Mr. Morgan. We know what happened with your other partner, Smith, and," Aaron gave him a sharp look and cleared his throat. "Maybe I better let someone else fill you in on the details." He glanced at his watch. "It's 10 to one. Our boss should be getting here shortly."

We sat in the conference room and waited. The guards cleared the remains of lunch and sat silently. About 20 minutes later, we heard the front door open and the sound of voices in the outer room. An older man, obviously in charge, stood in the door. He looked to be in his late 50s, perhaps 60 at most. He was of moderate height, dressed in a slightly worn gray suit and walked like a man who worked out daily. He smiled. "So, we meet at last! Matt, Lisa – you don't mind if I call you by your given names do you? You've caused quite a stir."

I picked up a slight east Tennessee twang in his voice.

"They've gotten me down here to see if we can get things straightened out in a way that meets everyone's needs."

I thought that was a strange thing to say. He continued, "I hope you'll forgive me if I just introduce myself as John. I know you've both been through a lot, and in one sense of the word, I almost feel like I should apologize to you, but you've got to realize that you've caused a whole lot of trouble for quite a few people, not to mention the murderous acts of your Mr. Morgan.

"I guess you want to know why we're holding you here instead of in a more proper detention facility. I guess you want to know what I do and why I'm here. Let me get that last part out of the way first. Our group, these men here and I, work for a unit of the Justice Department. I have an office and a title and a very good government salary, but I, we, don't exactly have job descriptions. We're all called special agents but in reality we're a group of problem solvers." He waved his hand toward the table and chairs. "Here, let's sit down. I think this is going to be a long afternoon. I need to fill you in on what's happened. You've got some very big decisions to make." He motioned for the guards to leave the room. "Shut the door on your way out. We'll call you, if we need you."

Lisa and I had said nothing to that point. We sat down. Lisa spoke. "Look, Mr..."

"John. Just call me John. I think you need to realize that the less you know the better off you may be." He smiled, benignly.

"OK, then, John. We know we were wrong and we've admitted that, but ..."

John interrupted. "Lisa, why don't you let me talk for a while? Let me tell you where we are in the investigation, what we know and what we don't, and what may be a good solution to a very sticky situation."

"Do Lisa and I need a lawyer here to represent us? We have that right ..."

"Oh, absolutely you do! And if you demand counsel at this moment, I will ask my men to deliver you back to the cell you left this morning and we will arrange for you to call your attorney, or have one assigned to you. But before you exercise that right, could I suggest that you hear me out? If your case gets in the court system, I'm out of here. You're both facing a *minimum* of 5 to 10 years in federal prison, and that's assuming that you can avoid a murder charge which could mean life – or worse. I want to see if we can't offer you an alternative. If you don't like what I have to say, we can stop at any time. It's your call."

Lisa and I looked at one another. I spoke. "OK. We'll hear you out."

John stared up at the ceiling for a moment, seemingly collecting his thoughts. "I almost don't know where to begin. Do you recall the myth of Pandora who opened the forbidden box and released sorrow into the world? In a sense, you two have opened Pandora's Box. My job is to put the lid back on, *if* I can. You see, kids, the world's an imperfect place. The government, your government, really does try to make this country a better place, but sometimes in doing so we have to take shortcuts, make compromises. I think we're in that situation. Let me start at the beginning. I'll tell you what we know, I'll tell you what we've found out, and I'll make a proposal to you. This is going to take a while, so let's get started."

CHAPTER
Fifty-Four

"You know, I've been in government service now for going on 35 years," John began. "I guess I should have retired, but I really like what I do. You see, I'm a fixer. I'm the guy who gets to attend to all those little problems that don't fall neatly in one slot or another. And you know what keeps me going? It's cases like this one. This has got to be one of the most bizarre situations that I've come across yet, but I'm going to see if we can't work it out.

"I've really got to give you kids credit. You know, you remind me of my own children. I've got a boy about your age, Matt. Has a degree in information management and works in Chicago. And my girl, Sarah, she finished law school a couple of years ago and is an associate at a firm in Washington. I can see how you got yourself in this situation. Hell, if I were your age, I'd probably do the same thing.

"I realize that they treated you harshly the first couple of days you were here. You can't blame these guys, though. They have this knee-jerk mindset that everyone's a terrorist until proven otherwise. They had the local security folks, the FBI, the domestic terrorist people and even their CIA liaisons smoking you over – trying to get you to admit to something more than a simple hunt for hidden treasure. You see, they *thought* that intruders were inside their security perimeter, but they had no idea where you were, or even that you were still inside. This place is just too big to guard every square foot. Once the storm passed over, they launched their little remote control airplane to fly a pattern near where they thought you might be. Well, it's apparently got infrared sensors and a video feed and it didn't take long before they spotted you and sent out what they like to call their 'Special Response Team.' Looks like they got there just in time to keep your lawyer friend from killing you two. By the way, the case against Morgan is airtight. The video taken from the remotely piloted drone picked up the whole sorry show. The guys were on their way by that time, but had no idea Morgan planned to murder you all and take the gold for himself.

"So you believe us?" I asked.

"Of course I do, otherwise I wouldn't be sitting here. Reports of incidents like this are routinely sent up to Justice, and when they got word of the full ramifications of what had happened, that's when they called my group in. We got here a couple of days ago. I spent yester-day here going over the transcripts and videos of your testimony, while I had another team thoroughly search your house, Matt. It's pretty clear you've been telling the truth. Lisa, my computer people tell me you're nothing short of a genius to solve those codes."

"Ciphers," Lisa corrected.

"Ciphers. Whatever you call them. What was I saying? Oh, any-way, they tell me you should be working for our side."

"I do," Lisa replied curtly.

"Sorry. Figure of speech," John said.

"What about Nick?" I asked.

"Oh, poor Mr. Morgan. He tried to lie his way out at first, but we told him about his situation and that we had him on video commit-ting a murder, and he just folded. Told us the truth, or at least what he tells us jibes completely with what you've said. Told us he'd sunk your Jeep into the river, Lisa, and that he planned to kill all three of you and bury the bodies in the grave that held the gold. Under other circumstances, he might have gotten away with it, too. You know what he was worried about? He kept saying he was afraid he couldn't get two boats stacked full of gold ingots safely back to the landing without tipping them over. Not worried about three murders, just how to get away with the gold. What a piece of work! Some of the hotter heads in the group say we could charge you as accessories to murder, but I personally think a jury would see you were in fact potential victims."

"What is all this about radiation," Lisa asked. "They stripped us down and scrubbed us raw and then kept hauling us to see this weird little fat doctor who kept looking for rashes."

"Now, kids, that's where the problem comes in, and if you want to know the truth, that's why you're sitting here instead of a holding cell in some federal building somewhere." John paused. "And that's why they called in my team. We've got a little problem there." He rose and walked over to the window, drawing back the curtain and looking out toward the forest. "You were born when, Matt? 1973?"

I nodded.

"And you Lisa, 1975?"

"Right."

"I guess you don't remember much about Vietnam. I do. I spent a couple of years over there on special assignment doing the sort of things you don't get to talk about, and earning myself a reputation that eventually landed me this job. It was a pretty rough time for the U.S. We were losing that war from day one, and the suits in Washington couldn't see it. Some of the things we did will never see the light of day, and rightfully so." He turned away from the window and looked at us. "Ever hear of Agent Orange?"

"I think so," Lisa replied. "Wasn't that an herbicide used to kill vegetation so the Viet Cong and North Vietnamese wouldn't be able to use the jungle for cover?"

"Right you are. Good at your history, young lady. Yeah, it was a big thing back then, and still is now. They used it for about 10 years, up until 1971. I've been told they sprayed as much as 10 percent of the entire area of the country. The tree huggers teamed up with the anti-war types to say that we were poisoning the forest and eventually got it stopped. Turns out they may have been right. There are still lots of vets out there who claim they were injured by Agent Orange. I'm not one to say, but I do know that it could have been worse. That's where we come in."

John walked over to the table and sat down again. "No matter what the government may have said publicly back then, they were very sensitive to all the anti-war and environmental rhetoric. The Defense Department started looking for alternatives that would do the same thing and not permanently damage the environment. Back in the mid to late 1960s somebody came up with the bright idea of using radiation. You have to remember at that time we were right in the middle of the Cold War. The nuclear weapon production line was going full tilt right here in the Savannah River Site. Now I don't want you to think I'm an expert, but I've managed to educate myself enough over the past few days to be able to understand the problem.

"You see, in the process of producing plutonium and enriched uranium for nuclear bombs, you produce a lot of other highly radioactive and extremely toxic byproducts. How to dispose of byproducts was an issue then, and still is now. One of the byproducts is an element named Cesium. A small amount of it is used for radiotherapy in cancer patients, but doesn't have many other practical uses. We end up having to bury most of it to get rid of it. Somehow or other, it was suggested that a radioactive isotope of the stuff would be a good thing to try as a possible replacement for Agent Orange and several other chemicals they were spraying over there. There was plenty of it right here to experiment with, so they picked out several remote areas and put out varying amounts of it to see how it would do in killing jungle vegetation. They were intending to use one particular isotope called Cesium-134. That has a half-life of just over two years, which means that the radioactivity drops off rather quickly. *But*, they needed a control plot for long term monitoring, and they wanted an isotope that wouldn't weaken over a matter of years. No problem, someone said, we've got lots of Cesium-137. That stuff has a half-life of 30 years and emits of lots of gamma radiation — there's your constant control source.

"So they tried it and it worked, to a degree. Killed off the vegetation very nicely. They actually considered using it until someone in the command chain came to their senses and realized that contaminating the jungle with radiation might just be worse than using herbicides. About that time, the whole defoliation program was cancelled, and the issue became moot.

"Now, here's the problem. These fellows here at the Savannah River Site are scientists, and among other things, they are interested in the long term environmental effects of radiation exposure. They decided to indefinitely continue the experiment with Cesium-137. They'd just top it off every year to replace that small amount of radioactivity that had been lost through natural decay. About twice a year, they've been going out in radiation suits, taking soil and vegetation samples and looking at the effects of constant high dose radiation on the flora and fauna of low-country South Carolina.

"Remember that white bucket that was sitting on top of one of the gravestones? Morgan said it had been kicked to the side in the process of digging up the grave. Said he didn't pay it much attention. Remember it?"

"I think so," Lisa and I both said spontaneously.

"That bucket contained a massive amount of highly radioactive Cesium-137. Enough to deliver a fatal dose of radiation in a matter of minutes."

Lisa gasped. I felt a sudden pang of nausea.

CHAPTER
Fifty-Five

JOHN WATCHED US INTENTLY while the meaning of his words sank in. I tried to speak but couldn't. After a moment, Lisa said, "You mean we are, are going, going ..."

"No, apparently not." John smiled a half smile. "The one word that keeps getting connected to your names is 'lucky.' For what it's worth, it looks like the plot to kill you is what saved you from certain death. Everyone's story is pretty consistent. You four found the grave, and almost immediately Morgan pulls his gun. You were then led over to the edge of the clearing and handcuffed to a tree. I was actually curious about that. Morgan's explanation was that he and Smith thought they could get the gold out by themselves, and they didn't want to risk you two turning on them like they planned to turn on you. They didn't trust you. No honor even among thieves."

"If things had gone as planned, all four of you would have received massive and certainly fatal doses of radiation. As it is though, only Mr. Morgan has met that fate. The stolen Confederate treasure has become his judge, jury and executioner."

"And us?" I asked.

"The technical people keep talking about millicuries of exposure, but the way they explained it to me is that in the few minutes you were near the source you had the equivalent of a lifetime of chest x-rays. It looks like the risk to your immediate and long term health is fairly minimal."

"So Nick is dying?" Lisa asked.

"As we speak. On a practical basis, there's not a lot that can be done. They tell me he'll last another week, maybe 10 days." John paused, evidently thinking about what he was about to say. "And if it makes you feel any better, he'll die an agonizing and painful death. A far less humane death sentence than the one he'd surely get in a court of law."

"What about the gold?" I asked.

"Good question. I asked the same thing myself. You see, Matt, the scientists that set up this experiment chose to put the radioactive source on top of the grave simply because the marble slab was a clean and convenient place to locate it. They had no way of knowing that just a few feet below were tens of millions of dollars in gold. For the last 30-something years those ingots have been blasted 24 hours a day with very intense radiation. They tell me that at this point, they're highly radioactive, but probably at some point in the future, they'll be safe to handle. I'm just not sure that'll happen in my lifetime or yours. Bottom line, though, the federal government has formally declared ownership of it all as confiscated property of the former rebel government."

"So what happens now?"

"That's up to you," John replied. "Let me give you two scenarios. First, for the sake of argument, let's say that the locals get their way. The FBI would take you into custody. There's a federal grand jury seated in Columbia at this very moment, and in less than 24 hours they'd have you indicted on a list of charges as long as your arm. The local federal prosecutor would argue, probably successfully, against bail, meaning you'd spend the next six months to a year in jail awaiting trial. News of this whole thing would of course leak out, and the case would be followed closely by the media. That would put all the more pressure on the DA to get a conviction, so he'd go for a long sentence to make an example of you two. He'd probably leave in the accessory to murder charges, knowing the jury might let you off on them while not feeling too much guilt about convicting you on a host of other counts ranging from simple trespassing to felony theft of government property. You might get out in 10 years, or in the worse case, you could both turn 50 behind bars. It's not a pretty picture. You better believe me; under normal circumstances, that is exactly what would happen.

"But let me tell you what also would happen. Remember the so-called 'Tuskegee Experiment?' It's a good example of what harm uncontrolled government research can do. In the early 1930s, government doctors in Tuskegee, Alabama, identified a group of black men with advanced syphilis. There was no good treatment for the condition at the time, and they wanted to follow their subjects during a period of years to see what would happen. Within just a few years, however, an effective treatment was found. You know what the scientists did? Nothing! Not one damned thing. They didn't want to interfere with their experiment. It wasn't until 1972 that shit hit the fan, when the media found out about it and made it all public. By that time dozens had died needless deaths.

"Same thing in this case. Can you imagine the media firestorm that would be created if word got out the so-called scientists here in this top secret facility have been leaving out dangerous radioactive substances to do nothing more than see how quickly they can damage the environment? Or that a study that rightfully should have been stopped more than three decades ago is continuing, and has already killed at least one man and could have killed all four of you?

"And that's not all. It would become public knowledge that not only is the security here full of holes, there is material perfectly suited for a 'dirty bomb' just laying about for the taking. That would interest a few terrorists, I'm sure. And think of the Civil War buffs and treasure nuts who would spend their every waking hour trying to see if there isn't some gold that wasn't found. No, kids, this is not the sort of case that needs to be pursued, or so say my superiors in Washington."

John paused. We sat speechless.

"So, let me give you the alternative scenario. You know, government is not perfect. It does some things well, and other things – how should I phrase it? – not so well. However, the one thing the United States government is very good at – and one thing I'm very good at – is cover-ups. A government is charged with enforcing its own laws. Sometimes it's not in its own best interest to do so. We rewrite history. We put a different spin on the truth. Things that shouldn't be discovered are made to disappear. Don't think it's illegal; it's not. A good example is the witness protection program. Sometimes, for the good of society, we trade freedom for information. We give murderers and Mafiosi new lives and a chance to start over in exchange for their testimony. Sometimes we offer freedom in exchange for silence. That's what I want to offer you.

"My superiors at the Department of Justice feel that prosecuting you will open Pandora's Box. I actually went to law school many years ago, and one of the beauties of our legal system is that justice takes place in the open. Except in cases of national security, civil and criminal trials are public proceedings. Yes, we could probably have you serve a decade or so in prison, but at cost to the reputation of our nuclear research program or the reputation and security of this facility? It's just not worth it.

"This is the offer. You work with us to make sure none of what has happened ever becomes public knowledge. We will allow you to keep your freedom in exchange for two things, your silence and your active participation in what can only be termed a cover-up. Interested?"

"My God," Lisa exploded. "People are dead and dying! How are you going to explain Doug Smith's death to his wife and children? What about Nick? He can't just disappear."

"We've been working on that, and I'm sure we can pull it off. The key is you two. You have to become part of the conspiracy. You will have to learn to lie. If anyone ever approaches you with the truth, you'll have to deny it."

"And what if we say no?"

"Then you're looking at federal prison for sure."

"For how long?" I asked. "How long will you have us under your thumb?"

"Well, assuming we don't take things to a grand jury, you'd theoretically be off the hook when the statutes of limitations run out – maybe 2 to 5 years for most of the likely charges. But, Matt, we can't have you ever tell anyone the truth. So I suspect that if we reach an agreement and you ever break it, the information presented to a grand jury will include a charge of murder. There's no statute of limitations for that."

"Murder! Are you kidding? You know we never..."

"Remember Agent Hall? You met him this morning. He's our staff legal person. He says we can build a pretty good case for a murder – maybe not first degree but enough to avoid the statute of limitations issue. After all, Morgan's going to die of radiation poisoning. You drew him into your conspiracy..."

"Morgan! He's the murderer, not us! You said you have him on video shooting Doug. We never ..."

"Matt, I hate to keep interrupting you, but look at it this way. Yes, Morgan is a murderer. Yes, he fully intended to kill you both. Yes, he has heartily earned a death sentence, but," John paused for effect, "that death sentence can only be imposed by a judge and jury. I don't think we'd have much problem with the argument that your bringing Morgan into the conspiracy and the subsequent events that resulted from it directly caused his death. Is that clear?"

John folded his hands on the table in front of him and waited for our reply.

CHAPTER

Fifty–Six

IT TOOK A MOMENT FOR THINGS TO SINK IN. I finally spoke. "You don't leave us much choice, do you, John?"

"I was raised in western North Carolina. In my little church, they used to talk about the concept of free will. The Lord put you here on this earth with a blank slate and the Bible as a guidebook. It's a similar situation here. You know what you should do, but what you *actually* do – and the consequences of your actions – is up to you." For no particular reason, it occurred to me I'd placed his accent a couple of hundred miles to the west.

"I don't think either Matt or I are particularly religious," Lisa said, "but we're not fools. Where do we go from here?"

"I thought you'd say that," John replied. He walked over to the door and summoned Agent Hall. "We've got a lot that needs to be done and not much time to do it. Yesterday, the Georgia Department of Natural Resources launched a search for a missing hunter from Walkerville named Douglas Smith. Morgan's absence has not raised any suspicions as yet, and I understand you two are up around Asheville taking in the fall leaves. But first things first...."

Agent Hall handed John a paper which he glanced at and slid it across the table to Lisa. "That's an incident report from the Asheville police dated yesterday, documenting the reported theft of a 2002 Jeep Wrangler, color Patriot Blue. You need to sign at the bottom right there." He slid a pen across the table. "That'll get you off the rental company's hook."

Lisa stared at the document, pushing it over so I could examine it. It looked authentic. "How can you ...?"

"I think perhaps you shouldn't ask too many questions," John replied. "Thousands of vehicles are reported stolen every day. The cost is built into the insurance you paid for. It may be that one day someone will find the Jeep in the Savannah River – maybe not. Either way, it won't be your worry after you sign that form."

"But the Asheville police, how can they ...?"

John interrupted again. "We have friends in police departments across the country. It's been posed as a national security issue. The report is real. There will be a limited investigation, the vehicle won't be found, the insurance company will pay, and the file will gather dust somewhere, lost in a storage box in a warehouse with other unsolved cases."

Lisa stared at him for moment, scribbled her signature on the form and slid it back across the table.

"Good," John said. "Now, Matt, you need to sign this credit card receipt from the Grove Park Inn. You guys checked in last Sunday and will be checking out tomorrow. You had a room in the old part, by the way. Great view of the city." He handed me an official-looking printout of a hotel receipt, documenting not only the room charges, but also drinks in the bar and two dinners on the Blue Ridge Dining Room. I noticed I had spent $1,867.97.

"How can you get away with this?" I asked.

"Big hotel. Lots of conventions. More than 500 rooms. No one would remember you anyway. I realize that you'd probably have stayed in a smaller place – maybe like The Mills Plantation – but this provides a better cover. Sorry about the big bill, but you can afford it."

"How did you know about The Mills Plantation?" Lisa asked. She seemed angry, as if a very personal space had been invaded.

"There're not many things we don't know about you two, considering the relatively short amount of time we've had to work on things. To specifically answer your question, the charge was on Matt's credit card. One of our agents interviewed the Mills. Nice family I hear."

"OK. What's next?" I asked.

"Got quite a few more forms for you to sign, but we needed to get those two done first to get the ball rolling for your North Carolina alibi. The fellows here are drawing up a statement for you both to sign. It pretty much documents the facts. You admit your guilt, and the government agrees not to prosecute, provided you adhere to the conditions we dictate. They're still preparing it, but should have it done in an hour or so. We need to run it by Justice, but someone is there waiting on us to get a draft to them. Assuming no one in Washington objects to the details, you can sign later this afternoon. Meanwhile, I need to get over to the hospital unit to see Attorney Morgan. I've got a few choices to present to him, none of which are pleasant." He rose to leave.

"What about Doug's body?" Lisa asked. "For God's sake, he's got a wife and two little kids. What are you going to do there?"

"We're working on it," John said, and left without further comment. I never saw him again.

WE SIGNED THE PAPERS. There were about a dozen of them for each of us. Release forms, acknowledgements, agreements and – for lack of a better word – a long confession were placed before us and the legal significance briefly reviewed by the stone-faced Agent Hall. We'd sign and a new form would appear. Lisa asked to keep copies, but her request was denied. It was nearly 6 p.m. when we finished. Supper appeared; fast food takeout this time with an unappealing choice of pizza or soggy hamburgers. We were offered packets of cellophane wrapped forks and napkins. Apparently our signing the papers had given our guards some sense of trust.

At 7 p.m., my guard, Aaron, announced we would be released the next day. "Matt, we'll be driving you back to Walkerville, and you, Lisa, have a 6:30 flight out of Augusta and on to San Francisco via Atlanta. Tom will be flying with you just to be sure you don't have any problems getting home safely."

Lisa looked alarmed. "But I'm not ready to go back to California. I need to go to Walkerville with Matt. I've got my clothes, my things."

"We've packed them all for you. They're in the Suburban. If there's something we missed, we can get it delivered to you later."

"Dammit! Right now, I want to be with Matt. There's nothing for me in San Francisco."

"The form you both signed said you agreed to have no contact with each other for a minimum period of six months," Aaron said.

"What!!" Both Lisa and I shouted at the same time.

"We didn't sign anything like ..." Lisa said, her voice cracking.

"I think you did," Aaron replied. "Let me get Agent Hall."

We had signed it. Page 14, paragraph 3, fourth and fifth sentences of the document entitled, "Statement of Facts and Confidentiality Agreement." We had agreed to avoid all contact with one another for "six months or for a longer period of time, the duration to be determined by the Department of Justice, should circumstances warrant. This determination shall be made solely at the discretion of the Department of Justice and/or its designated representatives."

Hall said, again unsmiling, "It's not too late. We can still take you both back to your cells and do this the regular way. It's your call."

I looked at Lisa. She was crying. "OK." I said, "We'll do it your way. But I want to be with Lisa tonight."

"We can't allow that. Spend some time together if you'd like, but we've all got a big day tomorrow so I'd suggest you try to get some sleep."

The guards left us alone. We talked for hours. I didn't know what I wanted to say, and wouldn't have known how to say it if I did. I told Lisa I cared about her; she told me she cared about me. I asked her what she was going to do once she returned to California. She said that she didn't know what she'd do or where she'd be. She paused and then added, "I do know one thing though. I'll call you as soon as I can. Promise." At 10 p.m., Aaron and Tom appeared at the door and said it was time to return to our cabins.

I kissed Lisa. They turned their heads away.

Fifty–Seven

I COULDN'T GO TO SLEEP. I tossed and turned for hours. The cabin was quiet. At 2 a.m. I quietly pulled on my clothes and eased open the door to my bedroom. The seating area was deserted. I slipped out of the room and had made three steps toward the front door when Aaron's voice said, "Need something, Matt?"

I don't know what time I finally fell asleep. Bright sunlight streaming in my window awakened me. I grabbed frantically for my watch. It was 7:45 a.m. I leaped out of bed and threw open the door. Aaron was sitting on the couch, reading a book and sipping on a cup of coffee. "Morning. Want some coffee?"

"Where's Lisa?"

He glanced at his watch. "They left for the airport several hours ago. Did you finally get to sleep?" I told him I'd had trouble sleeping. He gave me a friendly smile.

She was gone, and I'd missed saying goodbye.

"Take your time, but we'll head for Walkerville whenever you're ready," Aaron said.

I RODE IN THE FRONT SEAT of the Suburban this time. I noticed the government tags on the SUV had been replaced by North Carolina plates. Aaron's gun and earpiece communicator had disappeared. We left the Savannah River Site without fanfare. An armed guard in a gray Wackenhut uniform waved us through the gate. We traveled northwest on U.S. 278, crossed the Savannah River, skirted Augusta to the south on I-520, then turned southwest on U.S. 1 toward Wrens and Walkerville. Neither of us had much to say. We arrived at mid-afternoon. It was Saturday; the city square was deserted, except for a few tourists taking photos of the courthouse with its gingerbread ornamentation and a few teenagers huddled around two mud-splattered, jacked-up pickups.

Rutherford Hall, like everything else in Walkerville, was unchanged. My leased Explorer was still parked in the garage gathering dust. Aaron pulled in the driveway with some familiarity and stopped near the back steps. "Got your keys?" he asked. I nodded. "The alarm's on."

"How do you know?"

"I set it. Several days ago. We left our own code in the system, in case we ever need to get back in. Just thought you'd like to know." He took my bag out of the back and placed it on the ground. "You need anything before I go?"

"Not really. But thanks. I know you're just doing your job."

Aaron extended his hand. I shook it. "You're not a bad guy, Matt. Just keep your nose clean."

"Thanks."

"Then see you later," Aaron said.

I grabbed my things and started to walk up the steps when I remembered something. Aaron was getting in the Suburban. "Aaron. One question I forgot to ask. How did they know we were inside? We'd disabled the camera, the storm had knocked out their sensors, we didn't see any guards."

He hesitated. "I probably shouldn't say anything, but I will. The SRS guards had no idea you were inside. Their perimeter security completely failed them. It was the nuclear power plant on the Georgia side of the river. They picked you up on their video monitors. They thought at first the boats were just heading into the branch to get away from the storm, and they figured security over at SRS would pick up on your presence anyway. When you didn't come out after a couple of hours and when they saw no one had been there to check you out, they figured they better call their counterparts across the river and alert them. That's why they started searching."

"Damn! It never occurred to us."

"You can't think of everything, Matt," Aaron said and slammed the door. He waved as he drove off.

The house was cold and empty. It seemed to have acquired a musty smell I'd never noticed before. I threw my bag on the kitchen table and took a quick walk-through. The study was unchanged. I flipped on the computer and searched for Lisa's files on the Rutherford Cipher. They were missing. I struggled to pull back the table to look at the hidden vault. The three odd planks were still in place but now had been nailed firmly to the joists, the nail holes countersunk and camouflaged with wax to make them appear old. With a growing sense of fear, I rushed upstairs to where I'd hidden the gold ingot and the missing diary. Gone! All evidence the stolen Confederate gold had ever existed had disappeared.

The phone rang. I started not to answer it; I didn't want to talk with anyone. I was upstairs and away from the Caller ID box so I couldn't tell who was calling. But it could have been Lisa. I picked up the receiver.

It was my mother. "Matt, I'm so glad you're home. I guess you heard the news. They found Doug Smith's body. You had heard he was missing hadn't you?" She didn't wait for an answer. "I just heard it on the radio. He was duck hunting over near the Savannah River and apparently was shot in some sort of a hunting accident. They think it was probably a stray bullet. It's so sad, Matt. It reminds me of all I suffered when your father died. We've got to get over to help comfort Nan and the children. I'll ..."

I cut her off. "I'm sorry to hear that. We've, I've, been out of town."

"Oh, I know. I got the nicest postcard this morning from Lisa. Said you were in Asheville. I guess I should tell you, I'm sorry about what I said the other day. I'm sure she's a wonderful person, Matt, and I'm looking forward to meeting her."

"She had to go back to California," i said.

"When's she coming back? We can have a tea for her. I can introduce her to some of the other ladies in town."

"Soon, I hope." I changed the subject. "Mom, have you heard from Nick?"

"No, as a matter of fact I haven't. I called his office yesterday about some letter I got about some of the bonds in one of the trust funds, and his secretary said he was still off fishing. Seems like he does a lot of that these days."

"Oh," I said.

"They haven't set a time for the funeral, but you'll need to go with me."

I said that I felt like I'd been to too many funerals lately. The line went dead without the customary goodbye.

My mother's phone call reminded me that I hadn't checked Caller ID. Maybe Lisa had called. The "New Call" light was blinking. There were only two calls and both of them in the past 24 hours. Aaron and his crew had probably erased everything when they sanitized the house. I noticed the answering machine message light was blinking. I checked Caller ID first. In addition to my mother's number, there was one other that must have been received only minutes before I arrived. I recognized the area code of San Francisco. My palms sweated as I pressed the "Message Play" button. A familiar voice said, "Matt, I know I haven't talked with you in a long time, but I miss you and I just wanted to know if we could get together. I guess you probably heard I've been seeing Luke James, and, well, it's just not the same, so I was ...." I hit the "Erase All" button. It was Brandi, my ex-girlfriend from California.

I stayed at home on Sunday. The phone didn't ring.

CHAPTER

Fifty-Eight

I WAS AWAKENED ON MONDAY MORNING by Eula Mae, stirring around downstairs. I padded into the bathroom and shortly afterwards heard her calling, "Oh, Mr. Matt. You 'wake?"

"Yeah, I'm here."

"Where is Miss Lisa?"

"Back home in California."

There was a momentary silence. I then heard the stairs creaking. "She's coming back?" She was standing on the landing.

"Soon, I hope," I said.

I heard the creaks receding as she walked back downstairs.

Eula Mae had coffee waiting when I finished my shower and came downstairs. She was rearranging the canisters on the kitchen counter. "That alarm man Mike sure was mad at you. He called here Thursday and like to cussed me out. Said he saw them other out-of-town alarm people you'd hired after all he'd done done for you. Said he wanted to give you a piece of his mind. 'Course, I said I didn't know nothing 'bout it and he says he seen they truck parked in the yard on Tuesday or Wednesday, I forgits which, and that hell was gonna freeze over before he'd come around and help you like he did before. I hung the phone up."

I simply said, "Thanks." I presumed that was Aaron and his men.

"And I guess you done heard about Lawyer Morgan?"

My head snapped up. "No. What?"

"They say he got some blood disease, and he's been off getting treatment and it ain't gonna work and they brought him home to the hospital here to die, 'cause this is his home and he said if he was gonna die somewhere, he'd rather do it 'mongst friends instead of in some big city hospital somewhere."

"Eula Mae. How do you know this?"

"Pearlie Mae, my cousin, she works for Doctor Pike and she told me they called him yesterday to come down and tend to Lawyer Morgan when the ambulance brought him home."

"Where's he been?"

"Some hospital somewhere. Augusta, I 'spect. Getting treatments."

They were so, so efficient, I thought. All the loose ends neatly tied.

I STARTED TO GO OUT, but thought better of it. For some reason I didn't want to be away from the phone. My mother called just before noon. "Son, I just heard that Nick Morgan is very ill and is not expected to live. He's apparently been in the hospital in Columbia, South Carolina, getting some experimental treatment for a blood disorder. They tell me it's called aplastic anemia, and that evidently he's had it for a long time." She paused, waiting for my reaction.

"Really," I said. No tone in my voice.

"Matt, he's pitiful. He's dying, and he has no one. He has no children, no relatives anywhere around, and nobody close at all except for that sorry ex-wife, Donna, who tried to take all his money when she divorced him. He needs us. We need to be by his side. We need to support him in a time like this. It's the Christian thing to do. I want you to take me to the hospital so we can both visit with him. They say he won't last but a few days."

"No."

"We need to show that – What did you say?"

"I said no. You go. I'll stay home," I said.

"Matt, let me get something straight. You owe a huge debt of gratitude to Nick for all that he's done for you over the years. You don't know how much help and support he offered me after your father died. I was so alone in the world, so lost, and he was there for me when I needed him and I think it's only right that we should be there for him in his hour of need. Matt, I've never told you this, but after your father died I thought I was in love with Nick. We almost ..."

This time I hung up the phone. I felt sick.

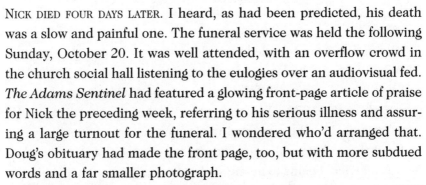

NICK DIED FOUR DAYS LATER. I heard, as had been predicted, his death was a slow and painful one. The funeral service was held the following Sunday, October 20. It was well attended, with an overflow crowd in the church social hall listening to the eulogies over an audiovisual fed. *The Adams Sentinel* had featured a glowing front-page article of praise for Nick the preceding week, referring to his serious illness and assuring a large turnout for the funeral. I wondered who'd arranged that. Doug's obituary had made the front page, too, but with more subdued words and a far smaller photograph.

Monday, October 21 was my birthday. On the same day in 1805 Admiral Horatio Nelson had been killed as he led his fleet to victory in the Battle of Trafalgar. An unsigned card with a California zip code arrived in the mail with the cryptic note, "Look in bedroom closet. Top shelf." Which bedroom — Lisa's?

I almost flew up the stairs to her old room. In the top of her closet, hidden behind an old pillow and a folded blanket, I found a small box wrapped in gold paper. I tore it open and found a $20 gold piece dated "1865" with a small unsigned note in Lisa's script that said, "I love you."

ON TUESDAY, OCTOBER 22 I GOT A CALL from Tom Grisham, one of the older lawyers in town. "Matt, I need to see you sometime this week in my office. It's about Nick Morgan."

I felt a cramp in my stomach. "Sure, what for?"

"He made you his sole heir. He's left you everything, Matt. His house, his property, his stock, his retirement accounts."

I was silent.

"Matt, can you hear me? Are you there?"

"I'm here."

"He was a very wealthy man, son. *Very* wealthy. I know you inherited a good bit from your Aunt Lillie, but ..."

"Why?"

"How's that?" He sounded very old.

"Why? Why did he leave everything to me?"

"Well, now, I don't rightfully know. I made Nick's first will out for him back in the 1970s. Right after your father died, as I recall. He wasn't married at the time and made you his only beneficiary. We updated the will several times, but he never changed it, even when he was married. Seems to me he said something about having pity for a fatherless boy."

"Or guilt." I was burning with rage.

"How's that? Oh, I forgot. He was with your father when the accident happened."

I decided to hold my tongue. "Yeah, I guess."

"Anyway, we need to get together in the next few days to discuss things, go over the estate and so on."

"We'll do that. I've been a bit stressed lately. Call me in a few days." I hung the phone up without waiting for a reply.

I was angry. So very, very angry. The walls of the house began to close in on me. I walked outside and paced in the garden. The air was cool, and small piles of fall leaves were accumulating, windblown against the hedges. I needed to get away. I got in my car and started driving, aimlessly. I drove north, stopping at a convenience store at a country crossroads to pick up a six-pack of beer. I propped a can between my legs and put the other five on the passenger seat. An hour later only one can was left.

I don't know if it was chance or design, but I realized I was in the hamlet of Warthen, north of Walkerville. I needed to stop, to take a break, to sober up a bit before I had an accident. And I needed to do one thing. I parked the Explorer on a shady side street and, carrying my remaining beer, walked down a wide path to the small community cemetery. It was a place of peace and rest. Huge elm trees, their leaves now yellow with the fall, shaded generations of dead. A garden of marble monuments lay before me. I threaded my way to the plot with freshly turned earth, now covered with masses of wilting flowers. A temporary marker from Davis Funeral Chapel was stuck in the earth at the head of the grave. It read "Nicholas C. Morgan. Died October 18, 2002."

I stood looking at the mounded earth. I popped the top on my last beer and sucked half of it down. I wanted to scream at him. I wanted to cry. I wanted to tell him how many people's lives he'd destroyed. I wanted to, do what? I finished my beer. I unzipped my pants. I pissed on his grave.

EPILOGUE

WE RECEIVED WORD IN EARLY NOVEMBER that Lance's murderer had been arrested. Or rather it would be more proper to say he'd been charged. It turned out to be his roommate. He was in jail on other charges and was overheard telling some story about stolen Confederate gold and the like. The police, who said retrospectively they had considered him the prime suspect all along, felt he knew more than he'd been telling them. He confessed after a couple of hours of intensive grilling. The fact he'd been withdrawing from heroin may have loosened his tongue.

I got the word from Uncle Jack, who in turn had been called by Chief Mathis, who was relaying word from the Columbia, South Carolina, police. Jack said he was glad it was all over, and that there had been enough sadness in this one small town for the year. I agreed.

He said my mother was relieved, too, that my name had been cleared of any suspicion. I said I was thankful for that. I presumed he knew we hadn't spoken since I refused to attend Nick's funeral.

Things became a bit more – or less – complicated a few days later, when we heard the suspect had been shot and killed while trying to overpower the deputy bringing him to Georgia to stand trial.

Two days before Thanksgiving, Mathis appeared unannounced at

Rutherford Hall. He was carrying a large sack. "I thought I should return these things," he said. "With Lance's killer dead, we won't be needing them for a trial."

Inside the sack were my clothes, some items taken from the house, and the still sealed evidence bag that contained the alleged murder weapon. I thanked him and he left.

In the kitchen, I opened the bag containing the other gold ingot, painted black and still encrusted with my cousin's blood. I washed it off in the sink, carefully rinsing the last remnants of red-stained water down the drain. I dried it with a towel and took it in the library where I used it to prop up one end of a set of leather-bound Dickens Collected Works.

Lisa still hadn't called.

DATE DUE

#47-0108 Peel Off Pressure Sensitive